The Glass Wall

The Glass Wall

A Superintendent Mike Yeadings Mystery

Clare Curzon

THOMAS DUNNE BOOKS
ST. MARTIN'S MINOTAUR ♨ NEW YORK

THOMAS DUNNE BOOKS.
An imprint of St. Martin's Press.

www.thomasdunnebooks.com
www.minotaurbooks.com

Library of Congress Cataloging-in-Publication Data

Curzon, Clare.
    The glass wall : a Superintendent Mike Yeadings mystery / Clare Curzon.—1st U.S. ed.
        p. cm.
    ISBN-13: 978-0-312-34963-9
    ISBN-10: 0-312-34963-7
    1. Yeadings, Mike (Fictitious character)—Fiction. 2. Police—England—Thames Valley—Fiction. 3. Thames Valley (England)—Fiction. I. Title.

PR6053.U79 G55 2006
823'.914—dc22

2006050122

First published in Great Britain by Allison & Busby Limited

First U.S. Edition: December 2006

10 9 8 7 6 5 4 3 2 1

Chapter One

The small man stepped from the lift, rang the apartment's door-bell and waited, his head close against the panels to catch any sounds of movement within.

Utter silence. No one came. Was no one left to come?

So it was real, what he saw from the road? *Thought* he'd seen?

It could still be illusion, his recurrent echo of childhood trauma. But that only happened when he balanced on the edge of sleep: the memory of torture, of being forced to watch while...

No. This time he'd been awake, stepping on to the kerb and looking up at the tall building he was bound for.

Who else had seen what happened? There had been no sudden panic around him, no screaming, no crowd gathering to point upwards to the penthouse window. With home-seeking traffic intent on beating the lights, and the sparse pedestrians burrowing against a sleety wind, was he the only witness?

Or was it – as he'd feared after the first transfixed instant – a re-enactment inside his own head, a half-emergence of something demonic his mind refused full memory of? And now the recurring nightmare was visiting him awake. A superstitious man, he half-believed Hell could be black-magicked on him from the other side of the world and more than half a lifetime away.

He knew again the same heart-clutching horror: gazing up at a height. And a body dropping out of the sky, turning over and over as it fell, this time silent all the way, disappearing finally from sight. Like frames of film in slow motion, while his body raced with terror. The same, but quite wrong, because this wasn't Sulu. No craggy mountains; just urban English streets, and for tropical heat a slicing wind carrying chips of ice to sting your face.

He leaned his forehead against the door frame, compelling sanity to re-establish itself, wipe out the past.

He drew in a deep, soughing breath, counting the heartbeats loud in his throat. Sort it. Act. Control the moment. And the door he leant on clicked open.

He rang again, received no answer, then exerted soft pressure on the panels and went in. 'Anyone here?' he called, standing in the hall, ready, if challenged, to explain that he'd found the door ajar.

Still silence, except for the central heating clicking into action, and behind it the low humming of a fridge. Even so slight a sound set his nerves aquiver. Tensed, he moved cautiously forward.

The hall lights were on. Every door of the apartment stood open. He was free to walk through. It was the sleet-laden wind driving in from the darkened lounge that sent him in that direction. He knew then he hadn't been deceived. Because a panel of the glass wall gaped open.

As he'd stepped off the pedestrian crossing, looking up, he *had* seen the old woman fall from her seventh-floor window. (But not into the street. The body would have landed somewhere behind the hangar-like building of the stationery warehouse.)

Now, all senses alerted, learnt skills took over. He ran, crouched double, into the room, again the boy insurgent trained to kill. And, instantly ice-keen, he felt the old feral passion, once second nature, sliding back over him tight as an outer skin. But today no knife in his hand.

And the room was empty.

This was wrong. The woman couldn't, unaided, have climbed over the guard rail and balanced there ready to jump. Couldn't, for that matter, have got out of bed alone, walked this far. Certainly her bent little claws would be useless, fumbling with the complicated lock that secured the sliding panel.

So if someone else had been here, where was he now? The other lift hadn't passed his, going down as he came up. Which left the staircase.

He ran back and craned over the rail, scanning the perspective of six double flights dropping to the marble-tiled lobby. Nothing moved anywhere down there. No sound came but his own taut breathing.

It was impossible. Someone must still be in the apartment, if only her personal carer. Someone who'd just killed the old woman, or had helped her to kill herself.

Silently he moved back into the apartment. In the hall he reached across the table for the ebony carving of three monkeys, curling his fingers round the smoother base. Steeled for action he slid into the passage, hesitated a bare instant to draw breath, and dived through the doorway of the first bedroom.

The air burst from his lungs in an aggressive roar and he stood there, his upraised arm an empty gesture.

Again this couldn't be. He let the carving drop as he sank on the bed's rumpled covers to take in the scene. Long moments passed while nothing happened. There was no sound. Nobody came. No doorbell rang. It was as though, entering the building, he had stepped outside present reality.

The tension slowly easing, his whole frame began to tremble, sweat drying on his skin. He recognized, and condemned, fear as possession by a demon. Forced himself to face it down, swore explosively and then instantly was ashamed.

There was no cause for fear. He was alone, and therefore safe. Nobody knew what had happened. There was no reason for anyone to rush in and find him there. All the same, he must protect himself.

He stood, smoothed out the rumpled bedding, returned the carving to the table in the hall, then went slowly back to the opened panel in the huge observation window. He leaned right out, peered all the way down; and by the inadequate lighting of the parking area could barely make out the body as a bundle of rags discarded among piled junk in the unused corner of the warehouse yard.

This window wasn't frontal to the main road but on the building's side, specifically designed to provide a view over the town centre towards the rolling Chiltern hills. Never meant for craning out to see what lay directly below. Such mundane commercial objects wouldn't interest those wealthy enough to buy property commanding such a panorama, although today, veiled in mist and sleet, the Chilterns were no more than a smear of indigo. He drew his head and shoulders back in, shook off cold rain.

He removed a tissue from its box on the coffee table and covered one hand as he reached to slide the panel closed. It snapped firmly locked. The wind ceased shrieking in.

On the glass to one side was a smear of blood, part of it etched in fine lines, like a palm print. The woman had bled before she fell; reached out to save herself. Never an accident.

He wiped off the stain, took a second tissue, spat on it and rubbed at the glass until it gleamed. He stood looking at the window, the glass wall that stood between him and violent murder. He carefully put the tissues away in his pocket.

He was satisfied that nothing showed now. It was as though nothing untoward had happened. He could not be blamed.

Next he must walk away, and no one would know he had been here. Except that he'd been expected. Nurse Orme had arranged it. He must do what he had come to do.

He thought back. At the street door below he had followed a neighbour in, some woman from one of the lower apartments. She would remember if questions were asked. She had keyed in the electronic code to gain entry and held the door for him, taking him for another resident. Later it could be assumed that someone had also let him into this apartment, because he had no key. Who would believe the door was left ajar?

But, being here, he must make his story fit the findings. It could be some days before the body was discovered in the walled yard below, and then why should anyone think it happened when he was anywhere near?

If later he was interrogated he had surely faced worse in the past. These people wouldn't threaten to cut out his tongue.

He went through to the kitchen, made strong coffee and sat to drink it, hunched in thought. The next move must be deliberate choice. He could leave the body to be discovered and deny any connection, or he could remove it by night to a safer distance, leading suspicion away. For that he would need transport. And he knew where cars stood unused overnight. He sat considering his options and what he must do to ensure survival.

He didn't know why he'd done what he did, covering up. Except from acquired wisdom. For so long he'd been wiping out traces of his own existence, the past being all bad. And what he'd just seen happen was already become a part of that badness.

He wished he had never been drawn in, because in Western society there could be no convenient ignoring of a violent act. The consequences would be a manhunt and punishment. He must be sure he wasn't caught up in them.

Over native superstition, experience had made him a fatalist. He knew that every move in life must lead to another, links of a chain that locked you in. It had always been so with him. And now, as some earlier action drew him into this present dilemma, he was for all time involved in another man's evil.

So where had this process started? What, and whose, was the decisive act from which this moment had become the inescapable consequence?

At the start, if he had turned down the woman's invitation, he wouldn't have received the nurse's offer and he wouldn't have come here, to be touched by this killing. Must he acknowledge that moment as the conception from which he'd been made destiny's fool?

She had not even been attractive. He had accepted from inertia, because a few weeks without disasters had lulled him into feeling safe. He had thought to learn something from her: how to fit into this alien world.

As though he was not picked out by fate for something worse.

He remembered the little black carving in the hall and how once he'd been told of the fourth monkey. See no Evil; Hear no Evil; Speak no Evil. The last one, invisible, and which the carver never dared to represent, was Do no Evil.

Chapter Two

The huge window spanned the room's width, facing north. An ideal apartment for an artist, but its owner never painted pictures, only acquired them. No sound penetrated its triple-glazing from the roadways, seven floors down. The market town, with its cobbled alleys and huddled half-timbered houses was shrouded with snow, masking irregularities, cancelling out period differences to leave a post-modernist statement of varying whiteness tinged with the orange of sodium lighting.

Only at the central island and its five mini-roundabouts was any movement discernible from up here. There, like black beetles, cars suddenly appeared, circled, spun off and were lost again in the universal pallor, leaving fine, dark tracks.

A single figure appeared on foot waiting at the nearest crossing, then hurried over. By the building's double doors she kicked snow off her boots and keyed in the entrance code. Tonight she chose the lift because she'd picked up supplies from Sainsbury's on her way back.

The penthouse apartment, when she reached that level, was warm and silent, its ceilings glowing faint orange from the outside light. No curtains had been drawn. All doors from the hall stood open except the one to Emily's bedroom.

Alyson dropped her keys on the octagonal table where they clinked against the little ebony carving. She unzipped and removed her boots, then went through to the kitchen where a blue light softly flickered.

Wearing a headset, Sheena was watching television at the breakfast bench. She looked up and raised a languid hand. Her shift report, written in biro, lay between her sauce-streaked plate and a mug with coffee dregs.

She stood, reaching for her fake fur jacket. 'I'll be going then. Still snowing?'

'It's just stopped. There's about four inches.' Alyson dumped the two plastic carriers, switched on an overhead light and picked up the report. The little that it contained raised no questions.

'Good programme this evening?' An effort to find common ground.

'Loada rubbish.'

Alyson smiled. So why watch? 'Good,' she decided, and switched off the screen.

The care assistant removed herself, stomping off in hiking boots. The outer door slammed and a minute later came the whine and swoosh of the lift bearing her down a further six floors to release.

Alyson opened the closed door, satisfied herself that Emily slept and returned to the kitchen. She shrugged off her sheepskin coat and began to restock the fridge and freezer: her routine switch from one life phase to another. Almost the *only* other. She could relax now and find herself.

She selected a handful of CDs and slid in *Gymnopédie*, simple and uncluttered like the huge room where she sat by the panoramic window to fork her microwaved chicken pasta. Then an old Cleo Lane blues, with Johnny Dankworth rippling in a mesh of notes like silver lace over her prune-dark wanderings. Two lovely people who belonged.

Staring out, she could see for miles, right up to the top of Winchmore Ridge over which hung cloud like a lump of potter's unworked clay, its underside tinged with the ubiquitous diffused orange. And immediately below, crudely brighter, the sodium street lamps stared unwinkingly, double ranked, marking twists of invisible terraces of houses or shops. A single dark patch gaping beyond the floodlit college was the river, sluggishly winding down to join the Thames.

She removed her tray to the kitchen, changed the music to Elgar's *Clarinet Concerto*, tuned it low, and reopened the one closed door.

'Hello, Emily,' she whispered. 'I'm back.'

She was still asleep, propped on three pillows and wearing her flower face: like a white violet. Later, in deeper sleep, when her jaw dropped, she would be Munch's *The Scream*.

Those weren't her only forms. At other times she could be ethereally beautiful, parchment skin stretched over fine facial bones. Sometimes, but rarely, she would smile, if her dream was a good one. Harsher facets would flash up when she exploded into sharp protest, wailed for someone to get her out of this, called desperately for Molly, Dolly, Martin.

And just occasionally she would actually make contact: a brief pause in her slow, progressive detachment from the present world.

This is what I do, Alyson thought, watching her: I keep people alive.

But today she hadn't. Old Albert Fennell had beaten her. It left an empty bed in ITU. Tomorrow someone new would be wheeled into his space.

She walked back to the room's wall of glass, and looked out on the snow, pristine, antiseptic, and blue-shadowed over the distant Chiltern hills. Cars crept silently round the broad traffic island and its five mini-roundabouts. Sheathed in ice, the central trees glistened like crystal candelabra.

She would leave Emily a little longer before the disturbance of bathing, anointing, feeding. For herself, under the window's compulsion, there was the silent night traffic, the lights, the snow. They were mesmeric beyond any television screen, or even the amazing pictures Emily had hung on her walls.

Only one tower block over-topped this stack of luxury flats above the BMW showrooms. On its completion the council had called a halt to cereal-box development, belatedly cherishing what was left of the snug Tudor-Georgian-Victorian town centre after post-war clearances. Beyond the long-fronted, five-storeyed college rose the hospital complex with its central block of eight floors.

Alyson looked across at its upper windows – some dimly curtained, some bright – and pictured the night shift settling to routine in the wards; the final round of thermometers and BP monitors; the volunteers' trolleys offering last drinks of the day: tea, hot chocolate, Ovaltine, Horlicks.

Her Intensive Therapy Unit was on the far side, ground floor, close to – but discrete from – the Emergency Department. *Crème de la crème*, the nurses there: all, like herself, lean as whippets, highly qualified, totally dedicated. And often, when they paused to admit it, just as alone.

But she had Emily, Gran's sister. Sometimes she thought that in Emily's fine features she caught a glimpse of her own dead mother, known only from an old photograph. For her that likeness had been the decisive factor when the family's solicitor sought her out to make their request. Demand perhaps, rather than request. (Who was it who said that the rich were different? How true.)

But once she'd seen Emily she knew she would accept. And the others were really no bother, never visited, seldom rang; simply provided the money; left her to manage.

Emily's family. Her own family, though more distant. They were strangers she'd grown up never knowing.

She wheeled the commode into Emily's room. 'Emily,' she said, stroking the back of one closed claw-hand. The little body was so light it took only one person to lift her, like a child. Emily came awake as she was settled on the porcelain seat. 'Cold,'she said, and pushed Alyson away.

Sheena Judd stomped across town to the Crown Hotel. The saloon bar was crowded, noisy and brightly cheerful; welcome warmth after the outdoor chill of minus four degrees Celsius. Roseanne, busy serving, gave her a sharp nod from the far end of the counter.

The new Filipino barman turned from a couple of guys and impassively demanded, 'Miss?' He was short, square-headed, his dark hair razored severely close; the white tunic with its red epaulettes starched so stiff you could cut your fingers on its creases.

'Vodka Martini.' She watched him dispense it and slide the glass across to her waiting hand. His face never changed. Over the eight days since he'd been taken on she'd never seen him smile. She wondered if it was perpetual sulk or just that he was as thick as a haystack.

'Have one yourself,' she invited on a whim. He stopped in mid-movement, reaching for a beer mat, but his features never changed. He nodded. 'I have it later.'

She supposed he'd simply take it in cash at the end of the day. Immigrants only wanted money. Silly to have tried to get a reaction. There were better things to spend one's hard-earned on.

He did relent though, coming back to her high stool when there was a break in serving. He ran a damp cloth over the mahogany counter. 'You a nurse?' he asked, assuming it from the hospital's nearness.

She grunted assent. Not a real nurse, but for a part of each day she did the same work, didn't she? He'd not know the difference. There were a number of tiny Filipino girls worked in the wards at various things. She supposed he was married to one of them.

'Yeah,' she said, drooping heavy breasts over folded arms and leaning close so that their swelling and darkly defined cleavage could not be missed. She watched his slatey eyes follow the movement. Still no outer sign of personal connection.

'What do I call you?' she asked, burrowing in the dish of peanuts for the really salty ones.

'Ramón.' He sounded more distant, as though forced to give something valuable away. Well, sod him then.

One last push: 'I'm Sheena.' Smiling suggestively at him, while his eyes still lingered on her exposed flesh.

'Nice name,' he granted.

'I'm a nice girl.' She giggled. Was it wishful or were things starting to warm up? She ordered the same again. She remembered then there'd been a volcano blew its top in the Philippines way back. Perhaps he'd been a child refugee, orphaned, lost everything. She'd never known anyone who'd fled a volcanic eruption. Kind of romantic. Maybe the wooden face didn't signify thickness. Enigmatic; wasn't that it? Oriental man of mystery.

'You live round here?' she probed.

'Here, yes.' He pointed at the ceiling.

'In the hotel?' It seemed so. Resident staff, he'd have been given some grotty little attic under the roof and worked like a slavvy all hours to pay for it. So maybe he was a loner.

'With your family?'

'No family.'

She considered this while he moved away to serve drinks at the far end of the bar. There'd been a lot of grumbling about immigrants and refugees. She wasn't really sure which were which; only that a lot were illegal. They slipped into the country from the continent and tried to lose themselves in the system, get unofficial jobs. God knows what they did about identity papers, National Insurance, that sort of thing. Fakes and forgeries probably. It didn't bother her that much, but she could see they'd find it a lot easier if they could become Brits. Which really meant marrying into it, didn't it?

She took a further look at him. Small, which was a pity. Clean, though. Nice square white teeth. Not much of a talker, but then maybe his English wasn't up to scratch. He had a job, even if a poorly paid one. A male immigrant, he could be looking for a wife to legitimize him.

Not that she'd want a permanent hitch. That short stint with Barney had put her off for life. But she needed someone to muck in with, bed with, share costs, hang around and make a fuss of her when she was down. Girlfriends were all right, but not all the way.

She could always pretend she was interested, string him along. Single men of her age weren't so thick on the ground that a girl could be choosy.

So why not? She'd got all the equipment. So keep it active. She could sound out Roseanne, the barmaid, about knowing Ramón a bit better.

Roseanne, less like a flower than a rather cute cartoon mouse, fiddled with a loose strand of hair while she swallowed the line a middle-aged police-court usher was handing her, grinned, displaying two long front teeth at its finish, said perkily, 'Well, you do see life, don't you?' and passed down the counter to where Sheena sat slumped. 'Hard day, mate?' she greeted her.

'Bloody awful boring. Still, it brings in the bread. I'd trade it for your job any day.'

Over her head a newcomer demanded a pint. Roseanne started to pull it, recognized the ominous sucking resistance, apologized. 'Just a moment, sir.'

She pivoted on her stilettos. 'Ramón, the barrel needs changing.'

Sheena, watching, caught the momentary flicker of some expression on the flat, square face. Had Roseanne's voice sharpened just then? Whatever, he turned away, went through the curtained doorway. Doing as he was told, like a good boy.

Roseanne, serious about her job, was engaging the newcomer in chat while his order was delayed. Sheena marvelled that she bothered. It wasn't that anything would come of it. Roseanne was in a long-standing relationship, even talked of having a kid, once Tom finished his management training at Halford's.

The newcomer was giving Roseanne the story of his life, and she grinning away as if it wasn't the far end of boring. And across the way someone else was hammering on the counter with the edge of a coin, impatient for service.

Sheena sniffed. So even bar work was mostly sweat and hassle. At least in her own job you didn't waste effort on the half-dead.

Sheena pushed her empty glass across the counter. Still with her listening face, Roseanne swivelled to apply it to the vodka optic, added the Martini and pushed it back into Sheena's hand.

'Speak to you later,' Sheena said, counting out the money, slid from the stool and took her drink to sit at a table by the window. She doubted the crowd would thin out, but she knew Roseanne. In duty bound, she'd come over on the excuse of collecting glasses. Liked to keep people happy, daft cow.

Oliver Markham sipped at his lager, making it last, telling himself he wasn't a real drinker; just for the moment needed an anonymous crowd to get lost in. Things were going wrong at work again. You knew when they started watching you that way. Then they'd produced that new woman and told him to show her the ropes. Part of the new policy of making magistrates' courts all mumsy-comfy. This time he could really be on the way out. Not that he wasn't shit-tired of the rotten job anyway.

Smothered in legal lists all day, keeping at bay the pompous and legally qualified while enduring the feckless and unruly, he relished this pub as halfway-house back to an empty flat. Relinquishing Roseanne (and it seemed she'd quite enjoyed the one about the mermaid and the bishop) he turned his back on the bright range of mirrored bottles to take in tonight's wallpaper faces.

Many were known to him; some of their names were too. They shared quite a number of personal histories he could quote if he cared to be indiscreet. These professional secrets in the safety deposit of his mind were little jokes to mull over in his private moments. 'Lord, what fools these mortals be!'

That was Oberon's line. Markham gave his tight little lean-cheeked smile. He'd rather fancy that part, seven feet tall, antler-crowned and draped in filmy woodland colours: one of the bard's most magical characters. Not quite Prospero, but then by the time he got to write *The Tempest* Old Will was almost out of this world.

What would he have made of this crowd here? The men – suburban hempen-homespuns, few of them commuters to London; at most two generations away from artisans, but considering themselves sophisticates. The town had grown faster than their wits. Their big adventure these days was a fiddled tax return; a weekend wife-swap; the family's holiday money blown on a three-legged dead cert at Newmarket. Smallest of small beer, the sort that ended up before him in magistrates' court.

And the women? He looked around – office escapees still tangling with Fred from Accounts or Ted from the next computer; the odd librarian delaying return to a grouchy husband or sullen kids. (No young talent, not at The Crown: there were brighter lights drawing them only streets away.) A couple of slags, and over by the window the Big Lump settling at a table with a fresh drink in her hand, hoping to mingle, pick up some interest. Bored and boring.

Well, he could bore her some more. As an old couple rose from her table he swung his legs from the stool and carried his lager across. 'Mind if I join you?'

Little welcome on the pudgy face, but she made room for him alongside on the padded bench. It amused him not to notice the move, sliding instead on to a chair that faced her. She flicked a glance back at the bar counter, making sure the Filipino noticed someone else was interested.

'I've seen you in here before.'

'Yuh. Just this last week or so.' She reached in her bag for cig-
arettes in a crushed packet, offered him one which he refused.
Then let him light hers from a disposable lighter. She wondered
why he needed it if he wasn't a smoker.

'I carry this for clients,' he emphasized as if she had questioned
it aloud; meaning to get across to her that he was a professional
man. Sheena, knowing exactly what he was, didn't rise to the bait.

'Not new to the town, though?' he probed.

'Me? No. Born here.' She spoke as if it was an infliction. She
waved a vague hand towards the door. 'Other side of town, but I
took on a – a patient close by. This bar's on my way home.'

If he was making out he was a full-blown lawyer, no reason she
couldn't be a qualified nurse. Ramón had swallowed it easily
enough.

'Agency nursing?' Markham sounded impressed.

'Private. One-to-one treatment. Very demanding.'

'Drink up and I'll get you a refill. You must deserve it.'

'Actually, I do.' She batted her short, blond lashes. 'It's been a
long day.'

'So what happens overnight? With your patient, I mean.'

'I have someone else for the graveyard shift.' She wasn't sure
she'd got the term right, but it sounded fancy.

'Nothing much to do then, with the patient asleep,' she amplified. 'And I'm on call at home, see, if there's a need to consult.'

'So it's a critical case?'

'A doddery old lady. Ninety-four next May, if she makes it to
then. Bedridden, special diet, but I have to get her sitting out. Do
everything. Purée her food. Still, you don't want to know.'

Actually he did. Anyone that old who could afford twenty-
four hour attendance would surely have made a will, maybe
appointed a proxy. He wondered which firm of solicitors had
drafted it. His court work made him curious about all legal mat-
ters.

'I'm surprised she lives in the centre of town. Must find the
traffic noisy, what with emergency vehicles from the fire station
and hospital.'

'Oh, you can't hear a thing up there. Enormous triple-glazed windows. It's so quiet it's spooky. Gets on your nerves. Still I've got my tranny and the TV.'

Yes. He could picture her polluting the silence with a ranting television soap or a tinny version of a DJ's histrionic enthusiasms.

'Up there' could only mean the block of luxury apartments above the BMW showrooms. It was the nearest to a residential tower that local planners had permitted. He knew the solicitor who'd dealt with the purchase of the fourth floor flat. The price had made him whistle. This very old lady who owned the penthouse had to be mega-rich.

He reached for the woman's empty glass, stood and took it back with his own to the bar, forgetting to ask what poison she'd been taking. But the barman remembered.

'Vodka Martini. After this she has enough, yes?'

'Just as you say. Mine's a lager, touch of lime.' He counted out the exact money, not begrudging the expense. You never knew when information gathered might be useful. The woman was trash but the connection needn't be.

She had swallowed her drink down before he was halfway through his own, but he wasn't to be hurried. 'So what do you young people do of an evening for entertainment round here?' he asked, presuming on his forty-odd years making her thirty-odd seem juvenile.

'A bit of this and that. There's the theatre, the flicks. Clubbing,' she added hopefully.

Slouching in front of the TV, he guessed. This one would go for the line of least resistance: supper out of a foil container courtesy of an Indian takeaway – unless she had the proverbial old mum chained to the kitchen sink, serving up bangers and mash on a cold, cracked plate.

'Have fun while you can,' he advised. 'For me it's a Hawaiian pizza, a large whisky, and more of the same I've been doing all day.'

'You take work home?' She didn't believe him. Maybe she'd noticed he had no briefcase.

'It's all on the home computer,' he said confidently. He tapped his head. 'What's not in the old noddle.'

Sheena wasn't impressed. He was a court usher. Sort of dogs-body, to her mind. And old with it. Forty-five if he was a day.

Because he'd planted himself down here Roseanne hadn't bothered to come across, so she was cheated of a good natter. And she hadn't had that chance to drop Ramón's name into the conversation.

'Look, I gotta go,' she said on impulse, gathering woollen gloves, scarf, shoulder bag, and lurching out under the table's rocking edge towards the standing crowd. 'Thanks for the drink. Be seeing yuh, eh?'

Gracious she wasn't, Markham regretted. He watched her push through towards the bar counter waving her fingers at Roseanne, go close, bob her head and exchange a few words behind one hand, giggle and be off.

He didn't like that. She shouldn't have giggled. She'd tossed her head in a knowing sort of way and Roseanne had grinned back, darting a look in his direction. A joke at his expense? He felt heat rise up his neck, knew his face was flooded with colour. Bloody woman making a mock of him. He clenched his right fist in his lap. The nails would have marked the flesh if they hadn't been nibbled away.

'Slag,' he said under his breath. The green-striped cotton dress below her fake fur jacket hadn't convinced him she was a nurse. Looked more like a lavatory cleaner.

Chapter Three

Alyson had Emily in the bath, gently pouring water over her shoulders when the buzzer sounded. Dr Stanford was late tonight: she'd more or less given up on him. She reached for the inflated rubber ring kept for emergencies and slipped it under the wasted arms. 'Just for a moment,' she promised.

The CCTV screen in the kitchen showed the familiar face upturned to the exterior camera for identification. She pressed the button for the street door's release, stood the apartment door open and went back to Emily's bathroom. She was lying back in the water, cooing like a dove.

When Dr Stanford stepped out of the lift she had Emily on her feet wrapped in a warm towel, transferred her to the wheelchair and rolled it alongside her freshly made bed. He followed them in and threw off his coat.

'Good evening, ladies. Alyson, you should ask for a mobile lift for getting Emily out of the bath. It's too much for one person.' His robust approach was belied by the dark smudges under his eyes. It had been a long day with some hard decisions.

'Emily's no weight, really. We manage, darling, don't we?' She completed the old lady's transfer to the paper undersheet of the air-bed and pedalled it up to working level.

Stanford adopted a hangdog expression. 'I suppose I'm too late for coffee?'

'Not if you can wait while I do a little something.'

He took a seat across from the bed and watched as Alyson cupped a hand for oil and began gently to massage the birdlike body. 'How does she seem?'

'Why not ask her?'

He spent a few minutes trying to coax a response from the old lady, but she had screwed her mouth into a tight circle and given herself up entirely to the sensation of being smoothed and stroked. At the end she expelled her breath in a long whoosh of contentment.

'Best...' she said. Then, after a few seconds' pause, '...part...of the day.'

'Brilliant,' said Stanford. He had seldom heard her say so

much.

'It is as Emily says: this is her best part of the day. And she is brilliant. You're right.' Alyson went back into the bathroom to wash her hands, calling back over her shoulder, 'Can you stay and talk to Emily while I make our drinks?'

'Right.' He leaned forward confidentially. 'Well, Emily, it's devilish cold outside. Quite a bit of snow underfoot, so you're lucky to be snug in here. And very lucky to have Alyson taking care of you.'

'Martin!' the old lady called out sharply, gazing blindly over his head. 'Martin, get me out of here!'

He reached for her hand. 'Sorry, Emily. I'm Keith, and you're really better off where you are.'

For the first time she looked at him, her eyes focused, but the moment passed even as her lips started to form words. The pupils wandered off. Her eyelids drooped. Another five seconds and she was sound asleep.

'It tires her out,' Alyson said, coming back with their drinks. 'Maybe she should have her bath during the day, but I can't leave it to anyone else.'

'How long will she sleep now?'

'An hour and a half, perhaps two hours. Then I'll feed her and she should get another four hours solid.'

'And you?'

'I'm geared to much the same. I'm a light sleeper. If she's disturbed I hear her in my room through the baby alarm.' She stood there, tray in her hands. 'Let's go through, shall we?'

He wasn't happy about the duties. 'That isn't good enough. Not on top of a day shift in ITU. You're overdoing it.'

She said nothing, knowing he didn't doubt her ability to perform at the hospital, but was concerned for her welfare.

He followed her into the large penthouse lounge, its lights dimmed to preserve the panoramic view, and they sat together looking down at the orange-lit snow, the diminished night traffic.

The town centre lay in a deep bowl which extended uphill on three sides. It made a natural auditorium and she was sometimes reminded of the ancient amphitheatre at Epidauros, imagining an orator below whose every syllable came up clearly to her. Which made the apartment's soundproofing doubly strange. The reality was something between looking down into a goldfish bowl and watching TV with the volume turned off.

Stanford was differently inspired by the scene. 'Toy town,' he said of the diminished streets. 'And you're Rapunzel in her tower.'

'I'm no prisoner. I come and go.' All the same, she admitted to herself, not a lot outside work.

In ITU there wasn't the companionship of an open ward. The nurses, individualists with families and outside interests, didn't party together. Few of her patients were ever capable of speech.

'How's Audrey?' she remembered to ask, not that there was any connection. Or not directly.

'Much the same. Scared, of course.'

At least he appreciated that. Some doctors became desensitized, even about cancer.

'She pretends it doesn't matter about losing her hair, but...'

'It must be very hard when you've been so beautiful. She still is, of course. But I can understand the horror.'

'There are other aspects she hasn't fully confronted yet. At least, I think not. Trouble is we don't talk. Never did really. Not about basic issues.' He slid both hands round the mug and lifted it to sniff at its contents. 'What's this? Ovaltine?'

'I'm not giving you caffeine at this time of night. You work hard too; you need to switch off.'

Wish I could do it here, he thought wryly: just curl up with my head on your gentle shoulder. I'd be good, really I would. For a while, anyway. But don't tempt me.

He sighed. 'Guess I'd better make tracks.' He swallowed the drink down, hot and milky. 'I'm off on a course in a couple of days. So after tomorrow I won't be in for a week. Dougie will cover for me, if that's all right. Anything you need, any change you observe, just ring him.'

'Right. Make a complete break of it, if you can.' She wondered what arrangements he'd made for keeping an eye on Audrey. She'd surely have protested at his need to be away from home.

She saw him to the door. Stanford left and she went back to the window, waiting until, a dark shape against the snow, he eventually crossed by the traffic island, stopped and looked back, face tilted upwards.

With the room dim behind her she doubted he could see her, but still he raised a hand, and she did the same back.

Mind how you go, Keith.

The little ormolu clock in the hall struck midnight. Tomorrow already. She went through to look in on Emily asleep. Her face was calm. She looked immeasurably wise.

In her almost ninety-four years she had known three generations, outlived their changes. What tales she might tell if only she were able.

Keith Stanford pulled the collar of his black overcoat up to his ears and trudged round the outer wall of the college to the hospital car park. His red Volvo was plumply quilted with snow on roof and bonnet. Abandoned there half the day, its locks had frozen over and his de-icer was in the glove compartment.

He hunkered alongside, breathing hard on the driver's door lock, then tried with the key. A few tactical wrigglings and the ice reluctantly yielded. He reached in for the plastic blade to scrape the frost off windscreen and mirrors. It took a few minutes with the engine running for the interior to warm, but he was in no hurry to get home. There had been three text messages from Audrey on his cellphone in the last four hours but it was pointless to reply. By now she should know how it went, emergency building on emergency; even more so in tricky weather like this.

Over the twelve years of their marriage she had never learnt how to cope on her own. Once, as a young bride, her dependence had delighted and flattered him, but his career didn't allow for the great chunks of time she demanded in his company. Nor had he managed to divert her interest elsewhere. None of the clubs or hobbies he'd suggested had kept her interest for more than a few weeks. It was much the same with acquaintances. The faces of women who appeared occasionally in his home were constantly changing. Those with positive lives soon ran short of patience with her, and she had wit enough to avoid any of her own kind requiring efforts made on their behalf. He was quietly ashamed that when her cancer had been diagnosed he'd seen it as yet one more tentacle she reached out with to bind him close. It was as well after all that they'd never had children.

As he drove it seemed that the stars were going out one by one. If it clouded over completely the frost would be less severe, and the forecasters had been warning of more snow. Audrey hated the winter, kept on about taking a break in Madeira, Florida, anywhere but Britain. He couldn't spare time to get away himself, and she refused to go on her own or with friends. By late May, when their holiday was booked, she could be weaker. Perhaps he could persuade the practice manager to grant him something earlier, on compassionate grounds. Not that that excuse would carry much weight with Bullock, his senior partner. And God only knew what extra time he'd have to take off when things reached the final phase.

The car was climbing towards open country. After the close-packed Victorian terraces had come more substantial houses set apart, then occasional dark woodland, bare orchards, ploughed fields. His own home had once been a farmhouse, seventeenth century, retaining many of the romantic features that delight house agents and prove less beguiling for modern living.

It was what Audrey had once set her heart on, but over the years so many alien elements had been introduced to the original structure that it now made him think of a wrinkled crone under layers of make-up and tottering on stiletto heels.

It appeared ahead through winter-bare trees; not just the porch light guiding him in, but every window defiantly ablaze as a rebuke to him that she was unable to sleep in face of his persistent neglect.

It would not be a smiling welcome. But then, he'd had that already, served up with sympathy and a nursery drink.

He was smiling to himself as he turned into the dip of the driveway. Then he saw the flashing blue lights and the cars drawn up by the entrance. Dougie was on the doorstep, pulling on his driving gloves, about to leave.

'Audrey?' Keith demanded, bursting from the car as it finished slewing on ice.

'Not as bad as it might have been,' his partner said shortly. 'I'm sending her into hospital for the night. I want Ashton to assess her.'

'What's she done?'

'Changed her mind at the last minute, fortunately,' Dougie said. 'Sat in the bath to slash her wrists, with her mobile phone alongside. I've fixed her injuries up, but she was in a right old pickle otherwise. Sedated now, but asking for you. You'd better go along with her, old chap.'

'Of course.' He turned towards the ambulance, then remembered the house and the lighted windows. 'Who's inside?'

'Mike Yeadings. He's just checking things out and he's got your spare keys, so you can leave it to him. His wife's with Audrey in the ambulance, but she'll need to get home for her children. A neighbour's minding them.'

'Right. Thanks, Dougie, for coming out. What a god-awful mess.' Ashen-faced he approached the emergency vehicle. The paramedic at the wheel hung out of the window. 'Sorry, doc. Your car.'

'Blocking the way. Yes, sorry.' He stumbled back to it, put it in gear and reversed into a clearing by some laurels. He switched off, put his face in his hands and waited for his shaking to steady. Then he walked over and climbed up into the familiar antiseptic smell which Audrey so detested.

'Nan,' he said to the woman seated beside the stretcher, 'this is so good of you. How is she?'

'Everything's under control,' was the answer. 'She'll be fine now you're here.'

'I had my mobile switched off,' he mumbled.

'Understandably. She tried your partner next, and then us.'

'Audrey rang you?'

'Nearest neighbours she knew would understand,' Nan said comfortably. 'She probably remembered I'd been a nurse once.'

Or that Mike is a senior policeman, Keith thought grimly. That would have been no coincidence. And no more than I deserved. God, why didn't I see all this building up?

Chapter Four

The first phone call next morning came at 10.15. Emily was lightly sleeping again after being washed, fed and monitored. Alyson had prepared ahead her purées for the day's meals, all blended to a regrettable sludge of varying brownish greys or foggy yellow, although nourishing and as palatable as possible. She slid their tray into the fridge and lifted the kitchen phone.

A woman's voice replied when she gave the number. 'I have Mr Timothy Fitt for you. One moment, please.'

There was a pause with a metallic *clank* and paper rustling while Alyson pictured the solicitor, small, fussy, myopic, his hands forever in nervous movement, searching, patting, sorting. She'd always thought of his name as a contraction of Fidget.

'A-a-ah.' A long-drawn sigh. 'Miss – er, Orme.'

'Mr Fitt.'

'Yes. Well, how are you, m'dear? And Miss Withers, of course.'

What could she say? – both fine?

'There is no noticeable change in Emily's condition, Mr Fitt. She's reasonably comfortable, given the circumstances.'

'No deterioration, then?'

Did he sound disappointed? She observed he didn't pursue further inquiries about her own health.

'Emily? No. In fact at times she seems briefly aware of her surroundings. If the family requires a full report I am sure Dr Stanford will be pleased to furnish one in writing.'

'No! No, no, no.' An initial squeak, descending an octave *diminuendo*. 'Oh no, not at all. I am sure your opinion will suffice without validation.'

Validation? Lawspeak, she supposed. Even in the negative it sounded slighting. She let a short silence build without demanding. Is that all?

'Yes. Quite,' the solicitor bleated. 'Well it was pleasant to speak with you again, Miss – er, er...'

'Orme,' she told him, and spelled it out.

'Exactly. Goodbye.'

'And perhaps "thank you",' she murmured for him as he cut

the call. It was uncharitable to despise him for the way he let others use him, but she had a nurse's acquired distaste for families who contacted patients through a third or fourth party, and the feeling leaked back on to him.

The phone rang the instant she replaced the receiver. 'Guess what!' invited Gina, trainee receptionist in A&E.

'No idea, Gina. Visit from a Royal?'

'Next best. Mega-scandal! New case for you in ITU. No less than Keith Stanford's wife Audrey. Seems she OD'ed on something heavy, probably diamorphine. The good doctor brought her in overnight and now he's gone off with the police.'

'Gina, discretion! I hope you can't be overheard.' The rebuke was instinctive even while her flesh rippled with sudden chill. She heard again Keith's voice; the words, 'She's scared…some aspects she hasn't fully confronted yet.'

Even as he'd confided that, his wife could have been facing up to the truth, trying to deal with her ghosts alone, and failing. But where had she obtained the drug? She wasn't allowed to administer it herself. Surely Keith hadn't been so careless as to leave the morphine where she could find it. And just when had she taken it? During the night, or so early that when he arrived home it was almost too late to reverse it?

He had sat on here, talking companionably, even relaxing a little, while just a few miles away Audrey could have been taking her own life. Had his returning so late made a near-fatal difference? Had she expected him to find her earlier? And was it a true wish to die or a further means of moral blackmail?

But Gina was a great scandalmonger and more often than not got her facts wrong. She would not have been given access to case notes and merely assumed the OD from Mrs Stanford's appearance when brought in. Despite the clerical trainee's guesswork, Audrey might be in coma, as a further stage of her illness. However it was, Keith must be facing the horror of suddenly losing her.

Alyson stared round the kitchen and it seemed to have changed in some indefinable way, tilted to a different perspective. Replacing the handset, she put her free hand against the wall to steady herself.

What was the next thing she'd intended doing? Run the vacuum cleaner round the apartment. It seemed not to matter now. She walked past where she had left the machine in the hall, and continued on to her observation point. Outside, it was snowing again. Large, lazy flakes like white feathers were already settling over the earlier fall.

She was due to take over in ITU at one-thirty. Three hours to fill and she'd meant to clean the apartment before Sheena arrived; but, even as she reminded herself, she seated herself close to the window and gazed down on the diminished world outside. She saw the ghost of a dark figure cross the road, step on to the further pavement, turn, look back and raise a hand in salute. Strangely, it had the fearful impact of finality.

She forced herself to leave the compulsive screen and robotically set about tidying the rooms. Sheena arrived in a flouncy mood, perhaps fantasizing as one of her pop-scene celebrities. Alyson had neither time nor inclination to humour her. There were no fresh instructions to issue.

On the way to work she picked up a plastic box of salad and some slices of smoked salmon, but still she was there ten minutes early. 'You've heard, then?' Bernice guessed as she entered.

'Gina rang me. How's our new patient?'

'Barely with us, but if you want to go straight through you could try talking to her. See if you get a reaction. She's lost a lot of blood.'

'Blood? What happened then? I heard it was an OD.'

'That'll be Gina, picking up the arse end of everything. No, Mrs S sat in a warm bath to slit her wrists, then rang round the neighbours for help. Including a senior policeman. Keith was in earlier. He's gone now to make a statement.'

Alyson knew Bernice would have accessed all information available. It was more appalling than she'd been led to believe. She shed her outer clothes, put her purchases in a sterile bag and found a place for it in the ward fridge.

Back in the therapy unit Audrey Stanford, ashen and limp, lay on her back in a bed where old Mr Fennell's had stood last night.

Beside it a blood bag and a saline drip were suspended from an IV stand. In the next cubicle was a young male crack OD who'd also been transferred from A&E overnight. Notes on him probably accounted for Gina's confusion over Audrey's condition.

On the whiteboard young Dr McLean's cabalistic signs recorded his monitoring of the young man's body fluids. Since he wasn't padding about between the five occupied beds she assumed he was in the broom-cupboard space of the designated restroom, sleeping off the rigours of the night. He'd have set his alarm in time for the next readings. Nobody could fault his devotion to duty. He was a puppy of the faithful-hound type, all bounding clumsiness and unbounded adoration for herself.

Alyson bent over the woman's bed. 'Audrey, it's Alyson Orme. You're with us in ITU and doing really well. Keep at it. We're all with you.'

There was no reaction. Alyson straightened and turned away. They needed Keith here. If he brought in his wife's favourite CDs they could play music quietly for her comfort, with the headset on her pillow. She wasn't strictly an emergency any more, but keeping her in ITU ensured a certain degree of privacy when all private rooms were in use elsewhere. And here the consultant from Psychiatry could observe her discreetly.

Where was Keith now? She imagined he'd gone home after seeing the police and would snatch a few hours of rest. Better not risk a phone call waking him. He would certainly come when he was ready, or ring in for a progress report.

Sheena Judd was feeling distinctly elated. Having left home straight after an early lunch with the declared intention of walking to work, she had instead taken a bus from the stop beyond her usual one (which could be overlooked from home) and got off at The Crown. It was the quiet before their midday rush and Ramón was polishing glasses. There was no sign of Roseanne.

'Hi,' she said, as if to an old friend.

The man's face stayed unmoving. 'Vodka Martini, yes?'

'Actually I fancy something different this time.' (Never let them think you're predictable, the style magazine had advised: to be unpredictable is to be feminine.) 'So what do you recommend?'

'Uh' That had foxed him: so, good!

'You try something I invent, perhaps?'

'I'll trust you, many wouldn't.' Being provocative for a change.

It came the colour of Mum's cough mixture. Not too far off the same taste too. Or what she imagined the taste would be, going by the smell. 'Great,' she lied. 'I could get hooked on this.'

It had the desired effect. Perhaps flattered, he left the polishing and rested his elbows on the bar counter opposite her. 'Roseanne not in?' she asked him.

'She come in at three. Relief me, yes?'

'Relieves,' she corrected him. 'I go on duty at one. When you come off, why not drop in and have a coffee on the house?' She beamed expansively. 'Actually dropping *up*'s more like it. It's the penthouse over the car showrooms. Hit the lift button for the seventh floor. Come up and admire the view. We're on top of the world there.'

He was looking inscrutable and that irritated her, counting on some reciprocal matiness. But behind the impassive, square features he must have been considering the invitation. 'Perhaps I find time after I finish.'

'Great. There's an entry-phone at the outer door. Just ring and whisper "Ramón" into it and I'll release the door lock.'

'I know how these things work.' Did the stupid woman think he had never been anywhere? She should have seen Hong Kong with its real towers. This female lump and her petty seventh floor!

Feeling she'd scored, Sheena drank up and pushed her glass back for a refill. Ramón glanced past her to two men in overalls who'd just come in, moved along the bar and served them. He didn't seem in a hurry to come back. Sheena raised her glass above her head and called, 'Pour it again, Sam.'

Of course he'd never heard of *Casablanca*. Instead she got more of the blank-eyed look as he repeated the drink. She glanced at her watch, frowned and downed the brown stuff in one. It seemed even stronger. She felt it hit, warm inside, and hiccuped. 'The mixture as before,' she excused herself jokily.

He nodded, again at sea with the quotation.

'Like it says on medicine bottles,' it was necessary to explain.

'Yes,' woodenly.

Not the sort for repartee, but perhaps that made him a man of action. 'Well, must be off.' She reached the door, turned, waved her brown wool gloves at him saucily. 'Be seeing you.'

'Indeed.'

She'd made it; won the promise of some diversion to get her through the boring hours of waiting on a near-corpse. Who could tell what impression the luxury apartment would have on Ramón? The style was a bit bare for her taste, but you couldn't escape the whiff of big money that came off it.

For once Sheena arrived with some enthusiasm for her stint of duty at Emily's penthouse, impatient for Alyson to be gone. The moment she heard the lift go down Sheena let herself into the nurse's bathroom and sniffed at the bottles. There was a new moisturising bath crème with a fresh floral scent. Running the mixer tap for water, she poured in enough to give a rich foam. (If Alyson noticed the lower level in the bottle she'd explain she needed a bath after cleaning up the old crone.)

Cosy afterwards in a new fluffy bath towel, she nudged with a toe her pile of cast-off clothes. In Alyson's bedroom she helped herself to a silky kimono and posed in it before the full-length mirrors of the wall-length wardrobe. She wished she'd let her hair grow, but it was more bother that way. She ran oiled hands through it now to make it stand up spiky, giving more height.

Still an hour and twenty minutes before she could hope to hear Ramón buzz from downstairs. The drinks he'd mixed for her were making her thirsty. Should she make herself coffee now or wait until he was there? At least get a tray ready; fill the kettle, find some biscuits or cake. Only, of course, Alyson didn't do sweet things. There were crackers to go with cheese, but they looked like something you'd buy for a dog.

With old Emily asleep and snoring on her back, she could safely go for a spot of shut-eye herself. She checked that her makeup had survived the bath – no call to wash above the neckline – and spread herself over the freshly made bed. The goose-down duvet smelled delicately of floral laundry freshener. She snuggled her nose in it, decided she might lose heat exposed outside, and eased herself under. She closed her eyes on the memory of Ramón's face, like polished cherry wood, smiling. Only he didn't smile, did he? Maybe, though, she'd find a way to get him going.

The buzzer stung her awake and she started up, couldn't grasp where she was. In her dream she'd been back home in the kitchen. Ma had been rowing with her over something and Uncle Chaz had stuck his oar in. Only Chaz had been dead a couple of years, lungs rotted away with those filthy old fags he never stopped smoking. She'd offered him a spliff once but he wasn't for changing. One of them was worth twenty of the stenchy stuff he used to roll himself.

She turned over, put both hands to her aching head, then heard it again. Ramón, she remembered. She hadn't meant to drop right off like that. Now she'd look a mess and…

She bundled the robe round her, retied the sash and ran to activate the door release and let the man in below. Would he remember it was the seventh floor? She didn't want anyone to see him on the way up. God, it was nearly four o'clock: she'd been out to the wide and felt all the worse for it. She stared in the hall mirror, pinched her cheeks to bring back some colour, and tugged at her hair. She heard the lift arrive and the soft susurration of the doors opening. The doorbell shrilled.

He had brought her flowers. They weren't much: a small bunch of those screwed-up, dark anemone buds that you could never be sure would open properly. Still, it was something, and she hadn't expected them. He was as deadpan as ever, but she'd admit he did seem curious, wanting to see everything, Emily's room included.

She left him in there while she went to fill the cafetière and could hear him opening cupboards and moving things about.

Still barely emerging from a dream, Emily came half-awake, impatient, consumed with longing for something indefinable, out of reach. It was like being young again and knowing a terrible need while unable to tell what it was her heart cried out for. If only she could see it, remember. She needed, needed...wanted so much. What?

To be free.

And then, in an instant, she was. As in a trance state, suddenly nothing was impossible. With no limits, no restraints, she was running through sparse autumn woodland, her face turned up to drink in the gentle rain; yet she had no face, no limbs, no body. Despite that she could feel it all. And it was wonderful. Such energy, such passion, such an overwhelming urge towards...

There was no future, no past, now was eternal, with the need to be running, to feel the cool fingers of rain stroking and tickling; to be at one with it and the woodland which now seemed familiar. And in a clearing ahead there was the ghost of a swing that hung on long chains from a tree, still gently swaying as if a child had just jumped off. Herself perhaps.

She looked down for her winged, shimmering feet, silver in the rain but immaterial. She was totally invisible. Just spirit.

A soul? No she mustn't believe in souls, the religious sort. It would be too awful if they were real and all that business about hellfire punishment.

Then, 'I am Emily,' she croaked defiantly, claiming what she suddenly knew was true. 'I am almost ninety-four years old.'

And the magic dissolved. She was back again in barely damped-down pain, frustrated. Trapped in a diseased body. In a square room with walls she couldn't see through.

Someone had come into the room and stood looking down on her. It was a man, a stranger, wearing a white jacket. She was suddenly afraid, closed her eyes, but could hear him moving about, opening and shutting drawers. She called for someone to come, to get her out of here. No matter who. Any of them.

She ran through their names but couldn't recall their faces. 'Martin, Dolly!' And there was another, but it had vanished from her mind. She opened her eyes. And the man had gone silently away.

Ramón joined Sheena in the kitchen, where he'd shed his parka on arriving, and carried the tray through to the front window, just like a waiter in a grand hotel. He looked like it too, still in his white tunic with the coloured epaulettes.

'So whatcha think?' Sheena demanded, offering him the snow-scene panorama with a sweep of one arm. He leaned forward to look down on the circulating traffic, then straightened to take his bearings from the perspective of distant hills.

'You can't see the pub,' she warned. 'It's behind that corner with the Natwest Bank on. That's the college opposite, and the hospital. Fire station's over there. You can't see much of the river. It's best at night. There's a patch of dark where the lights aren't.'

He nodded. 'And right below, at this side? A low building.'

'That's Elston's, a stationery and office warehouse. You would-n't have seen it from the road because there's a high wall all round, except for the side opening on Carlisle Street. The coun-cil have been trying to buy them out and build there, but they won't have it.'

'Wise,' he said. 'Worth a lot to keep.'

'I bet somebody'll have enough money for it some day.' Casually she lit up a spliff, acting sophisticated, but he scarcely noticed.

'It has a big car park,' he said. 'Empty, almost.'

'That's because they keep it clear for goods coming in. The delivery trucks are huge; come from all over Europe. So if other people leave their cars there they could get clamped. You often see a row going on down there with drivers who think they can sneak in and park for free. That's just in the daytime, though.'

But Ramón appeared to have lost interest. Sheena swirled the robe's overlong skirt off her feet and sat opposite him, offering a sight of chubby knee. She crossed one leg over the other to reveal a stretch of thigh, then discovered she couldn't pour coffee in that position.

'I do that,' Ramón offered. 'More my job.' He twisted the tray towards him on the low coffee table. 'You say how you like.'

'Hot and strong,' she told him, in time stopping herself utter-ing the trite old 'just like my men.' Something told her it would have been a mistake. 'You don't have to work overtime,' she said instead.

'Is no hard work here for you,' he observed, gazing around. 'The old lady call for other people. Not you.'

'Well, I'm all she's got here right now. Was she awake then?'

'No. I think she dream.'

'About dead people. All her lot are dead but her. She's as old as the hills.'

'She has no family?'

'*Miss* Withers. She never married. There are some great-nephews and nieces, I think. But nobody's bothered about her. None of them ever come to visit. Still, she's not that interesting. Tell me about you.'

That'll get him, she thought. There's nothing puffs any man up like talking about himself.

If anything, his face became more closed.

Chapter Five

Ramón drank up his coffee.

'That was good.' Which was true. Even this unappetizing woman couldn't ruin the superior Italian blend. He drew its aroma in through narrowed nostrils, to drown out the stench of her reefer.

She grinned smugly back at him. 'Nice place, innit?'

'That is good too.'

He was no conversationalist but she still had hopes of him. She'd leave him to make the first move. Maybe he was shy, strictly brought up. They were Catholics out in the Philippines, weren't they? And except for the blagging Irish sort, she'd always thought RCs a bit tied down by their images and rule books. Actually he was staring at her legs now. She swished the skirts of the silk kimono coyly back over her ankles.

And at that point the apartment doorbell shrilled. Not the buzzer from downstairs, so it had to be the doctor. He was the only one told the code for the electronic entry. But he'd never called out of the blue before. Always phoned ahead.

'Oh my God,' she blurted, 'it's the doc. 'He can't find us like this. You'll hafta hide somewhere.'

The Filipino gave her his deadpan stare. 'I talk to him. You go dress.'

'You can't...' But then why not? His uniform jacket was quite like one of the male care assistants at Alyson's hospital. Maybe he'd pass as one moonlighting.

The bell sounded again, with shrill persistence. Ramón reached up to slide open a panel in the glass wall and the wind rushed in. Sheena grabbed the tray and fled to the kitchen. With the door open a crack she could hear talking as Ramón let the visitor in.

It was a woman.

The voices were low, words indistinguishable. The woman was introducing herself, excusing her unexpected visit. 'On a sudden whim,' she said more loudly as they passed from the hall towards Emily's room.

Alyson hadn't mentioned any Health Visitor calling. She saw

to all that herself. And why let the woman know the street-door code? It was out of order. Sheena stood tense, gripping the edge of the door. They were in Emily's bedroom now and their voices no more than a murmur.

A few minutes passed and then there were footsteps coming towards the kitchen. Sheena shrank back in the space behind the door. But it was only Ramón.

'She smell the coffee. I make her some.' He started rinsing the used cafetière and resetting the tray.

'But who is she? What does she want?'

'To see Emily. Her grandmother, she say.'

'It can't be. Emily hasn't any family.' But hadn't she? There were great-nieces and great-nephews who never bothered to visit. Ramón could have got it wrong, no good at English, mixed up the relations. But not a granddaughter; couldn't be. *Miss* Withers after all. With a bastard child her generation, so namby-pamby, would have covered up with calling herself *Mrs*.

'That is what the lady say. Out the way, please. I need cup and saucer.'

She let him complete his preparations, smooth and professional. Waiter, barman or stand-in nurse. The woman, whoever she was, had accepted him without question.

Rachel Howard stared down at the old, old woman and felt nothing. It hadn't been like that as she'd entered the hall. Then so much emotion had flooded her that afterwards there was a void left. It was because of the carving, still around after so many years; still able to transport her instantly back into childhood, to all its lost glories and agonies.

She went back and picked it up, felt its weight and the hard, irregular outlines. The intricate carving, in dark, polished wood, was thought to be Chinese. As long as Rachel remembered, it had lived in the hall on the occasional table where Grandmother used to sort the post: three wizened little monkeys squatting in a row. One had its paws over its eyes, the second over its ears and the third over its mouth.

Since long before she learned that the three represented See No Evil, Hear No Evil and Speak No Evil, Rachel had seen the

carving as a lucky mascot and never missed touching it as she
went out of the house. At sixteen she had still done it, still smiled
recalling Martin's corny reaction to the description 'occasional'
for the piece of furniture it stood on: 'What's it do when it isn't
a table, then?' he'd demanded.

That first time, a Saturday, it had amused them all the long
walk to the library, making up stories of wild adventures that the
thing got up to when it wasn't on duty in her grandmother's
Victorian hall.

That last, awful morning she had missed touching it, passing at
speed because she was late and it wouldn't be Bert that day on the
school bus. When Bert drove he understood how she was held
back by Dolly at the breakfast-room window until the tea cup
was drained, even as she watched the bus turn in at Dimarco's
corner stop. Then he'd pull away and dawdle while she raced out
and ahead, scarf and school bag flying, to the bit where Kilmarnie
Lane narrowed with trade vans parked, and she could swing on
board as he footled through at five miles an hour.

Once seated, though, she was different, sophisticated, wordly-
wise, casual about the admiration of the giggling little third-for-
mers. She never finished homework on the journey, while they
swapped answers to Algebra or cribbed others' Latin translations.
Hers was all done properly at home, and most of it, she knew,
would be correct.

She felt bile rise in her throat, thrust the wretched object back
between a small brass gong and the framed photograph of
Arthur's Seat. The thing's power had run out that day when both
parents were killed in the light aircraft crashing on the Pentlands.
And Emily had taken over her life.

Ramón carried out the reset tray and found the woman in the vast
livingroom admiring the paintings. Sheena slipped out of the
kitchen, back to retrieve her clothes and sit waiting impatiently
on the side of the rumpled bed for sounds of the visitor's departure.

She had given Ramón her card, as a sort of justification for
barging in: Rachel Howard, with an address at some gallery in
Edinburgh.

'Scottish?' Sheena insisted when he showed it to her later. But Ramón knew nothing of British geography or accents. The only snatch of conversation Sheena had caught just sounded snooty. Anything else was left for Alyson to work out.

'What did she look like?' Sheena demanded. She'd need to describe the woman, as if she'd been there herself to let her in.

He said simply, 'Tall lady, very fine.'

'You mean well-dressed?'

'That, yes, too. Thin, very straight.'

'How old would you say?'

'Forty or more. Forty-five, but well...'

'Well preserved? Good-looking?'

'Like Emily, but black hair, younger.'

Surely that would be enough to satisfy Alyson, unless unluckily she was ever to meet the woman and be told who'd let her in.

'Did she say she'd call again?' For godsake, she was having to drag every stinking word out of the man.

'She telephone your boss.'

'Alyson Orme? Did she mention her by name?'

'She call her that, yes. I go now.'

She had overdone the inquisition and he was turning resentful. Well, let him. She'd wasted enough time on him already and she had to set the place straight again and get the old girl seen to. Just one more question, though, to be on the safe side. 'Did she say anything special?'

He paused, pulling on his parka, and thought. 'She is pleased with open window. Better than air condition. Good for invalid.'

'She actually said that? There was half a blizzard blowing in!'

'But it clean the air. I open it to kill smell of marijuana.' He treated her again to his blank stare and then took his leave.

'Kill old Emily, more like,' Sheena said aloud. Maybe that was what the family wanted. Rich old doll. She was making them wait too long for reading her will.

Alyson had lumbered herself with an umbrella. As she halted to open it outside the supermarket, a spike caught in the loop of the carrier over her arm and the handle tore, spilling out some groceries. She bit back on 'Sh –' and turned it to 'Sugar!'. Crouching to pick up the strays she heard a chuckle of sympathy.

'Let me help you,' said the man, bending to swoop on a packet of frozen duck portions and a box of eggs. His face loomed close to hers, handsome enough; good teeth; dark hair with a streak of silver at the temples. Standing up, he was tall too. All the ingredients for a fairground fortune-teller's extravagant promises.

A pity I've no time for fairy tales, Alyson thought cynically.

He was looking down at his hands. 'I'm afraid some of the eggs are rather bent. It seems you're halfway to an omelette. Just get under shelter here and I'll fetch you a fresh carrier.'

Courteous, and practical with it, she noted, thanking him. He strode off, returned happily waving one of the supermarket's tougher bags. She was feeling a fool by then, unused to being at the reception end of heroics.

'Thank you. You've been very kind,' she said firmly as he reopened the brolly and offered to carry the transferred packages. 'I've no distance to go at all. I can manage now.'

'I'm sure you can.' It was said smiling and, suspecting he was amused by her, she nodded coolly and moved away. She felt his eyes following her until the turn of the street, relieved at the nearness of the hospital. She'd likely not ever see him again.

She left it to Bernice when Keith came in to visit Audrey. He looked terrible, drawn and grey, seeming to have aged overnight.

'Have they been in yet from Psychiatry?' he asked before going to the bedside.

'No,' Bernice told him. 'They'll leave it until she's up. Luckily we had a free bed, since there's no single room on offer. It would be cruel to send her to an open ward.'

'Hello, love,' he said quietly, leaning over his wife. 'How's it going?'

His shoulders blocked out a view of her face. 'You gave us all quite a shock.'

Audrey said nothing. Punishing him still, Alyson thought, trying not to feel anger. There was no further chance to watch events because she was needed at the young OD's bedside to record his BP. Still in coma; the stomach pump had taken out almost all that was left of life in the skinny little body.

His name, according to a debit card on him, was Eric Allbright, but she doubted it was his own. More likely stolen. The signature on its reverse had been too adult. Suspecting the same, the police had taken it, but left the one crisp, unused note issued from a cash machine. A beat constable had found him overnight among the dustbins on a rundown housing estate. On the whiteboard the name was recorded with a query.

His heart rate was up a little. Encouraged, she removed the urine bag and labelled it with name and time, for analysis. They might be beating this one after all.

Bernice made instant coffee for Keith. He sat crouched at Audrey's bedside with the polystyrene beaker at his feet, the drink going cold. It wouldn't do much for him, Alyson reflected. Keith's accepted fix was a double espresso, even sometimes at night. He worked hard over long hours, must be dog-tired when he reached home.

Which was possibly at the root of Audrey's complaint. But not my concern, Alyson warned herself, shying away from any image of the Stanfords' intimate moments. She pulled on fresh latex gloves and went to look for the plastic sack containing the young addict's vomit-stained clothing. There was still hope of some clue to his background. If she could trace family or friends, a familiar voice might speed his struggle back to consciousness.

She pulled out the unlovely assortment: string vest, T-shirt, cut-off jeans and a thick, purplish sweater, socks, trainers. Surprisingly good quality, but nothing waterproof, she noticed. Usually derelicts brought in during the winter months had something to keep the weather out. She couldn't believe he had survived sleeping rough with just this lot. So he belonged somewhere indoors; maybe with a group who would wonder what had become of him.

There was a tapping on the glass panel of the ward door. Alyson removed her gloves, slid open the blinds and surveyed the young woman waiting outside. Through the intercom she asked for identification.

In reply a warrant card appeared: Detective Sergeant Rosemary Zyczynski of Thames Valley Police. Pretty and slim, with dark eyes.

'Come in,' Alyson invited. 'You might be the very person I'm looking for now.'

'Why? What's up?'

She had a warm smile, brown curls cut close, and a hooded anorak in burnt orange. About my own age, Alyson judged. And a sergeant, so – good at her job.

'Have you come about my mystery young man?'

Zyczynski considered her. 'Actually, no. My boss asked me to look up Mrs Stanford. He saw her before she was brought in. Took her panic phone call.'

'She phoned the police?'

'They're neighbours. I guess she meant to contact his wife, but they both went round to help. Mrs Yeadings was once a Sister at the old Westminster.'

'Thank heaven Audrey had enough sense for that.'

The detective nodded. 'It sounds as though you know Mrs Stanford.'

'Her husband's a GP. I met her socially through him.'

'I see. Look, don't let me hold you back. I know hell's always a-poppin' in here.'

'That's one way to describe it. Actually Keith's   Dr Stanford's – here with his wife at the moment. Come through and see him. But I'm afraid I can't let you question Audrey. Not at present, anyway.'

'Fair enough. A goodwill message from my boss will do for the present.'

Keith had looked up as he heard their voices. Now he rose and came across, smiling wearily. 'Z, you haven't come about my wife, have you? It was quite straightforward. Superintendent Yeadings could tell you what happened.'

'He did. He sent me to see how she is. Nan would have come herself but she's tied up with the toddler's sight and hearing tests.'

'She's going to be all right. From this, I mean. You know the cancer's terminal? The truth's really reaching her now. I'll have to spend more time at home with her.'

'I didn't know. I'm so sorry.' Her shock seemed genuine. In the awkward pause that followed, Alyson asked, 'So you know each other?'

'We meet professionally,' Keith admitted, 'when I stand in as police surgeon.'

Zyczynski nodded. 'I'll not get in your way, doctor. Try and get some sleep yourself. You look dead on your feet. Goodbye.'

On her way out she turned back to Alyson. 'You said you had a mystery young man. Is there anything I can do?'

'I'm not sure. The constable who brought him in as an OD took away a debit card he had. I doubt it would be his, since he's a junkie. I mean…'

'Not old or affluent enough to have his own account? So, he's nameless?'

'That's one problem. I was just going through his clothes to see if there's any clue. Would you like to look? That's more in your line than mine.'

'Why not? Can I take a look at him too? Maybe I've seen him hanging around with dealers.'

'It's family visits only, but he's out cold so he'll never know. Come on then.' They stood either side of the young man's bed. 'He's only a boy really,' Alyson said. 'What do you think?'

Zyczynski was frowning. 'There's something familiar, but I can't place him. Seen him in court possibly. Or at the nick when he wasn't quite such a mess. But maybe it's just a type. Don't you despair of them coming in like this time and time again?'

'Don't you?'

She smiled. 'I haven't your patience.' She leaned forward and read the ID card clipped to Alyson's pocket. 'Alyson Orme. D'you know, it was once a toss up for me between nursing and the police. I think I chose the right career.'

'I certainly did. Here, put some gloves on if you're touching his things.'

She left the policewoman to find out what she could. Keith was hovering at the door, ready to go. 'She won't have anything to do with me,' he said tightly. 'I might as well go home and leave her simmering.'

'And the course you were going on?'

'Can't leave, naturally. But while she's safe here with you, I can carry on working. Have to arrange, though, for when she comes out. See what the shrinks say.'

The one thing she wanted to ask was whether it had been a genuine attempt by Audrey to end her life.

As if he'd heard the silent question he said, 'It may just have been the proverbial cry for help. On the other hand she may have meant it at the time, then changed her mind.

'The saddest thing is that I'd do anything in my power to give the help she needs, only it's too late. Nothing left but TLC and see she's not in too much pain.'

'She's adamant still about the hospice?'

'Won't hear it mentioned. Quite final.' He shook his head. 'It has to be me. I must go through it with her. I guess that's what marriage is about. No alternative.'

'I'm sorry, Keith.'

'I know. Meanwhile, I'll be in to see Emily this evening, early as I can make it.'

She ought to tell him not to bother, but she didn't. 'I'll save you some supper.'

'That'd be nice. I'll ring you.' And he was gone.

Alyson returned to Rosemary Zyczynski and the plastic sack of soiled clothing.

'What do you make of this?' the detective asked, holding up a scuffed, once-white trainer. 'Did you happen to look under the lining?'

Chapter Six

The wind had backed during the afternoon, bringing Atlantic clouds and giving a brief, illusory sense of warmth. By evening the snow, no longer white, was being churned to unlovely slush. Drains, blocked with ice and debris, couldn't take the overflow. Car tyres hissed, flinging up sheets of greasy water to drench pedestrians waiting to cross at the traffic island. Among them Alyson ducked back as a wave swept up from a van that challenged their right of way. She made it safely to her own side of the complex.

Home, she thought, letting herself in; and had to smile at her own complacence. She hadn't a home. Not since Gran's death when at eighteen she'd come up to London, hub of the universe, to study nursing at St Thomas's.

This was Emily's home; yet Alyson had the illusion of belonging, because of the relationship, tenuous though it was. Emily being Gran's elder sister meant something when you'd no other family.

Sadly, the old lady couldn't last forever, but Alyson had never regretted transferring, qualified, to this Thames Valley hospital and moving in here on the solicitor's invitation. To be well paid for caretaking in a luxury pad was a bonus, and the hospital authority hadn't objected to her taking it on.

And then there was Emily herself.

She walked up the first three flights before allowing herself to take the lift. As soon as she opened the apartment's door she heard a chair pushed back on the kitchen tiles. Sheena came out excitedly to meet her, almost running.

'What's up? How's Emily?'

'Oh, she's fine. That is, y'know – just the same as ever. No, it's what's happened. She had a visitor. A Rachel Howard from Edinburgh. And listen – she must've known the entry code!'

Alyson put down the carrier bag with her purchases for the intended supper with Keith.

'Calm down, Sheena. Tell me exactly what she said.'

Round-eyed with importance, Sheena made the most of it: this haughty, tall, thin woman and her assumption she could do as she liked here. Forty or more, maybe fifty, Said she was some kind of relative. Well, Alyson must know what she was like, must have met her, because she'd been able to get in downstairs.

'How did Emily react?'

It stopped Sheena short. She'd no idea. Ramón hadn't said. Well, he wouldn't. Men didn't go in for other people's reactions. Especially old ladies'. Only, of course, she couldn't mention him.

'Oh, Emily was asleep,' she improvised. 'I wouldn't have her woken.'

'What time was this?'

'Between half four and five.'

'So she was sitting out?' Alyson looked hard at the carer. 'Sheena, you did have her dressed and sitting out?'

Better not lie too far: you could get in deep that way. 'Well, no, actually. She seemed so tired. Like I said, she was asleep.'

'But it's important, Sheena. I told you before. She needs the chair's support, and to be upright with her legs down, for at least a part of the day. Never mind if she dozes there.'

Sheena blinked her short, pale lashes. Thank goodness they were off the subject of the Howard woman. This was familiar stuff. You'd think Alyson really cared how Emily spent the day. Of course, however much of a bore she found the old girl, once she'd fluffed it that would be the end of the road for this cushy lifestyle. Alyson would be out on her ear, just like herself. Worse really. At least back at Mum's she had a roof over her head. Alyson would be really adrift.

'Did she leave her address?' Alyson was uneasy. Until now all communication had been through Mr Fitt. It must be he who'd supplied the entry code.

'Yeah. I've got her card here.' Sheena produced it, slightly smudged with makeup. 'Oh, and she said she'd be phoning.'

'Good. Thank you.'

'Did you know she was coming?' Sheena made it an accusation.

Alyson glanced up at her and wondered at her anger. What had Rachel Howard walked in on that had made her so uneasy?

'I've never heard of her before. She must be one of Emily's

family. I don't know any of them.'

'She said she was Emily's granddaughter. But she can't be, can she?'

Alyson considered. 'There's no reason why not. You say she's well over forty. That could be about right for age. I'm glad someone's taking an active interest in Emily at last. What a pity she was asleep and missed meeting her.'

Sheena was shrugging herself into her outdoor things. 'Gotta date with my boyfriend,' she claimed, presuming on her new connection with Ramón. He'd be on duty at the Crown anyway: captive audience more or less. She'd have to cut down on the Vodka Martini tonight though. It was working out expensive. Maybe she could get him to take her out sometime when he was free; to a film or ninepin bowling. It was too much to suppose he'd rise to a disco.

Alyson watched her go and listened for the sound of the lift taking her down. Sheena was proving less than satisfactory. She'd had experience looking after an arthritic neighbour and was a registered carer, but it didn't make up for her being incurably lazy. She made some show of observing hygiene requirements when under observation, but left on her own could be getting away with sluttish standards. Short of installing CCTV inside the apartment there was no way to be sure Emily was getting the service her money should cover. But going that far smacked of Big Brother. Threatened with that, Sheena would probably give in her notice. She wouldn't have been offered the job except that nobody else answered the advert. The hiring had been inevitable, so fire-power must be kept as the last resort.

Alyson made herself tea and let it cool while she prepared the vegetables for tonight's meal: calabrese, carrots and red peppers to accompany the lamb loin steaks and creamed minted potato. No pudding, but a choice of cheeses and Italian breads. Because Keith would probably come in chilled they could start with the supermarket's parsnip and basil soup zipped up with sherry and a pinch of cayenne.

He rang at a quarter past nine. 'On my way, if that's all right with you. Be there in fifteen minutes.'

Alyson smiled into the receiver. 'That's great. I'll open a bottle of red.'

Not just any red though: the claret Dr Moody had given her at Christmas and she'd never had sufficient occasion to break into.

When Keith came stamping and shivering in, complaining that it seemed colder than during the freeze she had a small table set up by the great window with its view out on the town's lights. 'Did you get any lunch?' she asked him.

He had to think, stopping in the middle of shedding his overcoat. 'I guess I worked through.'

'Empty stomach, so of course you're feeling the cold. It doesn't take a doctor to work that out. I've got hot soup ready to serve.'

'Wonderful. I'll just look in on Emily while you're at it. How is she today?'

'See for yourself. I've something to tell you when you come back.'

He wasn't long away. 'Didn't recognize me,' he complained drolly. 'Little short of spat at me. At least it's some sign of mental activity. What were you going to tell me?'

'She had a visitor today,' Alyson said, waving him to his place at the table. 'I wasn't here. Sheena saw to her. A Rachel Howard claiming to be Emily's granddaughter. And she let herself in below. So I assume Mr Fitt sent her.'

'It would have been courteous to warn you in advance.'

'Perhaps it was intentional, to catch us out. And poor Emily was left in bed all afternoon. No doubt I'll be hearing about that when the woman phones me.'

Dr Stanford shook his head. 'All the same I'd let Fitt know it's not on. There's no security if anyone can walk in on you any time they care to. If the family's suddenly showing an interest in our patient he should accompany the visitor, by appointment, when we're able to discuss her with them.'

'She could actually be a granddaughter, I suppose.'

'How much do you know about them?'

'Nothing really, beyond the little that Gran told me: just that her older sister 'got into trouble' and ran away when she was seventeen. Gran was only eight at the time and it was kept very quiet. Later she picked that much up from whispers among the servants. She was raised as an only child and barely remembered the rather magnificent young woman who'd gone missing. She did learn eventually that a baby had been born, a girl, but their father would never have Emily's name mentioned again in his presence.'

'Self-righteous old fool. God knows how many lives he spoiled by his obstinacy.'

'That was their way then. "Never darken my doors again" sort of thing. We may have swung too far the other way these days, but at least there's less prejudice. Children don't suffer the same stigma of illegitimacy.'

Keith considered. 'Even then he must have appeared a bit of a dinosaur. It would have been 1928, well after World War I, and things were beginning to loosen up. Even among the middle classes.'

'Whatever and however, it resulted in her being totally cut off from the family. It seems that both sides continued procreating until now only this Rachel and I are left to make what we can of the way things are.'

'And you see it as up to you to provide a happy ending.'

'Not exactly that. I just feel…'

'That you owe Emily something.'

'In a way. But she fascinates me; rather, I imagine, as she did Gran. You have to admit, Keith, there is something about her.'

'Something that makes her present nearest and dearest disinclined to take on caring for her themselves.' There was more warning in his voice than condemnation.

'That's partly it: as if all the way along she's been done down, cheated of her birthright. Which is hurtful. Why do you think that after all this time she still uses her maiden name? And insists on being "Miss"? I feel I need to make up to her for the past. Is that silly of me?'

'A tad fanciful perhaps, but kind. That's the main thing.' He watched her gathering their soup plates together and balancing them on one arm as she made room on the small table for their next course.

'No silver service,' she said, laughing. 'I think I'll dish up in the kitchen. It'll keep everything nicely hot. Come along and choose your vegetables, straight from the saucepans!'

He followed her, bemused. At home it would have been so different. Since Audrey had given up on normal meals he'd become accustomed to sitting alone, served by a silent Mrs Marsh, in a dining room heated only for the occasion by a single-bar electric fire. He would swallow what was presented, without tasting or appreciation, eager only to have done with it for the companionship of the living room's flaming logs or, more often, to go wearily to bed.

'This,' he told Alyson, 'is a rare treat. Thank you for taking pity on me.'

She turned back from the opened dishwasher, her eyes smouldering with something like anger. 'It's not pity. You know that.' Her eyes held his, challenging him.

'I think I do,' he admitted humbly. 'Only I don't know how to…' He held out both arms.

'No,' she said with finality. 'Say nothing. It's best. I was stupid to pick up on that. Forget it, please. *Please*, Keith. Let everything stay the way that it is. It has to be.'

He let his arms drop. Looked anywhere but at her. After a moment, 'What's for afters?' he asked, managing to sound like a greedy schoolboy.

'I'll see what I can find,' she told him, sharp and distant. But when she brought it to the table she was smiling again.

They were drinking decaff coffee when the call from Rachel Howard came.

Alyson took it on the lounge phone, signalling him not to go away. He listened while she explained herself to the unfamiliar voice, giving the hours at which she could be reached on home duty.

'Yes, all night, every night, from eight-thirty until noon next day. Of course it will be convenient if you visit. I look forward to meeting you, Mrs Howard. I'm sorry: *Miss* Howard, then. Yes, thank you. Goodbye.'

'Short and to the point,' she told Keith, replacing the receiver. 'She'll drop in tomorrow morning, before returning to Edinburgh.'

'I had already gathered they weren't a family to waste much time on sentiment,' he observed drily. 'Do you think she'll be suggesting we move Emily to a hospice?'

'I hope not. Surely in the little time left...and if she sees how comfortable Emily is here, among her own things...'

'Don't worry, Alyson. I shouldn't have brought up the possibility. Certainly if my opinion's asked I shall come down heavily on things remaining as they are.'

Nevertheless the conversation seemed to have cast a shadow that wasn't there before. Keith looked at his watch. 'I guess I'd better go back and look in on Audrey again, then get along home. Catch up on some of the sleep I lost last night.'

She brought him his overcoat, warmed from the airing cupboard. They said goodnight formally at the apartment door. No handclasp, no touching. Just a rueful smile from the man; a nod from the girl.

She stood long minutes in the dimly lit window until he appeared below, leaving the crossing. Then both raised a hand in salute, and he was gone.

Chapter Seven

Sheena had made straight for the Crown's saloon bar after work, eager to discuss Alyson's reaction to Rachel Howard's visit. Ramón was curiously deaf, and she had to insist quite loudly on him noticing her there. With her second half-pint she was past observing that she had an alternative, more interested, audience.

'Let me get you a drink,' Markham offered, as though he had just noticed her come in.

'I'll have a whisky,' she ordered rashly, avoiding the predictable, and after all she hadn't to pay for this one herself.

'Find yourself a table. I'll bring it across.'

It came as a double, accompanied by a mixer bottle of Canada dry. Markham, guessing she was a beginner at scotch, poured in the ginger for her. She tasted it experimentally and decided it was thirst-quenching.

'Did I hear you mention Rachel Howard?' he asked casually. 'I knew someone of that name once. Red-haired girl with a bit of a stutter. Would that be the same one?'

'Nah.' She gave him the description Ramón had passed on.

'From Edinburgh, you said? Some relative of your elderly patient?'

She stared at him, uncertain. 'Did I say that?'

'Oh, maybe it was the barman. He seems to have met her too.'

'Could've bin. Well, he was there, wasn't he?'

'Ah. Your guest, so to speak.'

Sheena guffawed. 'Bit of a giggle! She mistook him for a male nurse. Because of that uniform jacket he wears. I bet that's all the clothes he's got. Anyway, I let him deal with her, and she seemed quite chuffed with him.'

The desire to flaunt the burgeoning relationship was irresistible, but she stopped short of explaining why she hadn't dealt with the visitor herself.

She still couldn't get over how calmly he'd taken over. But that was how Ramón was, inscrutable and as if you couldn't rattle him. Yet something warned her that he could be very different, quite overpowering. A small man like him: it was odd. She'd once felt the same, sort of, in Wales at some enormous reservoir Dad had taken her to on holiday as a little girl. So calm. Not a ripple on its surface, but for weeks after that she'd sometimes wake up in a sweat after a nightmare about the Welsh dam bursting. All those thousands of tons of water lying there deceitfully still and then suddenly gushing out to drown the whole world, with her underneath it.

Markham seemed still to be pondering what she'd said. 'That's nice you can ask friends in. Your boss must be quite understanding.'

Sheena shrugged. 'Could be worse,' she granted. 'A bit stiff and snooty, though. Still it's only natch'ral, working long hours on me own, that I deserve a bit of comp'ny sometimes.'

'Nice for your friends too. Pity I don't yet count as one of them, or I could drop in on my day off, bring you something fancy from Patty's Pâtisserie.' He leered at her, gambling on the odd free drink having given him some sort of leeway.

'Yeah, that'd be cool, man.' The mix of drinks was getting to her. She amplified the attempted brother-speak with an extravagant high-five in an over-arm swing. It nearly had him off his seat.

'Right,' said Markham. 'Sadly, I have to be off right now, but I'll hold you to that visit as a promise.' He grinned, exposing yellowed, slightly overlapping front teeth, slid into the crowd, left by the street door and entered the lounge, careful not to be spotted through the shared serving space. It was one thing to oil what you want out of people, but another to stay and risk embarrassment because they couldn't hold their liquor. There were locals here who knew him. He had a reputation to consider.

Already there was an old fellow hanging around wanting to discuss an assault case that had come up last week and been held over on conditional remand for Thursday. In exasperation he'd let slip who'd be sitting then, with Jerome Alcock as Chairman of the Bench. It had plunged the questioner in gloom. 'Oh Lord, 'e's a right stinker. That'll mean the slammer, won't it? Eh, watcha think, Mr Markham?'

It was flattering to be appealed to, but he had to get the old ditherer off his heels. 'Bound to be,' he told him curtly. 'He'll not have a wax cat's chance in hell.' He turned his back on the man and pushed forward to pick up his order. He had drinking of his own to catch up on.

Not that tonight it helped. Especially after that reminder of work. It left him, if anything, more morose, depressed after all the hassle today with the flaming trainee usher following him around. Silly bitch couldn't grasp the difference between a pink form meaning conditional and a green for *un*conditional remand. Bloody useless housewife, but they wouldn't be happy until magistrates' courts were entirely run by women. Most of the beaks were females already, as well as both clerks and the main prosecution. No place any more for a man, except in the dock. He'd be better off getting out before they found something more to complain about in his "attitude". There were other ways to earn a living and keep a bit of dignity.

After a couple more pints, and making certain that Sheena had lurched off leaving the coast clear, he finally left the pub, turning up his collar in the street against what was now no more than spasmodic drizzle. Darkness offered comfortable anonymity. There was nothing further to check on back at the courthouse. Otherwise he wouldn't have risked alcohol on his breath.

He would have to watch it money-wise, though. Popping in for the odd lager was getting to be an expensive habit, especially when it included softening up the Lump for bits and bobs of gossip. Not that he could yet see what profit it could be turned to. Still, no harm in knowing a few details about a vulnerable old lady with a lot of money to dispose of. He doubted the Lump had even considered the full possibilities there. Doubted she ever considered anything except what went into her blubbery mouth.

He collected his car, an eight-year old tan Nissan, from the council car park, and drove the short distance to the yard of the stationery warehouse. The long, single-storeyed hangar showed lights from high-up windows and skylights, indicating that night staff were restocking shelves and making up orders. He turned in at the gap in the outer wall, passing the two vans and four cars legitimately parked there, and drew into the shadow of the blank end of the structure. From there, with the driving window lowered, he could crane upwards and focus on the penthouse apartment where the Lump was employed as a day nurse.

At that top level the whole wall on this side of the building appeared to be glazed from ceiling to floor, with some kind of low ornamental railing close against it on the outside. The whole was slightly luminescent, more perhaps from reflected moonlight penetrating broken clouds than from the faint glow within. On lower floors windows were brightly lit. Through some he could occasionally glimpse people moving about inside. Nobody here, it seemed, bothered to close their blinds.

Bitterly he recalled the dingy net-curtain culture of the streets he was brought up in. *Don't let 'em see what goes on indoors*! As if the loud rumpus from drunken brawling in the neighbourhood wasn't broadcast enough. Some home comforts!

When he was small that hadn't been the case with his own straitlaced, teetotal parents. Ma, long tamed by hellfire texts; knew better than to step out of line. Godliness through misery, that's what the old man believed in, with vicious canings for his only son at the slightest infringement of home-imposed laws. He still recalled the salty taste of the leather strap he silently bit on, writhing while his back was crisscrossed with weals after some villainy like riding his bike over the bedraggled grass patch his father called a lawn.

Then Ma had died when he was nine and things changed. There was a gap when the two of them struggled to get along on their own, until the Slag moved in, big-busted, dripping fag ash, shouting his father out, hands on hips and legs straddled, but giggling into the night while the old springs wheezed in what had once been Ma's bed.

By then there was plenty for the net curtains to hide, grubby now and one permanently askew with a hook come loose. Things were as brutal there as in any of the other houses, with his father unhinged by a mixture of lust, frustration and the demon drink he'd always railed against.

Long-ingrained fear had at least served to make Oliver one of the rare youngsters thereabouts with no criminal record by the time he was forced to leave school. He found work at the stationery warehouse boring and repetitive, but a welcome break from the home from hell. By seventeen he'd saved what he was allowed to keep from his pitiful wage, so in time he'd moved out and moved on.

He withdrew his head from the car window, wiping rain from his face with the back of one sleeve. From an open fanlight in the warehouse he caught the whine of a fork lift truck and above it a man's voice singing some indistinguishable pop rubbish, with another whistling along. Discipline hadn't been so slack when he'd started there at sixteen, burning inside at the injustice of not being allowed to continue on to college and study Eng. Lit. Every time he passed the enormous modern block now upgraded to a University Department he scorned the sloppily dressed kids he saw streaming through its gates. Undeserving scruff-heads, most of them. How much had they ever read, let alone enjoyed, of Shakespeare, Marlowe, Edmund Spenser? He spat out into the dark before winding up the window.

Waiting now to drive out on the main road he looked left and saw, beyond the car showrooms, a dark figure hurry from the smoked-glass double doors of the luxury apartments. As he watched, the man – a mature male by the way he walked – crossed by the mini-roundabout, turned on the farther kerb, looked back for several seconds and slowly raised a hand.

It seemed to Markham that in the dim penthouse window a shadow had moved across some low light-source – perhaps a shaded table lamp – and stood there for the same short period before moving away. He was too distant to be sure it was a woman who had raised a hand in reply, but he guessed it would be the one the Lump said nursed there overnight.

An outsider to their comfort-wrapped lives, he felt an urge to find out who the man was. All it took was to follow him as he rounded the college wall on foot. Security lamps in the hospital forecourt helped. The man entered by the automatic doors to Accident and Emergency. By the merciless lighting inside, his identity was in no doubt. Markham knew Dr Keith Stanford through an appearance at court giving evidence in a case of serious assault.

This entrance was closest to where his wife would have been taken after her suicide attempt. There'd been whispers that she also had some kind of wasting disease, but that might not be what had pushed her to the brink. Suppose she'd heard gossip that the good doctor was playing away from home. If so, Markham considered, he might get to learn something of Keith Stanford's bit on the side, whom the Lump had called Alyson. It seemed she was a hospital nurse moonlighting with care for the sick, rich old lady.

For Alyson next morning the first light breaking over the distant hills brought back that earlier dawn years before when the shattering phone call had come. So similar – with lemon streaks on the skyline and the underside of layered cloud faintly flushed rose – that it could be that same morning. Recalled from a weekend with friends in Somerset, she'd rushed home in panic to find Gran still alive. But only just. And all she'd managed to say – the last word Alyson had to remember her by – was her sister's name, *Emily*, gasped with such agony behind it. The sister she'd been deprived of all her adult life, but strangely dominating her dying mind as the only thing that still mattered to her. Such unnecessary secret grieving, when surely Gran could have sought her out before then and achieved a reconciliation.

Perhaps, wherever Gran was now, if she was anywhere, she'd be relieved that her granddaughter had at last done that much for her: found Emily before it was too late. And now, probably today, she was to meet her counterpart, Emily's own grandchild.

Her visitor, when she arrived at a little after nine that morning, was someone else entirely. Alyson had buzzed her in without checking on the monitor.

'Hello,' DS Rosemary Zyczynski greeted her. 'I hope you don't mind my contacting you at home, but I've something to tell you and guessed it might be a tad more private here than at work.'

'That's fine by me,' Alyson told her. 'Come in and let me take your coat.' She shook off the surface rain and went to hang it in the airing cupboard. As she did so she noticed that Keith's scarf was left there from last night. Perhaps he'd drop in for it later and bring her up to date on his plans for Audrey.

Rosemary followed her into the kitchen and nodded enthusi-astically at the offer of tea. 'Yes, please.'

Setting out the tray, Alyson was aware of the other girl taking in her surroundings. Well, of course, a detective after all. She remembered how she'd said she was in the right job, and smiled. It was the same for herself, so they'd more in common than being of much the same age.

'Let's go through to the lounge.' Not having many friends drop in, she was curious to see this room's effect on her visitor.

'Now *that*,' Zyczynski said, 'is really something.' She had ignored the art display, going straight across to the glass wall to gaze down at the traffic circulating the town centre. Then she looked across to make out the undulating line of the Chilterns against a lowering sky. 'How do you ever get any work done here? If you get my point.'

'I certainly do. The view can be quite mesmerizing. But sit down and tell me what brings you here. I'd guess it's something about my junkie patient.'

'Yes. How's he doing?'

'Awake now and much as you'd expect. Pretty groggy. We'll clean him up, ready for a methadone programme. But once the habit's started, I'm afraid... It's a familiar story.'

'Discouraging. Like some of our regulars at the nick. Actually I've come for confession. The key I found under his trainer's lin-ing reminded me of a similar one I'd seen. So I took it away with me to check.'

She saw Alyson's mouth open to protest. 'I know I'd no right. And I've brought it back. It's here. Professional nosiness, I'm afraid.'

Alyson held out her hand for it. 'No harm done, I suppose. It won't have been missed yet. What did you want it for?'

'As if you haven't guessed! I was trying to find the sort of lock it fitted. And I did.'

'Am I to be told?'

'It's for a safety deposit box, the portable kind. So naturally I'm curious about how this lad came to have anything of value that needed locking away.'

'More than curious. You're suspicious.' Her tone was dry.

'Wouldn't you be?'

Further discussion was interrupted by the buzzer sounding from downstairs. This time, Alyson noted, Rachel Howard wasn't making use of any code revealed by Mr Fitt. She went through, asked for identification and pressed the button for the outer door release, then returned to the policewoman.

'Don't rush your tea. This will be someone to see my patient, Miss Withers.' And she explained how this mystery relative had turned up on the previous day while she was at work.

She went out on the landing as the lift doors opened. Emily's granddaughter, breathing her name and extending a gloved hand, came out wrapped to the ankles in a full-skirted black leather coat and with a collar of fox fur up round her ears. As Alyson disposed of the garment alongside Zyczynski's she found Rachel Howard had preceded her into the lounge.

'Ms Howard,' she said coolly, following her and determined to be formal, 'this is...'

'Rosemary, Alyson's friend,' the policewoman put in quickly, avoiding further disclosure.

How'd you do,' said the visitor casually. 'Oh, you're entertaining. How cosy.' There was more than a hint of disapproval in her voice.

She ploughed on. 'I met the other nurse yesterday, of course, but I felt I must see you too as the senior in charge. I admit he struck me as quite efficient, even though foreign, unfortunately.'

Alyson, seldom wrong-footed, had too much to deal with just then to find a ready comeback. 'Make yourself comfortable,' she managed to invite. 'I'll get some fresh tea.'

'Coffee, actually. I do prefer that in the morning,' and the woman seated herself opposite Zyczynski whose lively brown eyes appeared to be missing nothing.

Alyson escaped to the kitchen. When she returned she had a look of determination on her face. If the Howard woman intended to treat her as mere paid help, then there were a few things they should get straight between them.

'I've been trying to work out,' she said, setting down the tray in a space Zyczynski cleared on the low table, 'exactly what you'd call the relationship between us. As granddaughters of two sisters, does that make us second cousins?'

Rachel paused in extracting a cigarette case from her crocodile handbag. 'I can't say I've ever considered it. There's been no contact between the two branches. We hadn't heard of you before Emily's little solicitor produced you out of a hat.'

'I can't say there's much family resemblance,' Zyczynski murmured, earning a hard stare from the newcomer.

No, Alyson agreed silently; but what had shaken her from the first moment was the startling likeness between this woman and Emily. And more poignant was that she so resembled the treasured photograph of Alyson's own mother. An older version with the same high cheekbones and dark eyes, though the blue-black of this one's sweeping wings of hair must surely be artificial.

I don't like her, Alyson had to admit. Already I find her quite detestable.

Rachel was about to light up.

'Sorry,' Alyson interrupted brusquely. 'I don't allow smoking near my patients.'

For a moment it seemed there'd be a freezing-out of the upstart employee. Then it passed. Rachel slid the case back in her handbag and crumpled the cigarette into a saucer. 'Perhaps I'd better look in on Emily while my coffee cools. I can't stay long. I'm getting an afternoon train back to Scotland.'

Which was disappointing. Alyson had so much to ask her. Escorting her to Emily's bedroom, she said, 'Gran seldom mentioned her older sister, but I know she missed her badly when she went away.'

Rachel halted. 'Was thrown out when she went to the bad, you mean.' She gave a little grunt of contempt. For whom? Alyson wondered. Or for what – convention?

'She was seventeen. Told never to darken her righteous father's doors again. Eunice, the bastard child, was my mother. At least when she grew up she managed to find herself a husband. Married well moneywise; but *he* was the real bastard!'

No doubt *this* time where the scorn was targeted. The elegant, sculpted face was vulpine with rancour.

Alyson could find nothing to say. She knocked gently on the bedroom door, looked round it to ensure Emily was covered up, and let her visitor in.

The old lady was awake, her emaciated, claw-like hands clutching the upper sheet. It was one of her more lucid moments. She took in the figure bending over her, seemed for a second almost to recall the face, then frowned with incomprehension. 'No,' she said, almost spitting. 'You can't have it. Go away!'

Her head turned and the familiar cry burst from her lips. 'Martin, Dolly, get me out of here!'

'Emily, it's all right,' Alyson comforted. 'We aren't staying.'

Outside in the passage, Rachel's calm appeared ruffled. 'Fitt never said she was as far gone as that. Alzheimer's, I suppose.'

'She's just very old. And tired,' Alyson defended. 'There are things I wanted to ask you. These people she cries out for sometimes, who are they? Dolly or Molly, and Martin?'

'My stepbrother and stepsister. Molly was their mother, my father's first wife. He divorced her to marry Eunice, and legitimize me. But Molly stayed on, in a sort of *ménage à trois*.' Again bitterness was back, destroying the cosmetic beauty of her face.

She stared at Alyson challengingly with her huge, dark eyes. 'Emily doesn't so much mean "get me out" as "let me out". When we all lived together and she got cantankerous they used to shut her up in a cupboard. Martin and Dolly. As a small child I was treated even worse.'

'That's barbarous!'

'They aren't nice people. Eventually Fitt stepped in; got himself power of attorney for Emily. I hate to think what he's milking off her estate. Both my parents had died by then.'

She shrugged, looking at her wristwatch. 'Can I have my coat now?'

When Alyson saw her out there was no mention of a second visit. Dazed, she went back to clear the crockery and Rachel's untasted coffee. She had forgotten the other woman still sitting there.

'Did you get all that?' she asked, sinking on to a chair beside her. Of course Zyczynski had. Rachel's voice, with its ringing upper-class authority and precise Edinburgh diction, would clearly have reached her in the otherwise silent apartment.

The policewoman said nothing, nodding.

'I wanted so much to meet her,' Alyson admitted. 'And now I heartily wish I hadn't.'

Zyczynski cleared her immediate paperwork, clipped together the papers relating to the committal case she'd be attending in court next morning and knocked on Superintendent Yeadings' open door.

'Ah, Rosemary,' he said, looking up. 'I was thinking of sloping off home for lunch. Is there anything urgent?'

'No, sir. Things are pretty quiet. DI Salmon's got a dental appointment, so he told me to report direct to you. And Beaumont's checking on our Misper's son and daughter-in-law again. He's sure they're holding something back. It isn't the first time the old chap's disappeared without warning. A widower, he wasn't happy about moving in with them.'

'Um. Family trouble. There's a lot of it about, unfortunately. And far too much of it lands on our plates these days.'

She guessed he was thinking about Dr Stanford's wife. He and Nan were getting pulled into her affairs, and he'd enough mixed-up lives to deal with here at work.

'There's no end to it, is there?' she sympathized. 'I ran into a funny little incident myself today. Involving a nurse I went to see about that young junkie I told you about yesterday.'

'Oh yes. How is the lad?'

'Looks as if he might recover. In which case we'll need to do something about the debit card found on him.'

'Yes. DC Silver's traced it to a local man. The owner hadn't realized he'd lost it, and he's not best pleased that fifty pounds had been withdrawn.'

'He was lucky it wasn't more. Anyway the boy had blown most of it by the time he was found stoned.'

'M'm, not surprising, given a drug dependency. See what you can do with him, Z. When he's fit enough to open up.'

Do *for* him was what he really meant. Z nodded. 'Alyson, this nurse I mentioned, may be better able to help there, if she's not too tied up with getting Mrs Stanford to respond.'

'Human, is she? You said she'd family complications too.'

So he hadn't missed that point. 'She's caring for her late grandmother's sister, who's ninety-three and bedridden. The old lady has a history of what sounds like abuse from her nearer relatives and was apparently rescued from them by the family solicitor. Yesterday her granddaughter turned up out of the blue and started checking up on the lie of the land. She took the opportunity to cast doubt on the solicitor's motives. The old lady's wealthy and mentally adrift. I was there to overhear all this. Her visitor didn't endear herself to me any more than she did to Alyson.'

'The ITU nurse is acting carer in her spare time? That's hardly recreational. Or expected.' His tone became dry. 'It doesn't fit the modern pattern of hospital life we get from TV soaps. They mainly consist of serial bed-hopping between medical staff. Nan gets furious about the slights on her honoured profession.'

'I guess Alyson's one of the old school, sir.'

'What age?'

'Much like mine.'

Twenty-eight, then, Yeadings reckoned silently.

Z explained that the only time the girl got outdoors was on the walk between work and home, with occasional detours to get in the shopping. She didn't even have a jogging habit. Probably got enough exercise from the double job.

'So is the old lady left on her own during hospital shifts?'

'No, there's a care assistant comes in. And that's another strange thing.'

She told Yeadings about the visitor's reference to a male nurse, when the only other helper was actually a woman.

'An emergency stand-in, perhaps? Or maybe the work's being profitably hived off at a lower rate.'

'Could be. But without Alyson's knowledge or permission. She was mystified, but didn't let on. The visitor had been mildly impressed by the man she'd seen on the previous day, and Alyson admitted to me that the real carer wasn't much cop.'

'Intriguing, but hardly within our remit.'

'No. Still, I may find out more from her when I chase up the young junkie. Just to satisfy my curiosity.'

Yeadings smiled to himself, reaching for his coat off its peg in the stationery cupboard. Young Z had a nose for oddities, not unlike himself. Good, so long as she didn't get herself personally involved. Wasn't it Sartre who said Hell was other people? Or maybe Gide. One of those French depressives.

When the policewoman had left, Alyson was hard pushed to catch up with her self-imposed timetable. With Emily settled and out in her chair, the purées prepared and her bedding bundled up to drop off at the launderette, she rang Sheena's home number and asked her to come in quarter of an hour early. There would be a cold lunch waiting for her in the fridge.

'It's not that easy,' the woman balked.

'It's vital, Alyson insisted crisply. 'We have something to discuss.' She laid down the phone.

Sheena, uneasily aware of what in all likelihood her boss was going to make a fuss about, compromised by coming in just five minutes before her usual time. 'Is it Emily?' she demanded abruptly on entering. 'What's the matter with her?'

'Emily's as well as she ever is. I thought you should know that your visitor of yesterday came to see me this morning. She'd been quite impressed by the male nurse she found in charge. Can you explain that to me?'

'Care assistant,' Sheena quickly corrected her. 'I was going to tell you, only all that about her claiming to be Emily's granddaughter put it right out me head at the time. I had to pop out for something, see. Medicine for me Mum, and the chemist would be closed when I came off duty. Well, this man had been recommended and I'd met him socially, like. I thought, jest for fifteen minutes, see. I knew you wouldn't want me leaving the old girl on her own. And as it happened he was free jest then. Anyway, as luck would have it – sod's law, like – that's when the granddaughter turned up and he let her in. So when I got back I let him get on with it and stayed out of sight. Didn't want her getting the idea the place was over-staffed, and that old solicitor wasting the family's money.'

She drew a long breath after the rushed explanation. Alyson didn't need the expression of proud achievement in Sheena's unnaturally round eyes to warn her that something had been put over on her.

'I don't see why this friend of yours – all right, acquaintance, then – couldn't have picked up the prescription for you. You're paid to be here, not bring in a substitute.'

'You said that Rachel woman thought he was all right. And she seemed choosy enough. Did I tell you she let herself in downstairs? That solicitor must've told her the code. Probably sent her to check up on how we're ripping them off. Only she could see we aren't!' She ended on a high note of triumph.

'She didn't need the code for the street door. Maybe someone was going out or coming in just ahead of her and she slipped by them. It does happen. I've done it myself, though the residents ought to be more alert to strangers. Did she attempt to let herself in up here?'

'No. She rang.'

Presumably the male care assistant had reported this to her. He seemed responsible enough. 'Give me his name, Sheena. If he's suitable and available I might need to use him sometime as a stand-by.'

The woman hesitated. 'He's called Ramón. It's Spanish.'

Alyson nodded. So probably an EU citizen; maybe he was looking for work locally. It would be worth paying him from her own pocket to get occasional time off. Provided he met requirements. She'd need to interview him.

'Can you give me his phone number?'

Sheena looked aghast. 'Er, I'd have to look it up.'

She thinks she's in danger of getting the boot, Alyson thought. Well, let her. It may smarten up her performance.

Alyson went for the phone directory. Strike while the iron's hot, she told herself. She watched while Sheena fumbled her way through the business section. It appeared the man hadn't a private number.

Sheena ran a finger down a page and read out six figures. She looked up, her face flushed. 'He's taken a room at the Crown,' she said. 'While he looks around, like. You have to ring there and ask for Ramón. Don't know the rest of his name.'

I'll do that when I get my meal break at work, Alyson decided.

Let's hope it finds him in and free. He might just walk across and see me at the hospital. It's just round a couple of corners. And convenient for here too, if he's suitable to take on.

Her call caught him at the break in his split shift. There had been a sizable pause while someone hunted him down, but when he answered he listened quietly to her explanation of who she was.

'I understand. The old lady. You look after her.'

'She's an elderly relative I'm very fond of. I want to be sure she's cared for properly. If you would be interested in taking on that responsibility from time to time, and you're not tied up with other commitments... Look, could you possibly come across to the hospital and see me in half an hour? I'll arrange to be waiting in Reception on the ground floor.'

He hesitated only a few seconds. Then, 'In half an hour,' he agreed levelly.

Good. He wasn't rushing into anything. Which was a responsible attitude. He could be a godsend.

She watched him walking up towards the plate-glass entrance: a small, stocky figure in a green parka, his bare head covered in black hair short and stiff as a clothes brush. There was something oriental about the set of his features. His square, flat face was impassive. She waited for him to reach Reception and ask for her. She held out her hand. 'I'm Alyson Orme. Let's find a corner where we can talk.'

He left it to her, waiting for her questions, then answering them slowly. Perhaps he lacked confidence in English, was short of vocabulary. But his pronunciation was good and he had no trouble in following what she said. Her main anxiety was that he wouldn't be satisfied with occasional work if he was looking for something permanent.

'Had you ever considered becoming a student nurse?' she asked.

He looked a little embarrassed. His gaze rested on her uniform. 'That's not for me,' he said simply.

She guessed he lacked the basic education to be accepted for training. 'Well, care assistants have just as vital a part to play.' She hoped it didn't sound patronizing.

'I give good service,' he replied, quaintly.

'Let's arrange for you to take a duty when I'm there myself. Then I can show you where everything is and we'll see how Emily takes to you. She can be a little trying at times, so you'll need to be patient with her.'

He smiled then, showing large, very white teeth, and almost managing to look handsome. 'I am very patient man.' His face resolved back to its moon-smoothness.

'Tomorrow perhaps? At eight in the morning?'

It was possible. He could arrange with Roseanne to set up the bar and he'd be back to relieve her as soon after midday as he could get away. He stood up and offered Alyson his hand. They had an agreement. It was some time later that she realised she hadn't asked him for references.

Oliver Markham slammed his locker door and shook out the folds of his black gown, his badge of office. He was the only officer of the court to be visually distinguished as a dignitary. Even the beaks were in collar and tie – or, more often now, twin sets and pearls. This set him apart, sent a warning message to the lowlifes hauled up to account for their misdemeanours.

A bitter smell came off the coarse cloth. Fustian. He savoured the Shakespearean word. A portmanteau of fussy, musty and cotton to his mind. Sour and mouldy to the nostrils. A salutary warning whiff of the slammer as an end of Justice.

He threaded his arms through the half-sleeves and went out into the entrance hall. The dratted trainee woman was there already, also gowned. 'Mr Markham,' she simpered. You're wanted in the back room. A word with the Senior Usher.'

Marcus Brent here today? That was unusual. Doubtless seeking his opinion on the trainee. Well, he'd tell him: hopeless. She just hadn't the necessary authority. Never would have.

There were three of them in a huddle: Brent, today's Chairman of the Bench, and that sloppy girl with droopy hair who was his Clerk. So it would be a legal point. But on his arrival the latter two withdrew.

It was utterly unexpected., unbelievable. A complaint from the public about himself. He listened at first with disbelief, then mounting anger. Who was getting at him?

And then as Brent developed the complaint it came back to him: the snivelling little shit pestering him in the bar yesterday. He'd wanted to know who'd be chairing the bench for the GBH committal case tomorrow. And what chance there was of the case being thrown out. And there'd been others within hearing distance.

God, what had he said to him? Anything, to get the little tick off his back.

Now it was being read out to him from a slip of paper the Senior Usher had taken from an inner pocket. He'd deny it, of course. He'd said nothing of the sort; retained a dignified silence. It was a blatant case of malicious falsification.

But, Brent said, there was an independent witness who upheld the accusation. Markham had not only given away the name of the Chairman for the coming case, but also his assured opinion that because of him the accused 'hadn't a wax cat's chance in hell' of getting off.

He must see, Brent pointed out severely, that he had prejudiced the case and maligned a magistrate. This was an extremely serious matter and an inquiry must be held into why the court's schedule now required changing.

'Look,' Markham insisted, 'we can go into this later. I'm needed in there right now. If you'll wait until after the session I can explain what really happened.'

'We'll discuss it now,' Brent said stolidly. 'Mrs Norris can take over your duties while the matter is looked into. Meanwhile you are indefinitely suspended.'

The room was vibrating with hot light. Markham felt his head fill with a rush of angry blood. It was intolerable that the untrained housewife should, even temporarily, take his place. He could kill the pretentious cow. And this sanctimonious creature standing here who thought he could humiliate him.

'You know what you can do with your fucking job?' he hissed close in Brent's face. 'You can shove it where the daylight never reaches. I don't have to stand this. I'm handing you my resignation.'

The man blinked and moved a step away. He had gone very pale. 'In which case,' he said quietly, 'I have no hesitation in accepting it.'

Chapter Nine

'Audrey Stanford is threatening to discharge herself.' Bernice told her when she returned to ITU.

'If she's well enough for that she shouldn't be with us. Have you paged Dr Ashton?'

'There's some kind of crisis in the Psych department. She'll be along as soon as she can. Meanwhile it's up to us.'

'To restrain her? Is she really serious, or is this for effect?'

Bernice shrugged. She'd clearly had her fill of this patient. Alyson nodded and went to apply damage limitation.

'Audrey, how are you feeling?'

'Bloody awful. What do you expect? Where's Keith? I want him to take me home. Get my clothes, will you. I told the other girl.'

'Dr Stanford will be in afternoon surgery just now. I'm sure he'll be visiting later. He's cancelled the course he was meant to be going on this week.'

'So I should bloody well think. Which means he could be here to fetch me.'

'Before we let you go home we'll have to make sure there's someone there to look after you.'

'Because I can't be left on my own? Try telling him that. Do you think he cares what becomes of me? It would have suited him if I'd died out there alone while he was off chasing his fancy women. It's not as though he'll have long to wait in any case. You know, don't you? I'm on my bloody way out.' Her voice rose to hysterical level. She reared up in bed, shaking, crouched forward, tense like a barking dog, weight on her balled fists in their dressings.

'You didn't bring any clothes with you,' Alyson said calmly. 'They took you out of the bath, wrapped in a towel.'

Audrey stared up at her, shaken into silence. 'Nobody cares,' she said bitterly.

'We all care,' Alyson assured her. 'That's what a hospital's about. That's why your husband works himself into the ground, because there are so many sick people depending on him just now. Believe me, we understand how it is for you, and we'll do everything we can for your comfort.'

'You can't understand. It isn't happening to you! You don't have the pain and the terror!'

Alyson sat beside her and reached to take her in her arms, but the woman screamed and tore with her nails at the nurse's face. She recoiled, feeling blood well out under one eye and roll down her cheek.

'Right,' said Dr Ashton crisply, entering on cue. 'It looks like a case for sectioning. I'll get someone else along for the paperwork.'

It had been a bad day in her department. In clinic an outpatient had viciously attacked a nurse with a chair, so they were one staff member down and the patient, a fourteen-stone diabetic, had needed to be admitted until his medication was regulated. Now they would have to take on this virago with suicidal tendencies. Which put paid to her hopes of getting home in time to read Jeremy his bedtime story.

She'd be in shit to the *nth*. She should have known better than to promise they'd finish the story together. Desmond would take on the reading and miss the whole point. Jeremy had identified heavily with Pirate Percy and would need the bloody ending skilfully edited. Why did the writers of children's books have to work out their repressed aggression on young, impressionable minds? It was her fault for having chosen that story, but it had been a good romp up to that point.

While her mind churned over her own misfortunes she felt the patient's forehead, took her pulse reading and decided that the temporary lull in violence was just the prelude to a second outburst. She would certainly resist an injection. Better give the sedative in something bland and syrupy. Slower, but safer.

'There, my dear,' she said emolliently, 'it only *seems* to help, getting het-up like that. But it changes nothing in the end except to give you a sore throat and use up your energy. Tell you what I'll do. Nurse here shall arrange for a porter to swish you off to another ward where I'm nearby, and we can give you our undivided attention.'

Codswallop, Alyson thought, gently dabbing at her cheek. She'll never get away with that. And as for undivided attention, that's exactly what we're about in ITU.

But get away with it she did. Audrey appeared to hang on every word, her eyes fixed on the psychiatrist's own. She put out a pathetic little hand which Dr Ashton briefly squeezed then dropped like a hot potato. 'Be seeing you,' she said breezily, and left.

At the door she grimaced at Alyson. 'Sorry about the implied slight. I'm the greatest admirer of what you get up to in here. Give a mild sedative by mouth and I'll send along a magic potion to cover the move. Then we'll see how she is after twelve hours' solid sleep.'

She tapped Alyson on the wrist and lowered her voice further. 'When Keith drops by suggest he keeps on walking. I don't think we want sight of him to fire her up again just yet.'

It was an hour and a half later that Dr Stanford appeared and he looked shattered. Alyson stopped him at the door. 'Keith, what's happened?'

'I've arranged to take indefinite sabbatical leave. It's deuced difficult because the practice is one down already with this flu outbreak. But anything else is unthinkable, the way things are.'

She nodded. 'I'm sure you're doing the right thing. If there's anything I can do to help…anything at all?'

He closed his eyes. 'What a mad thing to ask. Of course there is.' He fell silent, then picked up in a more controlled voice. 'When Audrey comes home there'll be no room in my life for anything else, but until then I have time to…adjust. Will you help me, Alyson? Is it too much to ask that you let me repay your hospitality? Perhaps we could have dinner one evening. If you could get free, of course. Drive out into the country to somewhere quiet?'

He watched her face. 'I'll deliver you home safely. Straight after, I promise.'

'I don't need your promises. I mean, I know…'

'You know me.'

'Yes.'

'Is that yes, you know me; or yes, you'll come?'

She looked at him evenly and made up her mind; whether for his or her own relief. 'Yes for both. I think I can get someone to stand in for me with Emily. In a day or two.'

'Good. You need to get out and see a little life. I'll leave it to you to arrange when. Sooner the better. Ring me, will you?'

'I will. But Keith, there's a message from Dr Ashton.'

'I've seen her. She's probably right to section Audrey. Is she still here?'

'Sedated. We're just waiting for a porter to move her.'

He nodded. There would no longer be any excuse now to drop into ITU, but Alyson had agreed to have dinner with him. And there was always Emily to visit and so keep seeing her.

On the way Markham had called in at the Stag to take aboard a couple of scotches to firm up his resolution, and then Baldrey had given him an overdose of much the same (but of a superior brand) after they'd concluded their discussion. The cramped little office was overheated, and as he stepped out into the street again the wind sliced through him, setting up a ringing between his ears. But he felt resilient. More than that. Jubilant.

He'd put it over on them all. He was proud that the convincing way he'd slagged off the feebly-run courts had evinced just the right kind of response from Baldrey. It confirmed the debt recovery company's experience of the judicial system's shortcomings. At least a third of the cases the bailiffs dealt with concerned, basically, unpaid court fines.

It hadn't taken long before Baldrey had grunted, 'I'm surprised you haven't considered a change of profession before. Something like ours, for example.' His little piggy eyes screwed up as he watched Markham's feigned surprise at the new idea.

'I might even get around to doing that,' he'd agreed.

The money Baldrey then mentioned made his salary as usher look more like peanuts, although he wasn't too happy about relying mainly on commission. Then a little more arsing around the subject and he'd allowed himself to be persuaded: he'd chuck in the usher's job and join Baldrey here dunning the debtors. Of course, he'd always privately thought bailiffs were the lowest of the low, lacking all the gravitas of his previous occupation; but someone had to lean on the defaulters. Repossession and eviction: they were the basis of effective law enforcement . He'd still be a presence to be feared and respected. Plenty of scope all round for satisfaction.

Ernest Baldrey slid the bottle back into the bottom drawer of his kneehole desk and kicked it shut. '*Fait ac*-bloody-*compli*,' he said with satisfaction. Receiving intelligence of the usher's spat with his boss had been almost instant on the deed. Markham's final fall from grace had been a long time coming and pleasurably anticipated in several quarters.

His inclusion in the team would nicely square it up: Tam Godfrey to do the valuations and Markham to lean on the defaulters. If not ideal, at least balanced. The man would relish having more scope to throw his weight about. The kerfuffle over his loose mouth in the pub had been opportune, leaving the ex-usher in the right bullish mood to take on the new job with plenty of stored anger.

Despite the cutting edge of the wind, Markham's step had taken on a distinct bounce. The lethargic, incident-free monotony of everyday life had been overthrown, as, shaken out of torpor, he'd suddenly faced an unpredictable abyss. To be disgraced and jobless was gross, indecent. It had filled him with fury. Then a flash of inspiration and an opportunity instantly seized. The whole tenor and tempo of life had changed. He recognized he was high on adrenalin and loved the buzz.

He had to celebrate, do something madly out of the ordinary, bask in a spot of admiration. Only he wouldn't be going near the Crown any more. Or not for a while. So what did that leave?

He strode tall, contemptuous of passers-by huddled in their collars to escape the vicious wind. Ahead rose the hospital tower and beyond it the block of luxury apartments. He remembered then the Lump and this wealthy old woman's penthouse she'd bragged about. He'd kidded he would visit, taking in something from the pâtisserie for her tea. She hadn't seen he'd been stringing her along, but it didn't seem such a bad idea now. He'd get a glimpse of the *dolce vita* at first hand.

The little shop's sugary fresh-bread smells were irresistible. He watched four chocolate éclairs being nestled into a pasteboard box and tied around with pink string ribbon.

Arriving at the flats, he remembered Sheena mentioning a CCTV camera at the door and, having buzzed, he held up the box at shoulder level towards it, fixing a wide grin on his face. Indistinguishable words burst out of the slotted steel box beside him and the doors were smoothly released with a satisfying click. He was in. Nothing to it. It was one of those days when he just couldn't lose.

In the Intensive Therapy Unit, having overseen removal of the sedated Audrey Stanford, Alyson went back to check on the nameless lad. Temperature normalizing, and his pulse was improving. He was a tough little beggar. The chances were he'd pull through this time and they could try him on the methadone substitute. She thought he was watching her under half-closed eyelids and she bent over, smiling.

'We need something to call you, if you're going to prove our star patient of the week.'

His lower lip jutted with defiance. He looked little more than a sulky child.

'Is there anything I can get you? Friends to contact?'

'Clothes,' he said indistinctly.

'You can't even think of going home yet. And where is home anyway?'

'I want my clothes.'

She thought of the key now returned to his trainer. 'They're safe where they are. As you are, with us. Just concentrate on getting stronger.'

He shut his eyes and she thought she saw a glistening of tears under the long, dark lashes. It was a relief that he hadn't come round violent and abusive like some.

Bernice muttered as she swept past the bed, 'Don't waste your time.' Resentful as ever of having to deal with self-inflicted injuries, she clearly still expected trouble over this one.

Alyson wondered what the safety deposit key had revealed to the woman detective. It could be a clue to the youngster's identity. She'd started to say something but then their conversation was interrupted by Rachel Howard's arrival at the flat and there'd been no follow-up. Rosemary Z's card was still on the hall table at home. It might be worth ringing her to find out more.

But first there were arrangements to make with Ramón. She must vet his performance of basic care duties before she dare risk leaving him in charge of Emily. As soon as her shift was over she'd ring him again to fix a time.

Sheena hadn't been expecting anyone to call on her at work, so she was slopping around in worn velvet mules and without makeup. Emily had been fretful ever since her arrival, spat out her purée and resisted being told to go to sleep. All the time that Sheena was washing her hair with Alyson's shampoo she could hear her moaning and muttering between the loud bursts of the shower spray.

In a towel turban Sheena put her head round the door and shouted, 'For God's sake, shut up you old bat!' The volume, if not the command, had the desired effect. In the ensuing silence the buzzer sounded for the street door. In the kitchen's CCTV screen, with distorted foreshortening, a confectioner's box almost obscured the leering smile and yellowed teeth of the man Markham who had bought her drinks at the Crown.

So he'd actually meant what he'd said about dropping round with some goodies. Bloody persistent, that one. A pity she didn't fancy him one bit. Was he really after a spot of nooky? She could hardly turn him down, but he'd have to see she was worth more than a couple of drinks and a bag of buns. 'Better come on up then,' she muttered into the squawkbox, and pressed the button to release the door.

He stepped from the lift red-faced from the biting wind and slightly wheezing, shrugged off his car coat and slung it over the back of a chair. Sheena considered the box he'd set on the kitchen table. 'You smell nice,' he greeted her.

It was more than he did. He must have been drinking solidly since he left court.

'Jest washed me hair.' She unwound the towel and let the wet rat-tails hang round her shoulders. She shook them at him flirtatiously. 'What's in the box?'

'It's for you. Open it. Thought you could make us some tea to go with it. My throat's as dry as a sandpaper jockstrap. Been talking a lot, fixing a deal.'

That seemed to interest her. She glanced straight at him for the first time, a look of calculation in her eyes. Hardly an attractive face, he regretted, with a tendency to acne and definitely pudgy. Not that he went for thin women. At least this one had rolling buttocks, and her fleshy thighs strained the tight nursing dress into horizontal creases. Not that she interested him, except she was there.

The tea arrived, two mugs with floating tea-bags and the milk already added. Carrying the box and with the discarded jacket nonchalantly over one shoulder, he trailed after her into the enormous lounge with the observation window. On the way he took note of the weird pictures on the walls. There'd been a short period at school when he'd been interested in art and joined the groups visiting London galleries. He thought now he recognized a kneeling Modigliani nude, or something a bit like it. There was also a small canvas pulsating with colour and roughly signed 'Vincent'. It seemed incredible that there should be genuine modern masters hanging in a private home in this pedestrian Thames Valley town. But the old bird who was dying was reputedly also extremely rich, so she'd hardly be satisfied with prints.

No use expecting enlightenment from Sheena. She was so ignorant and uncouth she'd not bothered to set out the cakes on a proper dish. He walked across to take in the view over the town and the distant rolling hills. Strange to be here where Dr Stanford's woman had stood watching for the last sight of him. Then he'd been the outsider, barely able to see in. Now, briefly, he was inside, commanding this amazing view; a reversal of circumstances symbolic of the way his fortunes were changing. The thought brought a wild surge of euphoria.

He reached out to touch the window. No slightest whisper of the half-gale blowing outside. Just sheets of toughened glass that isolated one sort of world from another: the haves from the have-nots. He knew which of those worlds he wanted and the need had become suddenly urgent.

He looked back at the Lump and his mouth twisted with distaste. He walked across and slumped into an easy chair beside her while she cut the string, opened the box and cooed over the contents. 'Ooh, loverly!' she crowed, and batted her short, sandy eyelashes at him. She reached for an éclair from the box and stuffed one end in her mouth, sucked at the cream-oozing pastry, eyes half-closed in bliss. He watched the pink, moist lips pucker and close around her prey; suck sensually at the gleaming chocolate.

The three remaining éclairs lay, phallic but flaccid, waiting to be gorged.

With a start Markham felt his own crotch respond, his prick harden, start to engorge.

He reached a hand in his jacket pocket for the half-bottle of scotch he'd meant for a celebration at home.

Stuffed full of cream and chocolate she'd be halfway there, then a tot or two and she'd go all giggly and girlish when he started, but stuff that. It was an age since the last time, the unsatisfying humping of a London slag picked up near King's Cross station.

He drank off half the tea in the mug she'd pushed across to him, refilled it from hers, spilling tea on the black wood of the low table, and made good her loss with whisky. 'Something to jizz it up,' he offered.

She grinned back with cream all over her mouth, and showed off by draining it in one go.

He leaned close, resting his chin on her shoulder, and slid an urgent hand up her skirt.

Chapter Ten

Next morning Ramón was buzzed in at eight-thirty on the dot, was shown where to hang his coat and followed Alyson into the kitchen for instructions. His white jacket was scrupulously starched and pressed, his fingernails short and white-rimmed. Alyson explained that Emily had already been washed and was sitting out for the bed to be changed. They should do that together.

Ramón followed her instructions deftly and lifted Emily back in, settling her against her heaped pillows. His movements were smooth, almost catlike.

'She'll be hungry,' Alyson said. 'I'd like you to reheat her purée and help her eat it. She finds a spoon difficult but it's important she tries for herself.'

That too went well. The man seemed familiar with a microwave oven and handled things in the fridge carefully. She explained how the purées were prepared and took him through the written timetable.

'She doesn't require a lot of entertainment. I talk to her but there isn't much response. She has music CDs already set up. She simply has to press a button on her control board. Same thing if she rings for attention. Apart from that you'll find she sleeps quite a lot.

'You wouldn't be expected to do any housework, just load the dishwasher and see to the laundry. Normally we do it here but the tumble dryer's waiting to be serviced, so perhaps you'd drop her bedding off at the 24-hour launderette when you leave. Sheena or I will pick up yesterday's later.'

He gave his oriental smile and nodded.

'Then I think it's coffee time.'

'I make it,' he offered and went unerringly to the right cupboard. She watched as he ground the beans and prepared the cafetière, ignoring the jar of instant. None of Sheena's shortcuts. He seemed almost too good to be true.

Over coffee she was able to draw him out a little. He'd worked in Hong Kong and Singapore, but came originally from the

Philippines, where his parents, both killed in the insurgent uprisings, had been doctors.

There was enough truth in it to satisfy them both. No need to explain that he remembered little of his real family who had been simple fishermen. Nor that, kidnapped as a nine-year-old, he'd lived for five years with rebels, raiding other islands and slicing throats as a way of life. When the Marcos soldiers overran their camp it was the doctors who rescued him from the bloodshed, took him to Manila, taught him civilized ways and employed him as their house-boy.

He was used to giving the sanitized edition. The full story was not for sensitive Western ears which knew nothing of violence and could not understand the imperatives of survival.

There was enough grimness in what he did reveal to keep Alyson from probing deeper. She satisfied herself that he could relieve her for the first part of her night shift with Emily on Sunday, from eight until midnight. She would ring in from ITU to check that he'd taken over from Sheena, then change at the hospital and go out to join Keith in the car park. There was no escaping a slight sense of duplicity in that, but she must be discreet for Keith's sake. And it wasn't as though she intended anything really underhand.

Ramón left at 11.40 with the bag of washing, in time to open the bar, and give one of the hotel's chambermaids a couple of quid to drop the stuff off at the launderette. He was pleased with the arrangements for Sunday, his free night, but it must be a one-off. He couldn't afford temping as a care assistant if it interfered with his job at the Crown.

Keith had dropped in to see Emily as Ramón was about to leave, and Alyson introduced them, aware of the way each was sizing up the other. It was Ramón whose eyes dropped first.

If Keith hadn't reminded her about the promised dinner she would have fought shy of bringing up the subject. 'I can get cover on Sunday evening,' she told him, 'if that would suit you.' His face told her the answer.

'Shall I pick you up here?'

'Could we meet in the hospital car park? I'll try to be there soon after eight.'

'Splendid. I'll book a table for nine.'

He found Emily quite chirpy. 'Visitors' day,' she said with her little twisted smile. Wryly Alyson thought it made her sound like a prisoner.

'You've done well lately for visitors, haven't you?' she said. 'Rachel your granddaughter, Ramón who'll look after you, and now your favourite doctor.'

'What did you make of the granddaughter?' Keith asked when they were again in the hall.

'I'd like notice of that,' Alyson said shortly. 'Sheena thought she might have been given the electronic code to get in, because she didn't use the downstairs buzzer. I don't like the idea that anyone can come up here unannounced.'

'If you think Mr Fitt gave it to her you should ring and tell him it's inappropriate.'

'Yes, I'd half decided to do that.'

'Decide fully, then. Security is essential. Emily might well get upset, from what I've picked up of that family.'

'It's my family too, remember.' She spoke lightly as though he was taking the matter too seriously.

'You know I don't include you. But do it now. Leave it another half-hour and Fitt could be out to lunch.'

She phoned from the hall, conscious of him watching her closely as she waited for the connection. 'Miss – er, Orme,' the solicitor greeted her. 'How can I be of help?'

He listened while she explained her uneasiness. There was a short silence, then his voice came back brusquely. 'I certainly have had no reason to impart the code to anyone. The number is kept in Miss Withers' safety deposit box at the bank. Nor has anyone had access to it. Unless, perhaps, for your helpers' convenience, you thought fit…?'

'No,' she said crisply. 'Dr Stanford and I are the only ones needing to know, because there's always someone on duty to let the other in.'

'In which case perhaps you will find that Miss Howard was let in by another resident who was using the outer door. However, I will point out to – er, the family that if they wish to visit, it must be by previous appointment made through me. Perhaps that will set your mind at rest.'

'That's very thoughtful of you, Mr Fitt. Thank you.'

She said goodbye, laid down the phone and explained the solicitor's offer. 'He'll think I'm just fussing.'

'Not at all,' Keith told her. 'It's not only Emily who's vulnerable here. He rightly feels responsible for the whole setup. God only knows what could happen if the wrong sort of people got in.'

Sheena, surprisingly, arrived early. Her face appeared puffy and red. Alyson hoped she wasn't about to go down with a cold. She watched as the care assistant peeled off her coat and rolled up the sleeves of her thick sweater in response to the flat's artificial warmth. As she surveyed the fridge's offerings Alyson noticed dark bruises on her lower arms.

'Are you feeling all right, Sheena?' she asked.

'Sure. Never better.' She put a hand to one cheek. 'Just a bit of stubble trouble from the boyfriend.' She rolled her eyes. 'You know how it is.' Meaning slyly that Alyson wouldn't. Opportunity was a fine thing.

'Right. I'll be off then.' She wasn't going to get drawn into listening to a blow by blow account of how Sheena had spent the intervening hours. Each to her own taste.

DS Rosemary Zyczynski carried her tray across the canteen and hovered over a table where two of the drugs squad were halfway through their main course. 'Can I join you?'

'Provided you don't chomp too loud,' said the man, a sergeant.

'Sure, me love,' said the woman, clearing her bulging shoulderbag on to the seat beside her. 'How's Major Crimes these days?'

'Keeping us busy.' Z emptied her tray on to the table, conscious of them examining her choice.

'The chicken's all bones,' warned Terry.

'That's the way they're made nowadays. I can take it. Actually it's your brains I really want to pick.'

'Like wow,' said Moura, impressed.

'There's a youngster in ITU at the hospital, a crack OD, can't be more than sixteen, and I'd like to find out his name. They haven't got a word out of him yet, which makes me think he isn't local and his accent could give him away. He's small; skinny as this chicken; dark, curly hair that might have had a decent cut a couple of months back; no body-piercings that I could see; blue eyes; eyelashes a Hollywood starlet would die for. Possibly homeless.'

'Could be any mug our clients deal to.' Sergeant Ross wasn't interested.

'Blue eyes and black hair,' Moira said thoughtfully, 'and possibly living rough. Which nobody'd want to in this weather. There's a little kid I've seen hanging about the Hollingworth Estate. Cheeky little runt, but I wouldn't say streetwise.'

'One of a gang?' Z asked hopefully.

'More of a natural loner, but he does mix. If anything I'd say the other lads over there have a healthy respect for him. They don't take liberties, for all he's a midget.'

'The one in ITU is certainly tough, the way he's hanging on. And staying desperately stumm. The nurses doubted at first he would pull through.'

'Tell you what,' Moura offered. 'There's a lad who just might open up about him. Geordie Moffat. He owes me one for doing a blind Nelson. I'll have a word. Ring you back, OK?'

'Stand you both a pint,' Z said, grinning. 'When you deliver, that is.'

Oliver Markham went across to the court buildings to clear his locker and deliver his formal notice pecked out on an old typewriter he'd adopted after computers took over there like an army of Daleks. He was supposed to give a month's notice but was content to lose out on wages provided he didn't have to turn up again. Let the housewives take over, scuttling about like clockwork mice, dealing out the wrong forms, sucking up to the Justices. He'd gone on to better things.

Now that his whole life had turned round he couldn't believe he'd been grinding on so long at the same old routine, with the same sour old faces, same stenchy drunks and car thieves and wife-beaters turning up time and time again. Sodding wankers who messed their shitty little lives; leeched on social services; made the state and the county and the dumb tax-payers shell out to provide a system that continually recycled the same sick parasites between street and dock and prison *ad nauseam*. And he'd been in their service!

Goodbye to all that. His new freedom meant he'd be paying back the feckless, dealing direct, hitting them where it hurt most – in material possessions which they wrongly considered theirs. Now they should see where it all led, as the bailiffs' men carried off the goods they'd conned and lied and thieved to make their own. Even the prospect gave him a sense of achievement.

Not least significant among yesterday's winnings was the matter of the penthouse. He'd gained entry to more than a rich woman's apartment. Driven first by a minor itch of curiosity, where had it led him? A sweat broke out and he felt blood flood his face at recall of violent sex on the polished wood floor, with the Lump struggling under him, batting him off and then suddenly rising to the force of nature, yielding, clamping her thick thighs about his heaving shanks, panting and clawing at him as if she'd suck in the whole of him in one go.

Proof, if ever needed, that when a woman said no she meant *yes-yes-and-more-more-more!* He'd given her plenty to remember him by. She'd not need persuading next time.

The new freedom didn't mean he'd escaped the inevitable hangover. His head felt like a football after a particularly aggressive game against Wycombe Wanderers. And there were some bad vibes mixed in with the smug sense of achievement. He'd slept fitfully, confused by flashes from the past, his first stolen sight of his father slamming the Slut against the passage wall and tearing off her knickers; the sound of their panting and groans as they abused each other. He'd watched, appalled, from between the banisters on the stairs, vowing it would never happen to him.

He shuddered. What he needed was a hair of the dog, but it was too early to be caught slinking into a pub, and there were no off-licences left in the High Street. There used to be three, but the supermarkets had killed them off. Now it was all house agents, hair stylists and no less than five charity shops. Booze was collected by housewives these days, along with their groceries, Harry Potters, nylons and tampons, from Sainsbury's or Tesco. Then doubtless doled out in whatever measures they thought fit for their menfolk. Bloody feminist invasion taking over the world.

Superintendent Mike Yeadings contemplated his paper-strewn desk. Hadn't the advent of computers promised to save the rain forests? Instead they spewed printouts with the velocity of a stuttering machine gun. There'd been a couple of days' respite when he'd almost caught up, then in quick succession an aggravated burglary, a possible suicide, and two suspicious deaths had showered on the team.

DI Salmon, still suffering the after effects of an infected lower jaw, was even more surly and unresponsive than usual. Apart from him, there was team gloom because Angus Mott, briefly glimpsed for his wedding to Paula, had taken only a three-day honeymoon and then returned to duties in Kosovo. There was zilch hope of his joining them for another eight months at least. Even then, Yeadings regretted, Angus would get promotion, which must mean a sideways move into uniform.

The radiator belched and in counterpoint someone rapped on his door. He barked out, 'Come,' and DS Beamont slid into the room, snow fresh on his shoulders like a bad case of dandruff. 'Had to leg it from the morgue,' he complained. 'Ruddy car wouldn't start. I've had to send DC Silver over with some leads.'

'Leave the lights on, did you?' Yeadings inquired with exasperating mildness.

'Got flagged down by a ruddy car park attendant at the hospital. Their ticket machines have seized up and he's demanding money with menaces.'

Enough to get Beaumont's quick temper up, Yeadings guessed. He'd have stormed off without a backward glance and the attendant would have paid back his rudeness by omitting to draw his attention to the lights.

'So, what of the post mortem? Does Littlejohn go along with suicide?'

'Looks like it so far, unless anything exotic turns up from toxicology. Most of the stuff already recognized could be obtained over the counter.'

'In the quantity required?'

'She could have gone on a suicide shopping spree. There are chemists enough in town to spread the order.'

'Visit them with her photo. Get times and dates. We don't want to make a mistake here. Then consult with Z. She's dealing with the family background.'

In his overheated office Timothy Fitt looked over his half-moon glasses at his secretary as she presented the correspondence for his signature. 'Thank you, Miss Philpot. Just leave it and I'll – er, run through it.'

He knew it annoyed her, just as he knew he'd find the work faultless. Nevertheless caution was an ingrained habit, and she'd been with the firm long enough by now to appreciate that he couldn't really help it.

There were eight outgoing letters, the final three almost identical and addressed to members of the Howard family. Martin, Rachel and Dolly, *née* Howard but now Shields, were advised that any approach to Miss Emily Howard should be by appointment only and made through the offices of Callendar, Fitt and Maltravers. Access would otherwise not be forthcoming.

It was blunt. It was firm. No point in being anything else with such a questionable set of people.

Chapter Eleven

It wasn't such a bad face, Markham considered, slanting the shaving mirror as he turned one flat, razored cheek towards what morning sunlight stabbed through a crack in the overcast sky. He overlooked the red streaks in his eyes that showed up the washed-out blue of his iris. They were just temporary. There were a few deeper lines than when he'd last examined himself so thoroughly.

Any indication of his freshly liberated libido? He practised a scowl. Impressive. That was the new line: dominance. Watch out; this is a hard man.

He hadn't meant to smile then, and the rictus startled him. Still, impressive; that as well. Even dangerous.

Monday couldn't come soon enough. The new job, the challenge. And in the meantime two whole, yawning days to fill. Of course there was the Lump. He dismissed a brief image of the pudgy, unlovely face, slack-lipped and framed by the nondescript, pale hair, the elephant legs. No way a welcome exercise for the eyes.

What had mattered was the humping, all she was good for: the enormous relief of tension, the sense of vindication. He knew he would be going back there, taking her again, seizing control to the full. She would be there for him and willing. But there was no immediate hurry.

Maybe next time he'd catch her leaving the building, give her a lift. So, to be boy-scout ready, he'd throw his old tartan rug in the back of the Nissan. Stop off somewhere quiet. With the engine still running, he'd have her strip off. The satisfaction of flesh against flesh, slippery with sweat. No clumsy fumblings with elastic and straps.

And in the meantime? Reward himself for the bold new moves in his life. Look at some cars? Think about something more eye-catching, in silver perhaps. A three-year old with low mileage. Not that he'd necessarily be buying right now, just surveying the market. He'd need to do something about the Nissan, spruce it up to get a reasonable exchange rate.

At present there was a rare kerb space almost opposite his one-bedroom flat. He was still using the council car park because nobody had thought to snatch back the electronic admission card. He went out to the back yard and routed behind the dustbins for the traffic cone he'd picked up a couple of months back. He dumped it outside to keep the space free, then set out on foot to retrieve his car and give it a bit of a sponge-off.

But that was when they spotted him and demanded the entry card back. Sourly he drove back and started a vigorous overhaul.

It was some weeks since he'd even emptied the boot and now he made a good job of it, working himself into an almost enjoyable sweat, squirting the interior with kitchen cleaner and polishing everywhere with an old shirt. He used two buckets of soap suds outside on bodywork and windows, finishing with a final slosh of clean water to rinse the whole thing off. The bloody thing had never looked better, even the day he bought it, five years back. Good enough to let it be seen when he did a tour of the Saturday second-hand market on waste ground down by the river. After that he'd have to find somewhere else to park it.

Indoors again, he made himself an instant coffee, drinking it standing at the sink, ready to leave in overcoat and gloves. As a last-minute thought he dug out his cheque book for the Halifax Building Society. You never could tell. Maybe he'd see just the bargain he was looking for.

DS Rosemary Zyczynski was late quitting her bed because there were only thirty pages left to read in the library book she meant to return that morning. She'd taken one look at the overcast sky, thanked heaven it was a free day, and taken her breakfast of cereal and coffee back to the warmth of bed. When the call came from Moura of the Drugs Squad she stuck a finger in as bookmark while she took the message.

Geordie Moffat had come up with a possible name for the OD case in ITU. The boy was a Micky Kane, a Londoner only recently arrived. He wasn't skin-popping, was a beginner on smack, 'just to keep out the cold'. Quite a toff in a way, Geordie considered, but a bit out of his depth.

Z thanked her. 'Your snout certainly came up with the goods.

I'll get on to it right away.'

'No snout. Like I said, it was just a *quid pro quo*.'

'Any time I can do the same for you...'

'Like getting me off on a murder rap? I tell you, it'll be for that swine of a chauvinistic sergeant I seem joined to at the hip. Though you needn't look far for alternative suspects!'

Z laughed, let the book fall on the floor and rolled out of bed. Now that she had a name for the teenager she'd drop in at the hospital, so they could fill in their paperwork.

She found Alyson had a free day, but Bernice told her the lad was stabilized and transferred from ITU to High Dependency, the adjoining unit. She went through and recognized him propped up on three pillows, scowling at the duty nurse at the central desk who monitored the bank of screens for her patients. He was still wired up to a drip, but otherwise seemed ready for the next phase of 'step down'. However pathetic he'd looked on first sight, now he was making progress. Tomorrow, she was told, he could be on an open ward.

Z dropped a couple of magazines on his bed and grinned breezily. 'Hi, Micky. How're things today?'

His scowl transferred itself on to her, then she saw the panic dart in his eyes as he caught up on what she'd called him. 'My name's Joe.'

'Whatever,' she said, shrugging. 'Hope I've hit on something that interests you.' She nodded towards the magazines.

He poked them apart with a rigid finger. 'Football,' he said scornfully. Apparently model aircraft were more in his line. He picked that one up. 'Thanks, anyway.' He sounded a tad ashamed of his surliness. Maybe had decent manners drummed into him way back. Less spiky now, perhaps he'd decide she'd hit on his name by sheer fluke.

'You work in this place?' he demanded.

'No. Just across the square. Civil servant. Anyway, can't stop. Got shopping to do.'

His sudden look of suspicion must mean he'd taken her for a social worker. Or was wary of the Probation Office.

'Benefits clerk,' she said cheerfully. True enough; she liked to think of the Job as beneficial. 'Be seeing you.'

Lying in the second bed from the nurse's station, Micky had watched the woman all morning and half the afternoon through slitted eyes, awaiting his opportunity. Everyone, he knew, was a creature of habit, and she no different despite the training. There had to be a moment he could use. She busily came and went, spoke to doctors or colleagues at the door, returned, checking the six beds, one unoccupied, finally the bank of monitors on her desk.

They were what bugged him. He'd have to wipe out the system, then he could manage the rest. All he needed was one minute when she was otherwise engaged. It came when a nutty old guy at the far end started plucking at his stitches. A triple heart-bypass, he'd been moved in during the night when there was a rush on ITU. The nurse went across to him, dealt with him like a schoolmarm. And then was distracted as a porter and nurse from A&E started barging in with a trolley and a patient for the vacant bed.

Micky swung his feet out, reached for the IV stand and started gently wheeling it towards the toilets. 'Gotta go. I'm bursting,' he protested as the nurse turned to block him off.

The trolley was now alongside the vacant bed and the other nurse waiting. 'Mind how you go, then,' the dragon warned, and turned her back as he slid past. A patient by the swing door raised himself on one elbow, but Micky scowled savagely and he saw fit to look away. With luck, no need now to tamper with the monitors.

He made it to the corridor. There were figures walking his way from the far end. He pulled open the neighbouring wood-panelled door. It was a walk-in linen cupboard. He tore the cannula from his wrist and steered the IV stand into the vacant space. Voices passed outside. When it was quiet again he ventured out.

Along the corridor two women in outdoor clothes were seated on stacking chairs outside a door marked X-ray, awaiting their turn. Hoping they'd accept that his hospital gown granted him priority, he nodded confidently and went through the swing doors.

He had entered a square ante-room having three cubicles with the curtains left open. They all appeared empty. In two there were neatly folded blue gowns on the seat, but the last had outdoor clothing hung from a hook on the partition wall.

From beyond a closed door marked *No Entry* he made out the radiographer's voice as she settled a patient on the table. From the opposite end a swing door opened and a ward maid started to enter backwards wheeling a small trolley of crockery. He whipped inside the further cubicle and pulled the curtain across.

Behind his neck he felt the cool touch of a leather car coat. He lifted it down, removed the check shirt and tweedy trousers hanging under it. They would have fitted a six-foot fatty, but they were all on offer. He had no hope of tracking down his own clothes removed when he was brought in.

He slipped on boxer shorts and string vest, bunched the voluminous trousers at his waist inside a belt that had no holes where he needed them, but the leather was soft enough for him to knot it at one hip. The check shirt was like a maternity dress and he stuffed it in to give himself bulk. Then, with the trousers tucked up inside at the ankles, he could rely on the car coat to cover any suspicious lumps.

The maid had trundled her trolley out into the corridor and now she was standing beside the two waiting women, chatting as Micky walked past, self-conscious at his bulk. If they noticed anything odd perhaps they'd accept it as teenage grunge.

He made it unchallenged to the hospital's main entrance and shuddered as the outer chill struck his exposed head. For a microsecond he regretted leaving the overheated ward, but liberty was sweeter. They could be searching for him already, haring around the corridors in panic, but Security would be slow to connect the X-ray outpatient's theft of clothes with a nameless teenager missing from High Dependency.

He was just glad he hadn't needed to pull the plug on the monitor system. It might have meant curtains for one of the really doddery old guys linked up to it.

DS Zyczynski had had second thoughts about passing Micky's name to hospital reception before dropping in at the nick to check on missing persons on the PNC. When she scrolled through records, his name flashed up as a runaway juvenile, aged thirteen, with an address in Wimbledon.

It sounded like a classy neighbourhood. So what had got into Micky that he decided to leave home some five days back?

A phone call to the Met could relieve her of further responsibility. The DC she spoke to agreed to inform the Kane family of his whereabouts and arrange a visit. Back here uniform branch were handling the theft of the debit card, but she was curious enough to chase up the officer who'd dealt with it. She found him in the canteen.

'This guy Allbright was right chuffed to have it back,' he told her. 'Refused to press charges. Yeah; said he must have dropped it, renewing his season ticket at the station.'

Nothing surprising there. That was where Moura's informant had said young Micky hung around. He could have picked the card up innocently enough, but it didn't excuse his using it fraudulently. Nor did it explain how he'd obtained the man's PIN number for withdrawing cash. It seemed the constable hadn't questioned Allbright about that.

Z doubted Micky Kane was used to sleeping rough inside the station perimeter. Drugs Squad should have been checking on any dealing taking place there, and wouldn't station staff, a cleaner at least, have had some idea of activities overnight? There would have been debris left behind: food wrappers or used needles.

'So this Eric Allbright's a commuter. Did he say where to?'

The constable stared at her. 'Nuh. Wasn't the chatty sort.'

A constable at the next table leaned across. 'Did you say Allbright? Bloke lives in Carrington Way?'

Between them they decided it was the same man. 'He's a nightworker at the stationery warehouse. Last week he reported damage to the nearside wing of his Vectra while it was parked in the yard. Working locally, what would he want with a season rail ticket?'

'Dunno. Mebbe he's got a day job somewhere else as well. What's the opposite of moonlighting? – sunlighting?'

The chat was degenerating into feeble witticisms. Interesting all the same, Zyczynski reckoned. Not all the tittle-tattle in canteen was entirely useless.

Checking up on the young runaway had eaten into her free morning. While in the building she might as well check in CID office whether anything fresh had come in.

A faxed pathology report was addressed to her, covering a post mortem she'd attended on an eighteen year old woman found dead in the family garage. As assumed then, the cause of death was confirmed as carbon monoxide poisoning, with no reason to doubt it being self-administered. She had also ingested a number of painkiller capsules with a considerable quantity of alcohol.

In which case, Z agreed, this was certainly a serious attempt, unlike the botched wrist-slashing by Audrey Stanford. Hers had been intended, if only fleetingly, as escape from the horror of terminal cancer; whereas this other woman apparently had a clean bill of health and no known reason to end a young life full of promise. Except that she'd been rather much of a loner, didn't mix with others in her final school year.

So how and why did she accumulate the capsules? Z asked herself. She couldn't have obtained that quantity in one purchase. And if not taken to deaden some physical pain, had she some overwhelming grief or guilt? Before the inquest someone really must look again at her personal history. And supposedly that chore would fall to herself.

Sheena Judd always resented working at weekends, but this Saturday Alyson had free from the hospital, so she stayed home to let Emily's carer go. Sheena caught a midday London train to go window-shopping in Oxford Street, intending to stay on late for a meal in Soho, to watch the passing nightlife from a bar stool, wander past the sleazy strip clubs, dreaming how she'd be taken for a model, at home among the bright lights.

Reality was otherwise. She examined a lot of fashion clothes she might have wanted if they'd been a quarter of the price, and even more that she wouldn't be seen dead in however throwaway the offers. Continuous tramping of city streets made her feet ache and swell. As for being noticed, she could have been invisible. Three gawking youths, turning from lurid pictures in a club doorway, jostled her off the pavement. She cut off a howl of pain as her ankle turned in the gutter. One looked back and made an obscene gesture with a finger.

Time to slope off home before things got really rough up here. The food at the Greek café had been fatty and now she was bloody well getting heartburn. She picked up a bunch of tired mauve chrysanthemums for half price from a trader closing down his barrow, turned on weary feet and made again for Oxford Street and a bus for the station. In the train she picked off the occasional brown petals and dropped them to the floor.

The flowers would still do to pass to Mum. Another gift from the new boyfriend, she'd say, like the single éclair left over yesterday and carried home as a trophy. Four would have made her sick anyway, and Markham had said he didn't do the cannibal thing, whatever he meant by that.

No harm in stringing the old girl along. A bit of a giggle getting her all excited about possibilities; not that anything'd come of whatever it was she had going with Markham. He might not be the total tosser she'd taken him for, but all the same...went a bit over the top like. Didn't know where to stop. She wasn't sure she was on for much more rough stuff, though it was good at the time. Maybe hold off a bit. Treat him mean and keep him keen. Or not so much keen as more careful. Let him give her some decent presents. And, if she kept on at him, maybe he'd take her out in his car.

Alyson Orme checked over the printout of her shopping list for the coming week and laid it alongside the telephone. The supermarket preferred orders for delivery taken off the website but she didn't subscribe to the habit; used a PC but hadn't a modem. It was hard enough to cram her life into twenty-four hours without such time-devouring pursuits.

She checked on Emily, who was sitting out, smiling dreamily, eyes closed and music playing in her headset. It was luxury to get the whole day here at the flat with her. They rarely shared afternoons together. Later she would drive her round all the rooms in her wheelchair so she could enjoy her pictures again. And if it hadn't tired her too much they'd end up at the observation window and have tea looking out at the hills. Until then there were jobs to do, and she hadn't yet brought up the morning's post from downstairs. Alyson went down, unlocked the penthouse box and slid out her letters. Among the junk mail and a couple of receipted bills was a belated and buckled Christmas card from an old colleague nursing in Barbados. She examined the postmark. Only five weeks getting here! It looked careworn enough for twice that.

There was also a hand-delivered envelope addressed to her and bearing the name of the law firm Callendar, Fitt and Travis on the reverse flap. Further instructions regarding Emily's welfare? She tore the envelope open. The letter, above Timothy Fitt's cramped signature, gave notice that a representative of Miss Withers' insurance company was preparing a fresh schedule for the art works in her collection. It would be appreciated if he could be accorded every facility to review the pictures. No likely date was given for his visit.

Alyson assumed she would be notified in advance by telephone, and returned to pin the letter on the kitchen notice board. It was time then to prepare a tray and set out Emily's purée from the fridge. She put everything ready before lifting the frail little body into the wheelchair for her revue of the collection.

In the hallway Emily gave a little cackle of mirth, pointing at a frame on the wall. It was a tinted ink drawing Alyson had always found distasteful. Among a random assortment of apparently metallic objects a skeletal human form could be discerned. Although fleshless, some muscles and ligaments remained, drawn out and attenuated like strings of chewing gum, to be draped over various angular shapes. Like some Picassos she'd seen elsewhere, there were misplaced features; an ear attached to the side of something resembling a fire iron; a single malevolent eye implanted in the neck.

Nothing remotely comic there: surely the outcome of a tortured mind. Many of the other pictures were dark in mood, but they seemed to give Emily pleasure. Perhaps she remembered the circumstances of acquiring them, when she'd run the Scottish gallery with her son-in-law. That was all Timothy Fitt had ever mentioned to account for the collection.

They were all by modernists. There was a calm, understated Cape Cod house signed by Edward Hopper; a prostrate statue and receding arches which she knew must be a Chirico; a continuous black line that wound through patches of runny colour from which you saw forms gradually emerge – a face, buttocks, a serpent, a flower. Then a broken window with the cracks radiating like a monstrance and, viewed in their sharp angles, the shadowy columns of a great, disintegrating cathedral.

Only at the entrance to the drawing room was there a reassuring patch of vibrant life, where three smallish oils were grouped; two street scenes with a Mediterranean feeling and a small blue bowl of mixed flowers on a white, drawn-thread cloth. On one of these Alyson made out the artist's name, Anne Redpath. Opposite them Emily put out a hand to stay their progress. She was smiling, but sadly.

'Some of my favourites,' Alyson said, encouraging her.

Emily nodded. 'I – knew – Anne.'

'In Scotland?'

'Edin – burgh. She – went away.'

That seemed the sum of Emily's intention to converse, but Alyson was pleased with her effort. She steered the wheelchair in front of the observation window. 'Of all the pictures this is what I love best.' She waved an arm at the darkening view as the winter sun sank into low cloud. A rare silver thread edged the tips of several buildings.

Emily leaned a little forward. 'Glass – wall. Safe – inside.'

'Safe and snug,' Alyson agreed. 'Let's have tea, shall we?'

Chapter Twelve

Sunday, February 3rd.

Because in all the months that Alyson had been looking after Emily she had never had an evening out, she was convinced something would force her to cancel Keith's invitation to dinner. At eleven on Sunday morning, when the phone rang, she was sure this had happened.

It was a stranger's voice asking for her. His name, he said, was Carlton Merritt. Mr Fitt would undoubtedly have informed her that he was revaluing Miss Withers' art collection on behalf of her insurers.

It so happened that he was at present in London preparing a new catalogue for the Wigmore Collection but must return to Amsterdam within two days. It was perhaps expecting too much to suggest he call at such short notice, but this afternoon was the only occasion he would be able to offer for at least two weeks. Since the premium renewal would be due by then it was inadvisable to let so much time elapse.

She saw his point. The drawback was that she couldn't be here herself when he hoped to call. Perhaps he'd assumed that, since it was the weekend, she would be at home to receive him. She explained her position and, picking up her hesitation, he immediately withdrew his suggestion.

His apology was so gracious and heartfelt that she felt loath to make problems. Sheena would be here after all, and the visit had been officially sanctioned by Emily's solicitor. Refusal could create difficulties with the renewal of the insurance.

'Could you tell me your time of arrival?' she asked him. 'I'll need to arrange with Miss Withers' carer who'll be on duty then.'

He assured her he needed no looking after, apart from an available socket for his laptop computer. He would be no trouble at all, and he understood from Mr Fitt the present circumstances of Miss Withers' condition. There would be no call to disturb her in any way. Perhaps four o'clock would be convenient?

It was agreed. Alyson wrote out a memo for Sheena, with instructions to provide Mr Merritt with a tray of tea. It could have been worse. The phone call she'd dreaded would have been from Ramón, saying he couldn't after all cover for her tonight.

Amsterdam, the man had said. It sounded an interesting city to be working from. He hadn't sounded Dutch; rather upmarket boarding school, with an underlying hint of the anglicized Scot. Which might well be how he'd come across Emily in the first case. Quite proper and a little old-fashioned, he conjured up a well-dressed, urbane, youngish middle-aged image.

With that minor hiccup settled, her spirits began to soar. She cautioned herself that this evening wasn't really significant: merely a return invitation for meals she'd provided for Keith when he'd turned up late and weary. This would be a one-off, never repeatable treat. In a few days Dr Ashton would have Audrey's condition sufficiently stabilized for her to return home or go some place where Keith could stay to look after her until the end.

And then? There was no afterwards, just as there never was at work when the patient was finally wheeled away. As far as a nurse was concerned her involvement was over; she must deny any personal loss. When Audrey was no more Keith, however grieving, would go on doctoring. And here there would still be Emily.

She looked through her wardrobe and selected the blue uncrushable silk. It would shake out at the end of her evening shift while her uniform went into in her locker. She pinned on the star-shaped brooch of pearls which had been her mother's. Simple enough preparations for the most momentous evening of her life.

Idiot, she told herself. It was a long time since she'd felt this way, as a student nurse going out to party in a crowd of youngsters. There had been moments of passion, even times she'd imagined herself really in love. But this was different: no more than a shared meal and the companionship of trusted friends. Nothing spoken between them, all understood.

Superintendent Mike Yeadings had set aside that Sunday morning for turning over the empty vegetable plot and digging in some potent manure. The noisome deposit had been delivered on Friday at the entrance to his drive while Nan had been out shopping. As a result both his Rover and her Vauxhall were now taking up kerb space, both out of range of the hose he needed for washing them down.

Removal of the offensive smell became doubly imperative when Nan declared baking priorities prevented her taking either to the car-wash. It was, he decided, becoming one of those days.

An ice cream van's dulcet chimes cut across their discussion. 'Papageno,' Yeadings announced drily.

'Pied Piper,' Nan corrected him with resignation. The children's noses were already pressed against the window panes. 'Mike, have you any loose change?'

He paid up grudgingly, fetched shovel and wheelbarrow and resigned himself to the fact that professional gardeners, if not CID superintendents, held their sabbath day sacrosanct from others' demands. As if to underline this principle the kitchen phone rang and it had to be his DI informing him that they had a body recovered from the river at Barham Marsh.

Salmon was already on the scene and had called in Zyczynski since she had a connection with the deceased. The DI was clearly put out and seemed to be blaming her for the discovery.

How connected? Yeadings asked himself, having hung up on the information. His woman sergeant had a number of friends he wouldn't care to hear of in the past tense, and certainly not if there were suspicious circumstances.

If his mind hadn't already been geared to a different kind of muckspreading he'd have thought to demand a name for the corpse. The obvious thing was to ring Z and ask, solicitously, what had happened.

Her mobile phone was turned off. Nan, returning from the ice cream van with two cornet-licking children in tow, demanded, 'What's up, Mike? I thought I heard the phone. They don't want you to go in, surely?'

'Not exactly.' He explained how little he knew.

'And you couldn't reach Z? Well, if it's personal...'

'You're right.' He was way ahead of her. 'I'll get over there myself and see what's up.'

Barham was a fairly new development on the edge of town,

with a number of council-owned apartment blocks and a small industrial estate built on reclaimed land. A stretch of greensward had been preserved on either side of the river and some pretence made of establishing a rowing centre.

'It's a lad, sir,' a constable informed him as he slid under the police tape securing the site.

So most likely an accident. There was always a certain amount of fooling about went on down here on a Saturday night.

Yeadings made out Rosemary Zyczynski alongside Beaumont on the opposite bank. She caught sight of him at the same moment, raised a hand and started to clump back over the wooden bridge in her green wellies.

'Someone known to us?' he asked in the recognizable phrase.

Her face was whipped red by the easterly wind. He couldn't decide if the brightness of her eyes was due to unshed tears. 'Just came across him this week,' she said shortly. 'A runaway teenager from Wimbledon called Micky Kane. Discovered locally OD, three days back. I left a report for you last night. His parents are due here tomorrow to see us.'

This was bad. 'How old?'

'Thirteen. I haven't heard yet how he got away from the High Dependency ward.'

'A runaway twice over. Now he's managed to drown himself?'

'It doesn't look like that. Somebody – something – had beaten his head in.'

Yeadings stared grimly across at the knot of policemen and the white tent being erected over a pitifully small shape on the ground. This day had started with shit and that was the way it was going on.

'Who identified him?'

'I did. DI Salmon called me in. They'd just pulled him out and I recognized him as a recorded Misper.'

'So this is the lad you saw when visiting Mrs Stanford?'

'Yes. I told you about the key hidden in his trainer. A friend has told me it's like one he has for a deposit box at his solicitor's.'

'Which one? That's not usual, surely, for legal firms to hold securities accessible by clients' key. Though I don't see any reason they shouldn't.'

'Callendar, Fitt and Travis. It doesn't mean they're the only firm to use the same make of key, but it's an unusual shape.'

'Is this Micky Kane known to them?'

'I hadn't got that far, sir. I'm hoping to see them tomorrow, before the parents arrive. It's unlikely a solicitor would discuss anything over the phone.'

'Go ahead anyway, though it may prove irrelevant. He could have picked the key up off the street. Or from someone's pocket. Like the debit card you mentioned before.'

Oliver Markham had to accept that, having been labouring in a rut these past few years, once he'd struck out in a new direction all kinds of minor options seemed on offer. He had three times changed his mind that morning about how he would spend the afternoon.

If he'd been able to clinch a deal on the new car yesterday he'd have intended giving it a tryout. Since that was off the cards until the bank opened tomorrow he felt disinclined to use the old one. Now it was spruced up he saw no point in getting it mussed. Unless, of course, to some purpose. For example there was nothing to stop him calling in at the penthouse and having another shufti at those weird paintings that might, or might not, be originals. Or even signed prints.

To do that he'd need some excuse, like inviting the Lump out for a drink and a drive. Then again, once he got her in the car there could be an entirely different act on the books.

It could mean losing his parking space outside his flat over the Oxfam shop, because if he left his traffic cone there more than half an hour it would be swiped as sure as pigeons' shit, and the council parking area was now barred to him.

So the Nissan would have to take its chances along with all the other garage-less crocks in the over-parked, non-permitted roads that brought in the lucrative council fines. He ruefully considered the drawback of being now on the wrong side of the official desk. So, once he drove off, Sheena Judd would certainly need to make his night out worthwhile, if not memorable.

In the meantime he put on his new leather coat and took himself off to air it along the river. He exited from his doorway between the Oxfam shop and the ironmonger's to turn left into the alley leading down behind the old Co-op building. There were crumpled drink cans in the gutter and discarded food wrappings soggily blowing along the cobbles, souvenirs of Saturday night junk-food grazers going home on foot. Once the residual stink would have been of fatty salted chips and acrid vinegar. Now, everywhere, stale spicy vindaloo assaulted the nostrils, ironically the new national standby. He made it a point of honour to despise Asian food.

He turned left towards Barham. Despite the biting wind there was a little crowd down by the jetty where the boats were tied up in summer. Mostly they were in the sheds now or padlocked to iron stanchions and upended for repainting. Occasionally some louts stove in the clinkers or sprayed graffiti over the fibreglass hulls. They'd had several cases of criminal damage brought up in court, but of late that novelty had dropped away.

Maybe it had started up again. There were police uniforms among the knot of people on the farther bank. They seemed to be fixing up some kind of screen. A white tent. He realized then he'd walked right into a serious crime scene. Recognizing the mortuary van that now coasted along behind him, he pressed forward, eager to glimpse the body.

Across the water the grass had barely been frosted. Now, even inside the security tapes, the grass was flattened and muddied by constabular trampings. He saw the DI who had replaced Angus Mott, and the man appeared to be fuming. Both detective sergeants were there, and even as he watched them their boss arrived by car on the nearer bank. The brown-haired girl sergeant with the unpronounceable name filed off, crossed over the bridge to meet him. DI Salmon scowled after her. This was intriguing stuff. Markham quietly closed up to catch the conversation.

'...just this week,' Zyczynski was saying.

Yeadings and the woman stood immersed in their discussion. Only an odd word here and there reached the eavesdropper's ears.

Suddenly the superintendent turned, aware of someone hovering in earshot. 'Ah, Mr Markham, what brings you here?'

'A Sunday stroll along the river,' Markham said with oily familiarity. 'I imagine it's different for you.'

There was no response to this. Both detectives were eyeing him warily, unsure how much he had overheard.

'Business, would it be?' Markham prompted.

'Ours exclusively,' Yeadings said crisply. 'I must ask you to leave now as we're shutting this stretch of the river off.'

He wouldn't have expected more. It was one thing to meet on a level footing in police court – or *almost* level; at least on the same side – but once outside it coppers played that game of Them and Us. Everyone a suspect. A race apart. So bloody superior. As if there hadn't been any dirty police linen washed in public of late.

Already more uniforms were moving in on them. Markham gave a wolfish grin intended as sardonic, nodded and turned away. At least his little stroll had proved eventful. He had no name for the body, but in connection he'd caught the mention of a local firm: a fresh conversational topic for his visit to the penthouse.

'Oh shit,' Sheena muttered as the entrance buzzer sounded. She had been late arriving to take over from Alyson and had won herself a chilly reception. There had barely been time for her attention to be drawn to the kitchen noticeboard before the nurse was away, reminding her that Ramón would take over from her at 8 p.m.

Now, recalled by the buzzer, she hurriedly re-read the note Alyson had left. This visitor must be the man about insuring the pictures. Merrill was it, or Merritt? She looked at the CCTV screen. He was staring up at the camera, cool and collected. Hadn't buzzed a second time. Nice-looking guy, dark hair greying at the temples, and a camel military-style overcoat that looked expensive.

She put on her fancy voice. 'Who is it, please?'

He gave the right name and she buzzed him in, rapidly checked her face and hair in the hall mirror, then went out to wait for the lift to come up.

Chapter Thirteen

Ramón stood stock-still at the window, working it out. It had been no illusion. A body had actually fallen from up here. In his mind the action ran again like frames of film in slow motion, the body turning over and over, arms outflung, legs splayed, skirts lifted by up-draught. And there had been no scream, unless the traffic sounds below drowned it out.

No. This time no scream, because she had been either unconscious or dead already before she fell. So, no accident; no natural death. There had been that unaccountable smear of blood on the glass that meant more. This was murder.

He leant his head against the glass, allowing his heart rate to slow as normality re-asserted itself around him. He took comfort from the petty domestic sounds of the apartment, the central heating breathing gently in synch as room temperatures began to level out. On the surface nothing showed that a panel of the glass wall had been left gaping to icy wind.

And who exactly had fallen? At first he'd assumed it was the old lady. But he had gone in to find her still in her rumpled bed, asleep on her back, nose upthrust, her face as sharp-angled and bloodless as a chicken carcase. So it was another woman. The one called Sheena, or else Nurse Orme who had given him the job. But she never came back until a little after eight, and tonight he was here to replace her.

Quietly he went back to Emily's bedroom and leaned over, feeling for the warmth of her hands and was reassured. Her pulse appeared as feeble and as scatty as ever, reminding him of a small beetle teetering over rough pebbles.

He felt unexpected relief that his first guess had been wrong. Not the old lady. She was safe here in bed. Everything could continue as it was, as it should be. Only her covers were disordered, one pillow fallen to the floor. He lifted it back and untangled the duvet from between her bony legs.

Emily alone here. Beyond her the penthouse had been deserted when he arrived: the carer not at her post to let him in, and the door unlocked. So she it was he'd seen fall from the window. The woman Sheena. He felt no regret. She meant nothing to him.

He had many times seen violent death; compelled to watch, or participate in action that led to atrocities. Most inevitable at the time, almost necessary, leaving him numbed. Only that first time had it had that devastating power, sapping his mind to leave him unable to erase its nightmare repetition.

For the moment those childhood images no longer crowded his brain. It was out in the street that the horror had seemed to be repeating itself. But he clung to the basic truth: that this was a *different* death. This time for someone never a part of his life. It hardly mattered whether she'd forced that end or been an unsuspecting victim. Nor would he reach for any reason behind it. Inexplicable things happened which were no concern of his.

Yet there was certainly danger, because, in this country killing must be accounted for. It wasn't always so for him. He had killed because he was under orders, killed in cold blood, unquestioning, and because you killed them or they killed you. No doubt then who the enemy was. Muslims or pirates or Catholics, they were as savage as each other, raiding, raping and laying waste the smaller islands. Only survival mattered.

Lately he'd begun to see it as a kind of madness; still sometimes in his sleep was back there doing it again. There were moments when he had to hold on to himself and fight down the demons, because memories crowded his head overfull and he knew what he had done, again heard the screams, saw the blood, the decapitations, the dead children left lying in the sun to rot.

He looked around now, reassured by the quiet apartment with its pale, rich carpets and the strange paintings on its walls. This was his present reality. Could he believe he'd madly imagined the other, the falling body, because once before when it happened he'd watched petrified, tight-bound and unable to move. He'd heard her high, attenuated scream as she was thrust out into space and fell, turning over and over until the sickening crunch of her bones on the rocks below. His mother, following her two youngest babies deemed useless; unlike himself who was nine years old and could be taken away as loot.

Sickened, he went through to the bathroom off the nurse's bedroom, and plunged his head under a shock of cold water. He buried his face in the soft folds of a towel. He shouldn't be here now; having no key, was not supposed to arrive until Sheena buzzed him in downstairs. Instead, alerted by what he'd seen from the street, he'd shouldered his way past a woman coming in, then found the apartment door unlocked.

And then, checking the front rooms, he'd missed whoever slipped out. Concerned with the open glass panel, he wouldn't have heard a lift going down. The one he'd used was still there at this level. He couldn't remember if the other had been there when he'd rushed past.

Get out, he'd told himself. Creep downstairs, all the way on foot; wait outside in the rain. Turn up at the right time, having collected the clean stuff from the launderette. Find no one to let him in, and finally go away. Leave Nurse Orme to puzzle over why Sheena wasn't here...

Or stay on. Let it seem everything was all right: that he'd come at the time arranged; that Sheena had let him in and gone on her way. He could simply get on with caring for Emily.

Going straight from the riverbank to the address she'd looked up in the local directory, DS Rosemary Zyzcynski found Allbright at home, relaxed, wearing sweatshirt, jeans and trainers. He'd answered the door himself and she caught no sound of anyone else in the house.

He was a physical type part of her remembered from child-hood. Recalled and loathed: the square body with arms and legs awkwardly attached at the four corners; slightly hump-backed; no neck and the heavy, cubical head hung forward like a bullock's stolidly enduring driven rain.

His impact on her was so strong that momentarily she was at a loss. Then training kicked in, even while she wondered that he could affect her. She identified herself and reminded him of the lost debit card.

'Yeah,' Allbright agreed, 'but I thought that was all settled. They said some kid picked it up and blew fifty off it.'

'And just happened on the right four-figure PIN number to

feed into the machine?' Isn't that unlikely, Mr Allbright?'

His eyes flickered, a lightning reaction out of keeping with the lumbering body. He gave a lopsided grin. 'Blame my leaky memory. Can't hold numbers, so I jot everything down. Must have pulled out the note I'd made, along with the card.'

She let enough silence build to let her doubt get to him. Behind the heavy face she could sense his resentment, but his features gave nothing away.

'Right,' she said calmly. 'Well, now that you have it back perhaps you'll be more careful in future. Keep the number and the card in separate places, as they advise.' She sounded total Plod. Let him accept her as a dumb female doing follow-up for a male colleague. She hoped she hadn't alerted him to being a suspect. It wasn't a formal questioning anyway or she'd have taken a second officer along.

'Maybe it's safer to cancel the card and apply for a new one,' he said, trying her out.

There would be no point: Micky Kane was dead, so couldn't misuse it again. Not that she'd any intention of telling him this latest development. Let him pick it up from local gossip or the next issue of the *Sentinel*. Even if Micky had lived, the remembered PIN number was useless without the card.

She left it at that, but the suspicion remained with her either that Allbright had given Micky the money for his fix, or – surely more risky – he had told him the number and sent him with the card to get the cash.

'You thought you might have dropped it at the railway station.'

'Really can't be sure now. Could have been a number of places.'

So he was recanting on that. Did he realize the station suggested his connection with the dead boy? She would need to be careful here, remain impersonal, because instinctive dislike was making her keen to lump some kind of blame on him.

'A pity you can't remember specifically.'

'It doesn't matter now. All sorted. I'll be fifty quid the wiser in future.' He gave a rueful grin. If he'd hoped it would disarm her, he failed.

The suspicion strengthened in her that the fifty pounds had

been to pay Micky off, and the man himself had trusted him with the card to draw the cash at the bank's wall-safe. But why should Allbright take such a risk? – unless he had some hold over the boy, so that Micky wouldn't have dared do more than instructed? He'd have had some good reason for returning to the man. Probably would have done so, if he hadn't been picked up unconscious from the overdose.

And didn't that mean that, as soon as he could get free of hospital, this is where he would have headed? If they applied for a search warrant would they find evidence of his presence in the man's house?

Maybe she was racing ahead of the facts. There wasn't enough against him to take such measures. Only her gut feeling, and that was too personal.

'Well, thank you for your cooperation, Mr Allbright,' she told him, making it sound final, but being far from satisfied. She nodded and turned back into the wind, conscious of him standing there staring after her until she got into her car.

It would be interesting to see whose face came up on the security film used through the cash-point peephole. Tomorrow, for starters, she would need to visit the man's bank and run it through. Also she'd make sure uniforms asked around for witnesses of any meeting between the two. Someone must have noticed Micky about the streets in the past few days, a boy of school age during term time. She would need permission from Upstairs for a sanitized post-mortem photograph to accompany an appeal in the local press.

With a murder case pending, there would be a wide area to investigate. It was essential to know how long the boy from Wimbledon had been in this locality, and what brought him here; whether he already had some connection with the town or simply been dropped off by some driver giving him a chance lift. Perhaps his parents' visit would clarify that, but they wouldn't be in a state for in-depth questioning straight off.

So, suppose her suspicions were right and Micky had been sent by Allbright to pick up the cash, what kind of association with the man did that imply? Not a charitable one, for sure. What services would Allbright have been paying a thirteen-year-old boy for?

Sadly, Zyczynski thought, Prof Littlejohn's post mortem examination might supply that answer. And where did the smack overdose come into the calculation? They must question whether Allbright was a dealer or supplier. Locally there was an established underground trade in drugs. A night worker at a warehouse where heavy goods vans called regularly over the hours of darkness – the man was certainly worth looking into.

It wasn't until that evening, as she watched an American thriller on TV involving a car chase round hairpin mountain bends that she suddenly knew why Allbright had seemed familiar and so odious.

He was the same physical type as the constable who'd shattered her life at the age of ten. He'd accompanied a woman officer to break the news of her parents killed in Italy by speeding teenagers in a stolen sports car. He'd been the one loudly announcing it to her aunt as she watched from between the railings of the stairs.

It was from that heart-chilling moment, when his face and body became indelibly printed on her mind, that nothing had ever been as sane and secure again. From that day, slowly she had grown to learn the uncertain boundary between adult authority and adult evil, until, years later, she'd dared face out the abusive uncle who'd offered the false security of his home.

In its way that encounter had been the setting-out point for where she was now, upholding the law, doing what she could to fight back at what was rotten. Allbright's likeness to the constable had shaken out the memory, but she had to make sure her present judgment wasn't affected by it. His physical appearance didn't make a villain of the man, any more than the crudeness of that constable had meant he'd intended inflicting pain.

Preparing for an early start on Monday, she was oppressed by a sense of guilt. She'd picked up Micky's case almost by accident, the only police involvement at that point; possibly the one who might have prevented what followed. If only she'd probed into his background when she'd seen him in ITU, reasoned a little further.

Preparing her report on her laptop PC, she stared at what she'd typed on to the screen. If only so many things – if she'd better used the time before he escaped from the hospital; if she'd been quicker making the connection with Allbright; if she'd talked direct with the boy's parents instead of leaving it to an intermediary in the Met. All of that, then she might have, *should have*, prevented it. His death, his innocent death.

At the same time wasn't that morbidly subjective? She tried to see what could be offered in her defence. He was a drug user, therefore to some extent self-destructive. A rebellious runaway schoolboy from what, so far, appeared a respectable, middle-class home.

It was recall of the white, dead face that condemned her. Micky hadn't deserved to end as he did, and from the first she'd recognized him as vulnerable. She'd felt shame, staring down at the sodden flesh already puffed from immersion, that she had forgotten the little brown mole at the corner of his mouth. If she'd had to describe him it would have escaped her. But she recognized it again in death, an inch to the right of the sharply sculpted gutter with its childlike up-tilt above cupid's-bow lips.

Within hours she would have to face his parents in their grief, and she hated what she must tell them.

Someone should pay for this. Herself, yes, but she hadn't been the one who'd made the decision and acted on it, taking the young life as if it had no worth. If that was Allbright – and she was more than half convinced that he was at least involved – then he should be pursued until he had nowhere to run, and prosecuted as heartlessly as he'd used the boy. Even then she'd not have atoned for it herself.

Towards the end of her shift Alyson Orme caught herself clock-watching. She'd been uncomfortably conscious of Bernice's raised eyebrows as she folded the blue silk dress into her locker together with the evening shoes. 'A night out with the girls,' she'd lied.

'Good for you. It's more than time you broke out. All work and no play makes Jacqueline a right old fart.'

'Thanks, I'll take that to heart!'

And when it came to a little short of 8 p.m. Bernice nodded to her to get going. She changed quickly then rang through to the penthouse. Ramón was already there and answered calmly. Emily was fine, he assured her. She seemed to have enjoyed the puréed rice and apple for her supper.

There was sleet on the wind as Alyson ran out huddled in her overcoat, and she felt the shock of puddled mush strike through the toes of her kitten-heeled shoes. But a flash of headlights showed Keith already waiting. He drove across the car park and flung the passenger door wide. The car was warm inside. The scent of his sharp aftershave blended with the pine air-freshener that dangled over the windscreen making her think of retsina and tossed Greek salad.

'I can't quite believe this,' he said, smiling into her eyes as she got in.

'Nor can I actually.' Then she laughed, leaned over and pinched his arm hard through the cloth of his jacket. 'But feel that! It's real.'

Immediately her earlier nervousness was gone. She had feared they would have nothing to say, both tongue-tied by the enormity of what they were doing, both so over-inhibited by a long-established sense of duty. But it was going to be all right. They should feel no disloyalty to anyone from an evening spent in each other's company. Good friends; simply that. Nothing must be allowed to spoil these special hours together.

Superintendent Yeadings confirmed that DI Salmon would be running the general enquiry into Micky Kane's death. Even before it was officially declared as unlawful killing he was making arrangements for setting up an Incident Room.

The facts they had so far were few enough. That morning, fifteen minutes before the police had been alerted, a pair of scullers from the college had seen the body lying face down under a few inches of water at the river's edge, as they went down to drop their shell in. The leather coat had weighed Micky down as the bulky trousers became snagged on a submerged tree root. The brutally crushed back of his head had floated, just visible beneath the surface like some grotesque Halloween mask.

A dog being walked on the towpath was attracted by the scullers' sudden interest, barked and threatened to plunge in after the body. Its woman owner recoiled, retching and, when her shuddering had steadied, rang the police on her mobile phone. All three witnesses had been driven to the nick to give an account of what they'd seen. Not a lot to work on, but it was a start.

Prof Littlejohn had already agreed a time for the post mortem. In the meantime they had Z's information on the boy to interpolate.

At a few minutes before midnight Alyson had been decanted from Keith's car at her door. He came round to steady her stepping down, clutching her coat about her with both hands. They had already thanked each other and there was nothing left to say. Just a quick pressure on her upper arms and then he watched her key in the number to gain entry to the building. She looked back before disappearing behind the smoked glass of the double doors. He put the car in gear to draw away.

He looked at his wristwatch. She was on time to relieve Ramón as arranged.

In the apartment all was still. Ramón stood up and padded out from the kitchen as he heard her come in, dropping her keys on the hall table by the ebony carving of the Three Monkeys.

He gave a slight bow, his flat face impassive as ever. 'All is well here,' he told her in a way that sounded old-fashioned.

'Of course it is.' She gave him a brilliant smile. 'That's neither less nor more than I'd expected. Thank you so much for stepping in like that at such short notice.'

'It happened that I was free. Perhaps I can be of use again.'

Alyson doubted there would be a need. Certainly no repetition of tonight, since Audrey Stanford would be going home in two days. But Ramón deserved encouraging. Now that she'd broken out once, perhaps she'd really organize a night on the town for the girls. Some of the nurses she saw in the canteen were worth knowing better. It wasn't good that they should see her as aloof.

'Perhaps,' she told him. 'Well, goodnight.'

She saw him out, then went, still in her overcoat, to look in on Emily who was sleeping with a little smile on her face. Alyson bent to kiss her forehead. 'Goodnight, Great-aunt. Sweet dreams.'

She didn't feel ready for bed herself, still too wound up by the excitement of the evening. Instead she poured herself fruit juice and went to drink it in the dark by the glass wall. Below, the town's guardian orange lights burned on. The occasional home-going car swept round the main island and disappeared between shadowed buildings.

Everything was normal, secure in a very wonderful world.

Chapter Fourteen

On Monday 4th February the Major Crimes team met early to discuss the death of Micky Kane. Computer printouts were already available covering the paperwork. A note from uniform branch on finding him slumped unconscious led to Zyczynski's report on his stay in hospital and was joined by versions of the body's riverbank retrieval from DI Salmon and DS Beaumont. The hospital had not, as yet, issued an official analysis of drugs the boy had originally ingested nor anything regarding his treatment there and state of health at the time he discharged himself. Superintendent Yeadings understood that an internal inquiry was being held to decide responsibility for his escape, also theft of clothing from an aggrieved patient undergoing X-ray treatment.

'Bloody careless. They've a lot to answer for,' DI Salmon declared sourly. 'Patients have a right to expect due care and vigilance once they're taken in.'

Yeadings wasn't going to let him get away with that. 'You'll find the hospital's responsibility ends when a patient discharges himself, with or without signing the disclaimer. Anything before that remains at present an internal matter and will not affect the conduct of our investigation. It's much to be regretted that the boy's decision resulted in his death.

'Uniform branch are calling house-to-house between the hospital and where the body was found. River Conservancy experts are to report on the most likely point the body would have been dropped in, but we shan't get far with their results until we have some idea of the time scan. Micky was reported missing from the hospital at 5.15 p.m. on Saturday, but that wasn't until corridors and nearby wards had already been searched. Their Security notified us at 5.40, by which time it was dark and the streets were filling with Saturday shoppers going home. From then until those scullers spotted him in the river yesterday morning, we have no witnesses, and so far no official time of death or estimated duration of being in the water. Merely the assumption that he was killed between dusk and dawn.

'There's a backlog of cases at the mortuary, due to the severe weather and a traffic pile-up on the M40 near Holtspur, but Professor Littlejohn will come in for this one himself. The first slot he can make is this afternoon at 3 p.m. Meanwhile DS Zyczynski, with a WPC, will be speaking to the boy's parents.'

'I'll go with her myself,' Salmon overrode abruptly.

There was a short embarrassed silence. Discretion and gentleness were not among the DI's notable talents. Yeadings intervened. 'I have another enquiry that's more pressing,' he said firmly. 'This debit card connection with the man Allbright. He needs to be kept uneasy. Take Beaumont and go over all the points of his story. He implies he knows nothing of the boy, so drop in the name Micky when he's least expecting it.'

'Do a Colombo,' said Beaumont brightly. 'Flasher's raincoat and all.'

'I've been to see him,' Z admitted. 'I'd come across his name from Uniform. As reported, his debit card was found in Micky's clothing when he was picked up unconscious. Apart from the card the boy had only a ten pound note and some silver on him. But the note was freshly issued. It could have been straight from a cash machine. When the card was returned to Allbright he checked his balance and claimed fifty pounds were missing. He took it very calmly.' She gave them the man's explanation of where and how he thought it had been lost.

'Your Micky Kane was a little thief,' Salmon said with a curl of the lip that implied the world wasn't worse off without him.

'What DS Zyczynski is questioning,' said Yeadings, already informed on the matter, 'is whether and how the boy acquired access to the bank's cashpoint. Either Micky had Allbright with him to key in the number – in which case the man would surely have retained the card; or Allbright had lent him the card and told him the number. In either case the man had a part in the boy's recent actions. He must come into the frame, if we find this is a murder case. We have to query every statement he makes.'

'There's something else,' Z went on . 'When I saw Allbright it was ostensibly to check he was satisfied with police handling of his loss. I did mention it was curious the boy had happened on the right access number, and he flashed the excuse he'd written it down, and the paper could have been along with the card in his jacket.'

'So the boy had picked his pocket for both?'

'If indeed Micky was a thief. Allbright had previously claimed he'd dropped the card, but the idea of theft seemed a quite acceptable alternative to him. Yet he still didn't want Micky charged.'

The DI appeared to be digesting this. 'Where's your report on that interview?' he demanded, scowling.

'Gone to computer. You should be getting it any time now.'

Salmon looked to Yeadings for a lead.

'There's the matter of the key,' the superintendent reminded Z.

'Which is still with his unclaimed possessions at the hospital, under the lining of his trainer. As we know, he escaped in clothes belonging to a male outpatient undergoing abdominal X-ray, because he couldn't get to his own in a locker at ITU. It's an unusual-looking key with a number on it, and could belong to a safety deposit box.'

'Also Allbright's?' the DI almost shouted.

'I wouldn't know. I thought better not to mention it to him, in case valuables were involved.'

'So, for all we know, this boy could have been running a Fagin's kitchen business all over the town in the time he's been with us. Why haven't Uniform picked up on this? And where has he been hiding up?'

Z fell silent, treating the questions as purely hypothetical. Salmon glared challengingly round the circle of faces for inspiration.

'Look, I'd better go and meet the boy's parents,' Zyczynski said, rising. 'I hope to make it for the post mortem afterwards.'

Mr and Mrs Stephen Kane had checked in at the *Pheasant* on North Hill where the houses began to thin out, and open fields were still covered by snow of pristine whiteness. He was the branch manager of a jeweller in Wimbledon and she a General Science teacher at the secondary school there. As Z had expected, they appeared respectable and comfortably off. Their car, one of only three in the hotel car park, and not having a local registration, was a dark blue BMW.

Hilda Kane, matronly, with grey-streaked hair flopping from a loose French pleat, faced the two policewomen tight-lipped, as she might a pair of year-nine miscreants. Her husband was more clearly in shock and Z was glad she'd decided to visit their hotel rather than face them in a police station.

'What can you tell us?' the man demanded nervously as soon as they were seated. The hotel had provided them with a small sitting room and now a waitress was bringing in a tray for coffee. Mrs Kane moved across to take over, while Z seated herself opposite and the WPC faded into the background.

'We just can't believe it,' the man said wretchedly, walking up and down behind them. 'Micky has never given us any trouble before.'

'Not more than you'd expect from a young teenager,' his mother granted. 'The usual sulks and fits of non-cooperation. He wasn't wild. Maybe a bit too quiet. All he wanted outside school was to take his dog for walks and to get into the tennis for the championships. He wasn't much of a one for football, although he had to play it, of course. He didn't belong to any gang or go out with other boys. He'd rather sit in his room and read or play with his computer.'

'Never mind that, Mother,' said the husband. 'Get her to tell us what happened.'

So Z explained how she had come across him in hospital after Uniform had found him collapsed in the street. 'We won't know until later exactly what he'd taken, but they'd sorted him out and he was making good progress. I had a word or two with him myself, took in something for him to read, discovered he wasn't interested in football but more keen on model aircraft.'

Hilda Kane stared at her fiercely. 'Did you say anything to upset him? He'd never had anything to do with the police before. He must have been petrified.'

'I didn't tell him I was police. And he wasn't at all upset. Quite quiet and polite. With hindsight I think he was already planning how to make his escape.'

'Wasn't that irregular? I mean, aren't you supposed to warn

people who you are before you question them?' The boy's father had stopped his padding up and down and turned to face her.

'I wasn't questioning. I'd gone there as a friend to enquire after someone else who'd been brought in the same night. A nurse in ITU mentioned Micky and I went along to say hello. Perhaps you would like to meet her. She's warm and understanding. I think she felt sorry for him, so young and on his own. She could probably tell you more about him than I can.'

'But he decided to run away? Again? And he was still unwell?'

'His treatment had barely begun, as I understood it. He just bolted. We've yet to discover why.'

'Nor why he left home in the first place,' his mother said tightly.

'I was wondering,' Zyczynski said after a little pause. 'When you run, it's either from something or to something. If everything seemed normal at home, maybe there was a compelling reason to go elsewhere. What had he taken with him? Did he expect to be away for some time or to get back before his absence was noticed? It was early morning when he was last seen, I believe.'

'It was an ordinary school day. I left in my car just after eight,' Hilda Kane said. 'I had some experiments to set up before assembly. Micky always walks, so I assume he left some half-hour later. It only takes twelve minutes.'

'The police asked me,' her husband put in. 'We left at the same time, at eight twenty-eight exactly.'

Of course, Z noted: a jeweller, he'd have a top-range watch and be a stickler for precison.

'And was Micky carrying anything?'

'His school bag. It seemed quite heavy, but then it almost always was. An open-topped duffel bag with a leather drawstring. I remember he swung it over his shoulder as he went past my car and I heard a buckle or something scratch against the bodywork. I called out for him to be careful. He stopped and turned round, and gave me such a – a funny look.'

The man's voice broke. He could hardly get the next words out. 'That was the last I...'

'Whatever else he had in his bag, he didn't take his clean gym gear. Which he would have needed.' Hilda spoke sharply, as if to demonstrate she was made of sterner stuff.

'So can we suppose he had already made up his mind to skip school, at least for that day?'

Micky's parents turned to look at each other, he wretched, she fiercely aggressive, almost accusing. Hilda nodded. Z assumed that their answer was 'yes'.

'One more question,' she said. 'Was he wearing school uniform?'

'Of course. Grey trousers and shirt; navy blazer with the school crest on its breast pocket; school tie with navy, turquoise and gold stripes; black lace-up shoes.'

Z recalled the clothes she had looked through in ITU: purple roll-neck sweater, jeans and slightly scuffed trainers. Clearly his own leisure clothes. So he had packed alternative gear and disposed of the uniform which could help identify him. Since he didn't have them or his bag when he was picked up unconscious, had they been taken off him or were they stashed away somewhere waiting for him to pick them up? Even having taken a change of clothes, it didn't mean he'd intended staying away. Getting rid of the uniform could have been simply the initial, normal gesture of freedom.

'Can we take him home?' Stephen Kane had been steeling himself for this moment. His voice came out like a rush of air escaping a balloon.

'I'm sorry. There are formalities...'

'She means the post-mortem. And then I suppose there'll be an inquest. When will that be, Sergeant? Because we must decide whether to stay on or come again.' Hilda was forcing herself into organizing mode.

Z explained that a date had yet to be fixed for the inquest, also that they would be asked to attend the police station and sign a statement. But first someone would be needed for the formal identification.

There was a silence. The man said, 'Oh God,' into his cupped hands.

'That had better be me,' Hilda said, her voice softening. She reached out and patted her husband's shoulder. 'I'll do it, Dad. It'll be all right.'

Z sat in the rear with Mrs Kane, with the WPC at the wheel although it was Zyczynski's unmarked car. They left the man standing at the hotel window staring at them as they drove off. Hilda wore her buttoned-up look again. 'Did Micky have any special interests?' Z asked. 'Hobbies or career ambitions?'

There was no answer. She doubted Hilda had heard her. At last, 'He never showed it,' the woman said almost absently, 'but inside he must have been really upset. Rags getting run over. His dog. I should have talked to him, comforted him; but boys can be so prickly. I was afraid of...being repulsed.'

In the penthouse Alyson rang Sheena after breakfast for a report on Carlton Merritt's visit, but there was no answer. Mrs Judd, hearing the phone ring as she was letting herself in hampered by her shopping bags, struggled to release the key from the door's lock. She clucked with annoyance, hearing the phone cut off as she reached it. She dumped her plastic carriers by the kitchen table, eased her aching back and dropped into a chair. When she had kicked her shoes off, she called aloud for Sheena. The girl was idle, still lying abed like that and letting the phone ring on and on.

It was after the kettle had boiled and she was dropping tea bags in two pottery mugs that she realized the girl's sleep must be unnaturally deep or she'd gone out unusually early. She stomped along to the bedroom next to her own and looked in. The bed was made up exactly as she'd left it the previous day. Sheena hadn't merely been late home, she'd been out on the tiles all night.

Little madam, not saying a word or phoning in! Mrs Judd fumed. So much for the boyfriend being such a gentleman! If she went on this way, throwing herself at him, she'd lose him for sure. No good could come of it. He'd take her for a flighty bit, and that wasn't the sort they married, unless they got cornered. But at least Sheena knew better than to go and get herself pregnant.

Not that marriage was quite what it was once reckoned. Youngsters weren't all that keen these days to get wed, even quite respectable ones. All the same, there was nothing like having a ring on your finger and people calling you Mrs. Keep a bit of distance between and you're more likely to get a lad who'd stick with something legally binding.

Besides, it'd be nice to have all the fuss of a proper wedding. Sheena had missed out on that last time, going off and doing that hole-in-a-corner business at a registry office with witnesses off the street. It'd be expensive, of course, but the girl must have something put by. She needn't expect it to come out of her Mum's pension, though she'd buckle to and help provide some of the goodies for the reception back here.

The uncles would expect to be invited, and a few neighbours. One in the eye for that snooty Mrs Parker whose slutty daughter had an illegitimate baby and nobody to father it. And maybe this time Sheena would settle down, have a baby of her own. It would be nice having a little one in the house again. The future looked crammed with possibilities.

Still no message from the girl, not even to say she'd not want a meal before going on duty. If she didn't buck up she was going to be late for work, and she'd need to drop by to pick up a clean overall.

Mrs Judd went back to the phone and pressed in 1471. The number she was given sounded vaguely familiar. She had herself connected. It was Nurse Orme who answered. So the previous call had come from her. Sal Judd was at a loss for words.

'Hello,' Alyson repeated into the silence, sounding short of patience.

'Oh, you rang me earlier,' Mrs Judd managed to get out.

'I was ringing Sheena. Is this her mother?'

'Yes. Well, she's not here at the moment. I'm expecting her back any time now.'

'I'm sorry to bother you. I thought she might have rung to say how she got on with the man from the insurance. But never mind, perhaps she'll get here a few minutes early. She can tell me all about it then.'

Mrs Judd's face screwed into a scowl. There was no way Sheena was even going to be on time.

'Sorry I can't help you, Nurse.' And that was a lie if ever there was one.

She firmly replaced the phone. There was a big row coming up and she'd no intention of being anywhere near it. If Sheena didn't look out she could lose her job. That's what came of letting a man get to your head. She'd really gone overboard this time.

Chapter Fifteen

'Look,' the man said, wrapping the towelling bathrobe more closely round him as sleet drove straight into his doorway, 'I've had all this from your lot already. For God's sake can't you get it into your heads that I'm satisfied little harm's done and I'll be more careful in future. So you can clear off. It's not easy being a night-worker, and this is my sleep time.'

It would be hard to decide, Beaumont considered, taking in Allbright's disagreeable face, squat body and mottled bare legs coated in long black hairs, to decide which of the two combatants was the uglier, though DI Salmon's purposeful expression might just give him the edge on the other.

'We're letting the weather in,' the DS observed mildly. 'How about us going inside, sitting down together and settling it for good. Then you can go back to bed.'

'Five minutes,' Allbright allowed eventually, scowling and winning outright on the non-beauty points. He stood back to allow the two detectives to go past. A rush of warm air met them from the hall radiator and sent shivers wriggling down the sergeant's back. He eased off his wet parka and dropped it on the quality carpet. The rest of the house looked quality too, he decided, as they were ushered through into a stainless steel and smoked-glass kitchen. Floor and wall tiles were pale lavender. A bit girly, to his mind.

Nightwork at a warehouse clearly paid a deal better than policing. 'Nice place you've got here,' he remarked flatly.

Salmon appeared less interested in his immediate surroundings and scorned to take one of the seats on offer. 'Mr Allbright,' he launched straight in, 'we are not satisfied with your account of the theft from your bank account. Particularly since examining the film taken at the cashpoint where the money was withdrawn.'

That was blatant bluff. All the team had examined the film. If Allbright had been present then he'd had the sense to stand well out of view. But there was no mistaking the way Micky Kane had glanced up before touching the keyboard as if memorizing a number or waiting for instructions.

Allbright's mouth opened but he checked himself in time. He could have been about to deny being at the cashpoint. His mind was working overtime to deflect suspicion. And he had no idea of the range of the video camera lens.

'Look,' he said, 'I wasn't quite straight before. The truth is I felt sorry for the kid. I saw him begging at the station; had a cardboard box he'd spent the night in. He never stole the money. I offered to lend him – well, give him, I suppose – something to tide him over and get him back home.'

'Fifty pounds?' Salmon sneered. 'He was a Londoner, only came from Wimbledon.'

Allbright shrugged. 'It was to cover a decent meal and his train journey, with a bit left over to cheer him up. I ran away from home myself when I was a bit older than him and I remember how godawful it was.'

Salmon took on a masterful stance. 'There was no cardboard box. Since the attempted rapes on women travelling late at night, there's been a regular security sweep at and around the station. No homeless hanging out there; no beggars.

'And you don't need to travel by train, Mr Allbright. You work locally, and beyond that you've a more than adequate car for the purpose, and a Harley-Davidson besides. It's because you've no reason to visit the railway station that you know so little about it. Now, suppose you tell us why you've found it necessary to lie to the police, and exactly what services you were paying this young boy for.'

Allbright looked more than scared. Almost sick. And Beaumont was impressed that the DI had already followed up on his registered vehicles.

'When did you first meet the boy?' Salmon pursued. 'How long has he been living under your roof since then?'

Allbright sank on to the breakfast bench. His bathrobe fell open to reveal more of the gorilla legs and the edge of striped silk boxer shorts. Not a pretty sight.

He was silent, staring at the floor, fists bunched, a tide of crimson rising up the bull-like neck to flood his face.

'While you're thinking up something suitable to tell us,'

Beaumont suggested pleasantly, 'how about a tour of the house, and in particular the place where he was sleeping.'

From that point Allbright put up no resistance. Micky had actually been allocated a single room of his own, and searching the wardrobe there produced a school duffel bag with Smiley stickers and a name tape on it. Inside were his neatly folded school uniform, two books – one on the night sky, the other a paperback thriller – a Parker pen and a well-thumbed notebook which Salmon pocketed for later examination. No change of underclothes, so perhaps the boy hadn't meant to stay away overnight. Nevertheless he had certainly settled in here. So much for Allbright's solicitous intentions to pack him off home.

'You can't take that stuff!' Allbright protested as he started putting the stuff together. 'It's Micky's.'

Now it was Salmon's turn to be caught with his mouth agape and the wrong words nearly out. He caught himself in time. Either Allbright didn't know the boy was dead or he was more quick-witted than his appearance suggested. Let the doubt stand for the moment.

'I must ask you,' the DI said sourly, 'to come with us to the local police station where you may be required to answer further questions.'

'Are you arresting me?' He sounded incredulous.

'Not at this point.' Salmon almost smirked. 'That's not saying that the possibility won't arise.'

Allbright rose from where he'd slumped on the bed and stared back with intensity. 'I prefer to make a voluntary statement. And I want my solicitor with me.'

'You have that right, Mr Allbright. Would you care to make that call now?'

He chose to do this from another room, although there was a wall-fitted white phone right there. Salmon nodded Beaumont towards it, and stood listening by the open door ready to give the sign to lift the receiver. Beaumont, adept at interceptions, complied.

Allbright spoke to a woman receptionist at Callendar, Fitt and Travis. After a certain amount of faffing and fussing while he explained his requirement, Fitt himself came on to explain unhappily that they didn't normally cover criminal cases, but he would send someone along who could advise him on how much, or how little, to admit when questioned.

At that point Beaumont replaced the receiver in synch with the man cutting off the call. Salmon strutted after Allbright and could be heard instructing him to get dressed.

Wrapped against the weather, a tight-lipped Allbright climbed into the rear of the unmarked police car, having been denied his own. 'We shall provide a lift back,' Salmon intoned, 'if that becomes necessary.'

Alyson Orme sometimes claimed that, like any ITU nurse, she was good at management by crisis. This time she knew she was out on a branch and alone. Two further phone calls to the Judd house had produced progressively surly negatives from Sheena's mother.

'I honestly don't know what she thinks she's up to,' the woman said in final exasperation. 'It's having this new boyfriend. It's quite gone to her head.'

'Do you mean she's still missing? When did you last see her, Mrs Judd?'

Sal Judd thought back. 'Yesterday midday before she went off to work. She was looking sort of pleased with herself. Like she was planning some treat.'

'And she didn't come home last night? So maybe we can reach her through this man friend. Can you give me his number?'

'I don't know it. Nor who he is neither. Well, you know what girls are these days. Never tell their mums anything.'

Rebuffed, Alyson said goodbye, rang off and dialled Ramón's number. She would need him to cover for Sheena since she didn't appear to be coming in. Time was running out for Alyson to be at the ITU herself.

Again at the Crown hotel someone was sent to find him. When he came on she explained the fix she was in. 'Did Sheena say what she had in mind for yesterday evening – where she was going?'

'No. She tell me nothing,' he said cautiously.

'Did she ever mention a man friend to you?'

'No name, but – there *is* a person interested, I think.'

'Yes?'

'He visits. I find coffee things used. Two mugs.'

'Ramón, I need someone to fill in for her. Emily can't be left alone and I have to get to work. I could be late already.'

'You want I come? I regret, impossible.' Over the phone her silence got to him. 'I work here. In hotel.' It sounded like a confession.

'I see, but surely someone there could replace you. I have nobody at all. You know how helpless Emily is.'

'Emily, yes. I am sorry.'

'I will pay double. If you could arrange...'

He made up his mind then. Monday lunch service in the bar wasn't heavy. It was mostly regular drinkers who only wanted a stuffed baguette or crisps besides. Roseanne could manage on her own and he would give her something extra. Also today's duty manager had his restaurant lunch brought to the office, and probably slept it off there afterwards.

'I arrange something. I come in half an hour.'

Alyson drew a deep breath of relief. She thanked him and rang off. When she was connected with ITU she found Bernice was already in charge.

'Well, if it can't be helped,' she grumbled, 'I'll expect you when I see you. Are you sure it's not a mammoth hangover from last night?'

'No mammoths in it, pink or otherwise,' Alyson assured her. 'I don't do hairy monsters.' Suddenly her spirits had soared. Crisis over. She'd been near panic point a few minutes before at realization of what fragile arrangements kept Emily going. Somehow she'd have to organize a back-up system, though it wasn't yet clear how. Perhaps an agency nurse.

There was no chance to exchange more than a greeting when Ramón arrived. As she dodged through the traffic on her way to the hospital it struck her fully what he'd said about the hotel. He was actually employed there. That was why it took time to find him when she rang. He didn't have a guest's room with a phone, but would live in cramped staff quarters. And he had that only because of the job. He could have put it at risk by pulling out from whatever duties he was responsible for that afternoon.

She felt a rush of sympathy for the little man. It wasn't just the offer of double pay that had made up his mind. She remembered his voice softening as he said, 'Emily, yes. I am sorry.' Real regret. It could be he already felt some bonding with his patient. There had been none of that with Sheena. If only he could take her place on a permanent basis.

She scuttled into the unit, locked away her outer clothes and went through to confront Bernice's raised eyebrows. 'Panic over,' she assured her, pulling on plastic apron and latex gloves. 'Now, what's new here?'

The wind had turned north-easterly, slicing with Siberian savagery. 'Too cold to snow again,' Beaumont predicted as Z stepped out of her car at the mortuary door.

'I'm not sure that follows.'

'Aw, leave me some sort of comfort. I've had all morning with the Charm Fairy and just left him grilling Allbright.'

'How's it going?'

'He's a definite maybe. Let's go in.'

Z watched him throw down a half-smoked cigarette behind him and grind his heel on it. Something had started him off again. It seemed he'd given up on the nicotine patches too soon. Or there was some new irritant in his home life.

'How's the family?'

'Huh! None-too-subtle extensions of female empire. She wants the living-room redecorated. The boy's dormant at present. I haven't dared ask after his grades. How's your love life?'

'Also hibernating. Max has gone to Iraq. Doesn't really need to. He just wanted a wider view of things, so he's with the Americans up north.'

Beaumont gave a sympathetic grunt. Max wasn't the investigative kind of journalist but his commentaries on everything from the use of loofahs to the human condition made lively reading. 'He'll be all right,' he assured her. He knew as well as she did that serendipity was the real enemy when terrorists were involved.

They removed their coats and went to join the mortuary attendant who was readying the body. Professor Littlejohn appeared from the ante-room snapping on his surgical gloves. 'A bright good afternoon to all,' he boomed.

Opposite the two detectives the coroner's officer took up standard police at-ease stance as the pathologist clipped the mike to his apron.

'We have the body of an adolescent male.' He raised one eyebrow at his assistant who promptly reeled off height and weight measurements.

'He appears to be fine-boned, lean, but well nourished. No obvious disease or disablement.' He droned on, only looking up and nodding as the swing doors opened to allow Superintendent Yeadings to join them.

'Lividity over the chest and abdomen indicate that the body was left face down on a solid surface for a period of well over two hours after death and before immersion. So we can exclude drowning from the actual cause of death.

'We'll look at the head injury. Can I have him turned over?'

The boy's water-bloated features had sickened Zyczynski. She had a poignant image of him in the hospital bed, vulnerable but trying to act cool, as kids do when burying emotion. To see him now was worse than expected. And now, when he was laid face down, the shattered skull made the breath catch in her throat.

The examination proceeded at a brisk pace, Littlejohn as ever interspersing his commentary with rumbles of song, half-voiced and half lost in his beard. There were more negatives: no possibility that injuries were self-inflicted; no needle marks apart from where, in hospital, the wrist cannula had been inserted for the IV, and a single puncture when his blood was tested; no river water in the lungs, therefore, again, no case of drowning. There was no evidence of long-term drug abuse and homosexual activity.

Littlejohn looked up and stared pointedly at his audience. 'The present anal tearing was recent.'

'Rape?' Beaumont demanded harshly.

'Certainly rough handling,' the pathologist allowed. He grimaced ironically at the over-eager DS. 'We have nothing to indicate whether consent was given or not.'

Z felt a surge of anger. She drove her fists deep in the pockets of her jeans and blinked hard to keep her eyes from brimming. If it was Allbright who'd done this to an innocent she couldn't hate him enough.

There was more to endure as Littlejohn opened the body. A young boy she'd briefly met and felt some sympathy for became dehumanized before her eyes. Despite the chill conditions of the room she felt stifled and longed to get into the outside air. But at last it was over. No startling new discoveries. They must wait a day or two for the lab's toxicology report, which would possibly confirm what was discovered from earlier samples taken in the ITU. Micky had been found with a mixture of drugs in his blood-stream, which included smack and ecstasy.

Outside, it was already dark, frost making the lights seem even brighter. They stood in a subdued little group. Centrally Yeadings huddled, bear-like, in his winter crombie. 'Better get off home now while you can,' he advised. 'We'll meet up for an 8.30 brief-ing in the morning. DI Salmon will task the extended murder team.'

Keith rang through to ITU at about four, and it was Alyson who took the call. 'I've dropped in to take Audrey home, but there's time to snatch a coffee first. Can you take your break now?'

'In ten minutes?'

'Splendid. Thanks.'

I shouldn't have agreed, Alyson thought. This is getting addic-tive. Another *last time*.

She fixed it with Bernice, went down by the stairs and found Keith at a corner table in the staff diner with two cappuccinos. He was contrite.

'There have been so many loose ends to tie up before I take leave that I couldn't even get round to seeing Emily. Another day would have helped, but Audrey's desperate to get home.'

'That's all right,' she told him. 'If Emily needs anything I'll give Dougie a ring. She won't care for the substitute but I'll try to explain.'

They drank their coffee in silence, surrounded by the subdued babble of staff chat and the scraping of chair legs on the wood block floor. Then, 'I think I need your advice,' she said. 'Well, not so much advice, because I may not take it. Opinion, certainly.'

'I'm intrigued.'

So she told him about Sheena's unexpected failure to turn up, and how she'd had to call Ramón in.

She paused before diving in. 'I'd like to take him on full-time. He seems so much more reliable, but he has a bar job at the Crown and it's live-in. It means he'd lose that. There's room enough for him at Emily's and it would be good to have someone else always on hand. What do you think?'

Keith frowned. 'I can't say, because I've never met him. You should really find out much more about his background. You say he's a foreigner. Has it struck you his papers may not be in order?'

'He's Spanish I think, so, as an EU citizen, there should be no difficulty about a work permit. He seems a private sort of person. I doubt he'd get under my heels.'

There was a silence while Keith considered the pros and cons. It would halve the weight of duty Alyson was labouring under, but having an unproved man move in presented unknown risks he didn't want her to take.

'You're uneasy because he's male,' she said. 'Look, nowadays men and women are flat-sharing on an equal basis all over the place, and it's taken for granted. And if I'm in charge, the boss figure with power to sack him, he's not going to take advantage of the situation, is he? In any case he may turn down the offer out of hand.'

It was clear she'd made up her mind already, had merely used him as a sounding board. All the same, he wanted to protest.

She rose to go. 'I have to get back. By the way, we still have your scarf. You left it behind. If you ever get out shopping or whatever, drop in and pick it up.'

Shopping: all he was reduced to now. It angered him, and he simply nodded as she took her departure.

Allbright hardly needed the solicitor with him. His stonewalling had Salmon fuming inside. Micky was a young vagrant he'd felt sorry for and so offered him somewhere to stay. After that, 'No comment'. They had reached a solid impasse when a constable knocked on the interview room door and handed in a note. Superintendent Yeadings had phoned in the salient points of the post mortem findings.

Salmon clucked with satisfaction.

'There have been developments,' he told the man opposite. He stood up.

'Stanley Allbright, I am arresting you on suspicion of the sexual assault of a minor.'

Chapter Sixteen

A summons to Kidlington to consult with the ACC (Crime) kept Yeadings from Tuesday morning's briefing. Without him his Major Crimes team assembled in the CID office to compare notes before joining what Beaumont termed 'the rabble' of their extended murder-case personnel. Most of the chatter ceased on the instant as the DI and his two sergeants entered the prepared Incident Room.

News carries fast in an Area station, and expectations were high since a suspect was already cooling off in a cell between questionings. By five that afternoon the twenty-four hour rule would apply: he must be either charged or released. Nobody had any doubts about which way it would go.

'Right,' DI Salmon snarled, facing the crowded room and identifying himself.

'As you should all know by now, we are concerned with the violent death of a thirteen-year old boy, Michael Kane from Wimbledon. It's to be a full scale murder hunt and there's plenty of hard graft for every one of you. Our victim's on the books as a runaway and a drug OD who discharged himself from the General Hospital Saturday, stealing another patient's clothes. He was still wearing them when his body was recovered from the river by the boathouse yesterday morning, less the shoes. But the lad didn't drown. Somebody clocked him from behind and split the skull. The blunt instrument hasn't yet been found.

'All the stolen clothes were several sizes too large. The shoes would have been almost impossible to walk in naturally for any distance. They haven't turned up among Micky's own clothes at the house of the present suspect, so we can't prove he ever went back there.

'I want those shoes found.

'It's likely that between leaving hospital on Saturday afternoon and being pulled out of the river on Sunday morning he returned to the house where he had been in hiding for an unknown period during the week he was missing from home. And where – ' he glared round the room –'it appears he was sexually abused.

'A warrant has been obtained overnight to search that house and all property belonging to one Stanley Allbright. That includes his car and motor cycle which scientific officers are already examining. We shall also be tooth combing the stationery warehouse where he's employed as night stock-controller, its precinct and all vehicles used by that company. The place will be sealed until the examination is completed and all the workers questioned.

'We also need to speak to hospital staff and any patients who may have seen the boy leaving the hospital; likewise shopkeepers and anyone about at the time he would have been crossing town at dusk. So oddly dressed, he'd stick out like a nun at a Wembley Cup Final. Copies of his photograph in school uniform will be available at the end of the briefing. Everyone is to take one.'

He glowered round the assembled uniform and plain clothes officers. 'We want no slip-ups on this, no half-done jobs. Every smallest scrap of information is to be passed in, irrespective of your private opinion of its worth. No matter what grotty rubbish you have to turn over, it is to be done thoroughly. This kid comes from the Met's patch, so their eyes are going to be glued on every move you make or clue you fail to suck up.

'Allocations are the responsibility of Sergeant Wimpole; and Sergeant O'Neill is Office Manager of the Incident Room. I shall be leading the active investigation, under Superintendent Yeadings as SIO. Any questions?'

The abundance of information must have floored them. Or maybe the DI's aggressive manner put off anyone willing to put up a hand and volunteer as bright boy of the class.

'What d'you think?' Beaumont asked Z as they filed out.

'Comprehensive,' she allowed. Privately she considered Salmon had missed a chance to appeal to family men with kids of their own, and present a more sympathetic image of the dead boy. But then, sympathy was a word that never got within a mile of the man.

Next it was Beaumont's turn to sit in with Allbright who had dismissed his brief as useless, relying on his own ability to repeat, 'No comment' until decision time on charging him. Z, familiar with the DI's stated dislike of women trailing around getting in the way, had no difficulty persuading Salmon to let her follow up a line of her own. She began by calling again on Micky's parents at their hotel to make sure they understood the outcome of the post-mortem examination. She knew Yeadings himself had already visited them with a woman constable to break the findings gently.

Z found them still at late breakfast, dazed by events but holding themselves together. They were pathetically grateful to see her again. 'There's no useful purpose to be served by staying here longer,' Hilda Kane said, 'so we've decided to get back – back home, and try to take up our lives where we left off. Thank God for work. Maybe we can bury ourselves in that.'

'I'll be in touch with your local police,' Z told her. 'I know they'll keep you in the picture, and I'll phone you myself on any developments.'

'We want this fiend put away for a very – long – time, ' the man said grimly. 'I'm only sorry they've not brought back hanging.'

Z nodded sympathetically. 'There shouldn't be any further disturbance for you at home. I suppose the local police searched thoroughly through Micky's things there once he'd been placed on the Missing Juveniles list?'

'Took his bedroom nearly to bits.' Today Micky's father was asserting himself.

'I remember you said Micky spent a lot of time up there. Did he use a computer for his school work?'

'All the time. Hid his head in it like an ostrich. Surfing the net and all that, as kids do nowadays. Don't know why I ever bought him all those useless encyclopedias.'

'Did the Met – the police – take the computer away for examination?'

There was an awkward silence. 'They did suggest it. Well, *demand* it, really.' Now he sounded embarrassed.

'But I couldn't let them have it. Micky had entered a lot of information for me on it. Private stuff, to do with the business. So I took the whole workstation downstairs and told them it was our family computer which Micky just used for school essays. So it's still with us, only I put it back in his room, because it's of no use to me, unless I learn how to work it. Of course Mother's a dab hand, uses one all the time at school for preparing lessons and keeping records. But she wouldn't have time to take on my affairs as well.'

And perhaps for that the boy was dead. Z took a deep breath. There was no call to hammer the point home.

'I'm sure you'd master it in no time,' she consoled him. 'And you could speed the process by joining an adults' IT evening class.'

'Do you think so? Yes, I might try that. Something to – to fill the time, you know.'

'I'm wondering,' Z said. 'Since he was surfing the net, we could use it to discover his pet interests. And perhaps he joined a chat line, as many students do, for an exchange of ideas. There may be friends he's made that way who knew what was in his mind at the time he decided to go away. It could provide a clue to what he went looking for.'

'But not what happened to him! He didn't deserve that. No child ever does!' His mother's anger broke through at last, but her husband was still groping for information.

'You mean it's all still in the computer? Everything he was working on?'

'Yes, for anyone who knows how to get it out.'

'Do you?'

'I think so. Unless he's used some very obscure password to secure his private zone. And in that case, we do have experts who can get through to it. Of course there's still all your business stuff in there…'

'Oh that doesn't matter. Not now. But, at the time, handing the computer over seemed an invasion of privacy. We didn't know how serious it would all become.' His voice broke. 'I've been foolish withholding it. After I'd moved it to my own room I couldn't admit I'd lied to the police.'

'Suppose I drive back after you and take a look? Or bring it back here for our computer experts?'

They looked at each other. Hilda's mind was already made up.

She nodded at her husband.

'Right,' Zyczynski said. 'What time were you thinking of leaving?'

Oliver Markham hadn't been enjoying his start in the new job as much as he'd expected. So far it had consisted of hanging about to keep observation on what appeared to be an empty house. He craved action and, if possible, opposition. He sat slumped in the passenger seat of Tam Godfrey's Ford Mondeo, glowering through the frosted mist while the other man, dour and uncommunicative, sucked at boiled sweets and read a magazine on antiques.

'You get a lot of valuable old stuff to deal with, then?' Markham demanded finally to break the silence.

Godfrey grunted. 'There's no harm in hoping.'

That seemed all he was prepared to offer. Except that, reminded of the other man's presence, he held out the limp bag of sticky sweets, appeared unaffected by Markham's scornful rebuffing of the gesture, and resumed his reading.

This was one godawful waste of time and ability, Markham fumed. He was eager to wade in, challenge the wretched defaulter with a list of accumulated debts, lean on him a little as a matter of principle and set about distraint of his goods to an appropriate value.

Today no amount of knocking on the paint-blistered front door had raised any reaction from within the Victorian terraced house, but Godfrey was adamant that the man was at home, declaring that he 'felt it in his water'. Markham, having overindulged on strong coffee at breakfast was rather differently afflicted, and the need to correct this was from minute to minute more pressing. Eventually he eased himself out of the car. 'Taking a turn around,' he told the other, and set off down the alley at the side of the house. Turning left, he found a pathway between the two rows of back-to-back houses and duly relieved himself.

Zipping up, his body temperature having plummeted witheringly, he peered through the dilapidated fence of the house he took to be that of his quarry. At that moment a dark-clad figure climbed through a first-floor window and let himself down over an extension roof into the yard. There he pulled a pedal cycle out from under a tarpaulin sheet and set about trundling it in Markham's direction.

The necessary paperwork was, of course, in the car. Boiling with frustration, he had to retreat, noting in which direction the cyclist set off at speed once he reached the outer alley.

Markham hurried back to inform Godfrey. Their pursuit was balked by the one-way road system the town council had in their wisdom imposed, and which the cyclist was able to flout by using pedestrian paths. It took several circuits of the town centre before they again sighted the escapee, coming on him face to face and swerving to cause him to wobble off into the gutter. His expletives, as he picked himself up and brushed off his knees, were repetitive and obscene.

'Oh Lordy,' Godfrey said, mildly exasperated, 'we've got the wrong bugger. This is our man's brother.'

The fiasco didn't improve Markham's enjoyment of the hunt. They waited a further three-quarters of an hour with himself posted in the cold to keep an eye on the rear of the premises.

'Right,' Godfrey finally decided, 'he's holed up for the day, with little brother sent out for the shopping. But with his known nocturnal habits, we'll get our chance later.'

In offering the job, Baldrey had made no mention of hours of work. Glumly Markham now faced the prospect that they were possibly unlimited and mainly of the unsocial kind.

Godfrey broke for lunch at 1.15 after a visit across town to a housewife in a more upmarket road. Her original fine of £30 for illegal parking, plus a late payment charge on the court fee, plus the company's fee for debt collection, plus Godfrey's personal commission on fruitless visits to date had run the debt into what she saw as astronomical figures.

'Plus Value Added Tax at 17.5% on the lot,' Markham joined in, taking grim pleasure in dealing the final blow. 'In all, that comes to £468.88.'

Appalled, she wailed like a banshee. No way could she screw this amount out of her monthly housekeeping. And she dared not tell her husband. He'd scalp her.

'Sorry, love,' Godfrey commiserated. 'It don't just go away if you ignore it. Next time best tell your hubby right at the start before it mounts up.'

Staring as she twisted her hands together trying not to blubber, Markham decided he remembered her from his usher's days. Her or a dozen other stuck-up, over-painted tarts exactly like her. At last he could draw some satisfaction from what he was doing. No longer impotent to implement the decisions of the court, he now wielded real power. Momentarily at least it seemed worth sacrificing the robes of officialdom.

Again Tam's decision was to return in the evening, by which time the stupid cow should have warned the husband that settlement was overdue and the final amount still climbing. Which obligation lessened the heart-warming sense of achievement; but Markham decided the encounter deserved some reward. He suggested a liquid lunch in the nearest bar.

'Half an hour, then, if that's what you're after,' Tam Godfrey granted. 'Only don't come back with a boozy breath. Myself, I dig in here with a sandwich and a flask. I've too much respect for money to go pouring it down a pub drain.'

Not that he restricted himself to tea or coffee. Markham didn't miss the label on the single malt that accompanied the foil-wrapped package. It seemed Godfrey was a snob in his drinking as well as his taste for antiques.

The Barley Mow Inn was only round the next corner. Anything was better than the Crown, where Markham was too well-known in his earlier profession, and the place was awash with images of the Lump.

It wasn't his fault that the thing with her had gone sour on him. She shouldn't have led him on, then repulsed him. Still, it'd done her no good in the end. He'd shown her, like any red-blooded male would, just how futile it was to resist, teasing him with shouting 'no' when she was clearly mad to get more of the same. It had really got his rag.

All the same, he'd never gone out of his head like that before, and in a weird way the red-blurred images of Saturday night evoked unease along with a defiant sort of warrior pride. He had-

n't full recall of how he'd left her. Which was as well. He would-
n't dwell on any of it. She was history, wiped out of his life, and
he knew to avoid her kind like the pox in future. All women were
a disaster. He'd recognized that even as a child and needed none
of them.

He followed the lager with a whisky chaser, then repeated the
dose as weather-proofing and to underline his growing contempt
for Tam Godfrey with his penny-pinching, petty interests.
Working in tandem with him was restrictive. If Bradley wanted
results he'd best switch his new man to cases on his own.

Deliberately Markham watched the clock hands mark up fifty
minutes before he downed a final scotch and took his time
returning to the car, where Godfrey, poor sap, was quietly dozing.

Ramón was feeding some kind of fruity pap to Emily and conscious of something new in her eyes as she observed him between
mouthfuls.

'You do this yourself now,' he suggested, reversing the spoon.
She fitted her stiff little claws around it and wobbled the next
load into her rounded mouth. That was better. It took some of
her attention off him.

He couldn't stand the staring. There was no way of knowing
what, if anything, was going on behind those unblinking, washed-
out blue eyes. Because she was different from others, so old and
with some faculties missing, he felt an almost supernatural per-
ception in her silent gaze. As compensation. In the way that
those who were blind had their other senses sharpened.

Could she discern things about him that he hid from others?
He knew he must be more careful with her, not to let secrets out.
Yet there was safety in her not talking. If she began to guess, per-
haps he could even tell her things, explain himself.

She pushed the spoon towards him and he guided it into the
slosh of fruit and custard. It seemed she was hungry. He steadied
her hand on its way to her mouth.

'A little walk?' he suggested when finally she pushed the bowl
away. He gently wiped her mouth and guided her wheelchair
towards the kitchen, where he removed the tray fixture and

unloaded the crockery and spoons into the dishwasher. Her eyes followed every movement.

Then they began a solemn promenade through all the rooms, pausing where she pointed or made some gurgling comment on pieces of furniture or the strange pictures that covered her walls. One smallish oil painting in particular, like a confusion of barbed wire and amputated limbs, she laughed at, and he unhooked it to place it in her hands where she cuddled it to her and stroked the rough, impasto surface.

He let her keep it on her knees as he parked the chair by the glass wall. She gazed out. How much did her flawed sight allow her? Was she aware, across the town's rooftops, of distant, white-frosted fields and above them the blur of charcoal streaks that were winter-bare woodland?

Whatever she saw, she seemed contented. He watched her eyelids grow heavy as she succumbed to sleep. He pulled the tartan rug up over her knees and hands, gently removed the picture, rehung it and went to look again at the room Nurse Orme had offered him.

It was perfect. Painted in apricot and white, with a wide bed that gave gently under his weight as he sat on the covers. No shrieking springs. Pale wood furniture, and in one corner a glass-walled shower with a seat in it. Everything looked unused. A real beginning.

All this he could have if he accepted to work here full-time. She had offered ten pounds more each week than he received at the Crown. And all meals would be free.

He was superstitiously afraid to accept. So much promised could invite misfortune.

He remade Emily's bed, bagged the linen and cleaned out the room. When he went back to the glass wall she was awake and smiled at him. She looked so wise.

He knelt beside her. 'Do you know about me?' he asked.

Her face said nothing. She was waiting.

'I am bad man,' he confessed. 'I did bad things.'

Her eyes engaged his own. He saw a new depth in them. 'Bad,' she said aloud, and struggled to get out something more. He watched her, nodding encouragement.

'Bad.' She nodded. 'Wicked. Wicked…woman.' She laid a small, cold hand on his.

He believed her. He knew then he would be accepting the job on offer. He would stay and look after Emily. They were two of a kind.

Nothing must threaten his claim on being here. The woman Sheena would not return, but at any time her body could be discovered. From the flat's huge window he had kept watch on activity in the yard below on Sunday night. Three cars had parked close to the blank warehouse wall, switched off their lights and waited. When a fourth turned in from the road the occupants all got out and gathered until the last arrival joined them. Then together they grouped at the small door let into the loading bay. They would be night staff setting the place up for Monday opening, and this last man would be the one entrusted with the keys.

Lights came on in the single storey building, visible through its skylights, as the four men went in. From then on Ramón had observed no activity until the arrival of a small closed van some twenty minutes later. This drew up in the darker, nearer end of the yard and doused its lights.

Anxious to see whether anyone should get out and investigate the near corner where the body had fallen, Ramón stayed on to watch, but there was no further movement. Some five minutes later a long, dark-coloured saloon arrived, to be greeted by a single flash of headlights from the van. It reversed before smoothly drawing up opposite, so that both drivers faced each other. Its lights too were extinguished.

He guessed the windows between must have been lowered, because an arm reached out from each and it looked as though an exchange of packages was made. The two vehicles remained together while some kind of conversation took place. Then the dark saloon drew away, switching on its lights as it reached the exit. Another few minutes passed before the van followed, turning left where the other had gone right.

This had been risky enough. Ramón recognized a drug delivery. He knew he must get the body away. Despite the frost, slow decomposition would already have begun. The meetings could be repeated. It took only one of the men needing to relieve himself in the darkest corner and the corpse could be discovered. The police would be called in. They would look upward to the penthouse. In the ensuing investigation he could come under suspicion himself.

Once the cold spell broke, however well hidden among the rubbish, the body would swiftly become evident. Sudden nausea overcame him at memory of bodies' stench decomposing in tropical heat. He had thought he was free of all that, but, unbelievably, the ghosts of the dead had followed him here to this quiet place with the two vulnerable women.

He knew what he must do, for the safety of them all. There was an old tan Nissan parked below which had been there since Sunday and seemed abandoned. He could use that to transport the body, wrapped in one of the plastic sheets they used for Emily's bedbaths. He would find some safer place of disposal. He had only to wait until Nurse Orme came home after eight and relieved him.

Chapter Seventeen

The Kanes' house at Wimbledon was much as Z had imagined it: a detached Edwardian villa with a double garage, gravelled parking space and a front garden mostly given up to glossy evergreens. Its paintwork was a startling white which mocked the grubby remnants of snow shovelled off the driveway. Inside it was all decorum and conventional taste of the Eighties. There were no fresh flowers. The only scent was from furniture polish and floor wax.

Micky's bedroom showed that he'd inherited, or at least bowed to, the domestic outlook of his parents. Books, used but in good condition, stood in formal rows on the shelves, ranged according to subject. No magazines. Above the workstation with computer, screen, printer and modem, hung the only indication that the room's occupant wasn't adult. This was a 3x4-foot print of trial-bike racing. Inside the floor-to-ceiling cupboards hung a second set of school uniform and two formal suits. Underwear, T-shirts and jeans were neatly folded, as laundered, on labelled shelves. Three pairs of well-polished, laced shoes lined up like guardsmen below them. Bundled on the floor in a back corner, but clean, was his sports gear.

His schoolma'm mother must have blessed her stars that she'd a son with none of the obviously laddish predilections which she would surely condemn elsewhere. Instead, there'd been a compliant half-child, half-adult, making no outrageous demands, but who could also, secretly, be a small, compacted volcano ready to blow. His death, and the manner of it, was something she had yet to face in full.

Z felt it was a house not to linger in. 'Is there anyone who could come and stay with you for a while?' she asked the woman.

It seemed there wasn't. As a family they'd been self-sufficient. Or thought they were. Their plight was familiar, but still unimaginably sad.

All the way back to Thames Valley, with the boy's computer in the car boot, Zyczynski tried to throw off her unease about what she must find when she logged on. There would surely be some clue to whatever had lured the boy away. She took the equipment home with her, put coffee on to perk and started right in. It took some half hour to hit on the password, *Explorer*, which concealed his obvious interests, and that only after she considered the only title on the bookshelves that hadn't some connection with school. It had been a paperback, Douglas Adams's *Hitchhiker's Guide to the Galaxy*. The link was tenuous but it did give access to his emails.

She admitted she ranked as little more than an IT lamebrain, so it was time to hand over the computer to the nerds at Area HQ. But she'd found a connection.

On line Micky had chatted with only three other boys, two of his own age, but one, Hutch, claiming to be seventeen, who had corresponded over a matter of weeks. Their correspondence had been increasingly slangy and personal, while the others trailed off. This survivor was almost certainly the Pied Piper whom Micky Kane had skived off school to meet. But no musician, this one. His instrument of seduction had been a Harley-Davidson bike. The enticing details of its power and performance, eagerly lapped up by Micky, had been followed by an invitation for *Explorer* to come and try it out. Hutch would guarantee him a ride home by pillion, if they could arrange a meeting over land line. That final message was dated twelve days back.

The change to an open invitation should have warned the boy, but it seemed Micky hadn't heeded. Nothing new there. Chat lines were proved an increasing danger, a channel for seduction where the predator was invisible, allowing the victim no means of checking claims on screen. Anonymity could tempt the most innocent to describe themselves as something they fell short of. Children, once abducted, were abused and murdered by older men posing as teenagers. This overprotected boy had gone that way, dazzled by the Harley-Davidson vision.

Which must mean a sure lead to their suspect, Allbright.

She thought of the boy as she'd seen him in hospital, although sick and injured, attempting to play it cool. But, underneath, surely desperate and ashamed at how he'd been betrayed.

So why, when he escaped, had he gone back to his abuser?

He'd had no choice. All his gear was left at the house, stuff he'd need to get him home.

Perhaps he'd supposed that in day time Allbright would be away. Maybe he'd lost account of time and forgotten it was a weekend. Had he imagined he could simply retrieve his bag, go home in his school uniform, pick up life where he'd left off there, and no one be the wiser? How could he hope to account for the days he'd been gone?

Allbright had to be the abuser. But the search of his home had turned up no computer. It must exist at some place he had frequent access to. Which pointed first to the stationery warehouse where he was night stock-controller. Every piece of equipment there must be examined to pick up his connection with the boy.

She left her coffee to cool where she'd poured it, returned the boy's computer to her car and drove straight back to the Area nick.

By Wednesday morning Oliver Markham was getting wised up to the job. Because it involved so much hanging about in the open he'd invested in a couple of heavy fleeces and a black leather trench coat that not only kept the wind out but suggested here was a toughie to deal with.

He'd taken some pride in his new (or new to him) 4x4, but on the second day of sporting it in a low-life area he'd picked up a double line of scratches along one side which could not have arrived by accident. He still owned the tan Nissan, at present dumped in Elston's warehouse yard, because buying the 4x4 had been a private deal with no part-exchange on offer. Now he decided to use the old car for when he didn't accompany Tam Godfrey on repossession visits, or at least until he could find a buyer.

Having hopefully placed his traffic cone in a temporary space near his front door and cursed any scrote who might dare remove it, he walked to pick up the Nissan after an abortive visit to a council-tax defaulter near the warehouse yard. He'd happened on a moment when several vans were picking up bulk orders of stationery and little notice was taken as he drove out of the yard, having removed a note from under the windscreen wipers threatening wheel-clamping on any second unauthorised overnight stay.

A decorator's pick-up which had received a similar note had stalled on pulling out in front as he tried to leave. Markham hooted for him to get clear. The driver gestured back through his wing mirror, revved up and drove straight into the radiator of one of Elston's own covered trucks coming in.

It was Laurel and Hardy to perfection. The heavier vehicle rammed back the pickup, springing the catches on the tailgate as it struck into Markham's front bumper. As Elston's van reversed, the pickup sprang forward, the tailgate dropped and a five-litre can of putty-coloured matt paint toppled out on the tarmac.

Markham roared and dived out to examine damage to the Nissan. The bumper looked only scuffed, but he'd lost a sidelight and there was no way he could avoid the puddle of wet paint in front. At that moment, as grinning faces from the warehouse began to gather to enjoy the general discomfort, his mobile phone trilled inside the car.

He climbed in to take the call, his face like thunder. Ernest Baldrey was demanding why the hell he hadn't reported in on his morning's progress. Markham started to grind out an answer, then, as the Elston's lorry gave way ahead, he reversed a couple of yards, seized his chance and swept round the stranded pickup before the space could be filled. All the way out to Mardham village for his next call he was growling curses under his breath.

The approach road past the watermill had no speed cameras, but it was a built-up area lined by cottages and street lights. It so happened that a probationer constable named Higgins had fallen foul of his sergeant and been sent to familiarize himself over the required distance with a hand-held speed-check apparatus and a rather untidy-looking WPC. After observing seemly streams of traffic droning past, the speeding Nissan could make his day. He strode out into its path, held up a forbidding hand and was almost struck as Markham stood on his less-than-perfect brakes.

Hiding his satisfaction under a mask of stolid officialdom, Constable Higgins called the driver out, examined the loosened front bumper, enumerated the car's failings and added to them the offence of driving at 61 mph in a 30 mph area. Markham slightly moderated his language, but his face was flushed and the PC fancied he discerned the effects of a liquid lunch. The breathalyser was produced, which confirmed that alcohol was present, although just inside the permissible limit.

After this minor disappointment Higgins insisted on his right to throw the whole book at this wanker. He again recited the list of road offences already committed: speeding, faulty front light, a bumper now hanging dejectedly just short of the road and failure to stop within the required distance. He peered in through the misted windows, then proceeded aft, demanding that Markham should open the boot.

Who knew what illegal treasures might be concealed inside? Stories circulated among old hands back at the nick included a long-dragged-out murder hunt solved by a routine traffic check on a motorway. True, it had included the examining copper being shot dead on the job, but then maybe that was the sort of exaggeration legends acquired. And anyway the likes of PC Higgins could hardly expect the dizzy heights of bodies in the boot, Class A drugs, or even terrorist guns.

Scowling, Markham did as he was told, looming as formidably as his black leather allowed. Young Higgins peered in the boot, poked about, suddenly froze, then straightened stiffly.

'What's this, then?' The fine hairs on his neck went rigid and an icicle seemed to drop down inside his back collar. Slowly he drew out a tartan travel rug caked at one corner with dark brown deposit. His eyes widened as the man in the black leather trench coat suddenly moved in on him.

Shopping on her way to afternoon duty, Alyson Orme passed the police station as Z was driving in at the electronic gate. The DS lowered her window and cheerfully wagged her fingers. 'How are things with you?'

'Not so hot,' the nurse admitted. 'My assistant's gone AWOL and I've taken on an unknown in her place. To live in. I thought he was an EU citizen, but now he tells me he's a Filipino. I should have picked up on the oriental looks. How can I check he's not an illegal immigrant?'

'Can't stop to talk now,' Z warned her. 'Give me a buzz in twenty minutes and I'll have all the details for you.' She put the car in gear, waved again and entered the police yard.

A lucky meeting, Alyson decided. That takes one load off my mind.

As soon as she'd sorted things in ITU she would put through a call to the number Z had left with her.

Yeadings waylaid Zyczynski as she hurried past his open door carrying Micky's desktop computer. 'Where did you disappear to yesterday?' he demanded.

'Wimbledon, with the Kanes,' she told him. 'I brought this back. Mr Kane wouldn't allow the Met access to it. And it's come up trumps.' She treated him to a Cheshire Cat grin, which he matched with a grim smile of his own.

'Can't be a bad thing. Let's take it to the CID office and get a printout.'

Only Beaumont was in there, poking at a keyboard with deadly concentration. He broke off as they came in and booted up alongside.

'Micky Kane's chat line,' Yeadings promised. All three bent to the screen as Z brought it up. They watched in tense silence. At last, 'Harley-Davidson,' Yeadings breathed with religious awe.

'It has to be Allbright,' Beaumont accused. 'All we need now is to find his record of the conversations.'

The internal phone rang. Beaumont reached for it and held a hand over the mouthpiece. 'Zyczynski, it's for you.'

The woman DS waved it away. 'I'm out.'

'No,' Yeadings said. 'Take it.' He listened as Z excused herself to Alyson for not having the needed information to hand. 'Can I ring you back?' she asked.

Alyson seemed doubtful, but finally agreed.

'Germane to our present inquiry?' Yeadings suggested, and Z was compelled to explain the difficulty over Ramón.

'She'll need to check his work permit and contact immigration. Better let her have their details at once, before any harm's done. And what's this about a missing carer? How long has she been gone?'

'I'll get the full story when I talk to her. It may be nothing. The woman seemed pretty lackadaisical anyway. She may have decided to take a job elsewhere.'

Beaumont was now busily gathering the chat line details from the printer. Yeadings grimaced at its harsh chattering. He quickly scanned the first page. 'I think I'll leave you both to it.'

Rather than risk disturbing work in the ITU, Zyczynski copied out the information Alyson required, slid it into an envelope and decided to walk across the town centre to deliver it herself.

Just as well. A phoned interruption would have been the last straw. Bernice, normally cool and competent, was rattled by the latest readings for a heart-lung bypass recovery, and Alyson was doubling for everything else in their end of the unit. 'Take a seat,' she hissed in passing. 'Be with you when I can.'

Z waited, dropping the sheepskin coat at her feet. With the high temperature required here and the sheer exercise of intensive nursing, small wonder the staff were lean as whippets. Eventually Alyson was free to take her through to the kitchen and switch on the kettle for tea.

'It's all in here,' Z told her, handing over the envelope, 'but my boss overheard and wants to know about the missing carer.'

'Oh, Sheena!' Alyson sounded disgusted. 'Her mother thinks she's gone off with some man friend. Not that she has a name for him.'

'So when did she disappear?'

'It must have been Sunday night. I haven't seen her since I handed over to her that afternoon. And Ramón was to follow her, taking on the first half of my night duty with Emily, from eight. I had a dinner date.'

'And nobody has any idea who the man friend is?'

Alyson hesitated. 'It's possible Ramón may know something. It was Sheena who introduced him here in the first place. Otherwise I've no contact. Actually, as far as I'm concerned Sheena's no great loss – if Ramón turns out to be legit. That's my main concern. I must have someone reliable for Emily.'

'And for yourself, if he's to live in. Mind if I have a word with him? Just about Sheena.'

'Go ahead. He's with Emily right now. Only don't scare him off, or I'll really be in a hole.'

'I needn't mention I'm police. Thanks, Alyson. Maybe we can meet up for a drink sometime?'

'I'd like that. I'm not sure I should ask, but have you got anywhere about Micky?'

'It's early days yet, but we're hopeful.' She would have liked to say more, but real proof was still lacking. It depended now on what IT experts could extract from computers at the warehouse.

Ramón had not been warned to expect visitors. He frowned at the monitor that showed a young woman looking up directly at the entrance camera. She appeared respectable, bare-headed, with a cap of soft brown curls; dark eyes; really pretty. She stood hugging a silver-grey sheepskin coat to her against the cold wind. 'Who, please?' he demanded through the intercom.

'I'm Rosemary, a friend of Nurse Alyson Orme's. She said I could ask you about Sheena.'

'Sheena not here. I not knowing where.'

'Look, we're a bit worried about her. Can I come up and talk?'

'I suppose.' He sounded doubtful, but she heard the lock click as it was released. When she took the lift up to the penthouse she found him already waiting at the apartment door. He waved her through to the lounge where she found Emily in her wheelchair, seated by the huge window and watching cloud shadows racing over the distant hills.

'Miss Rosemary, Miss Emily,' he introduced them.

The old lady surprised her by shooting out a bony hand to be shaken. Z took it gently and smiled.

After a short pause she said, 'Ramón, how can I find out who this man is that Sheena has gone off with? Surely you have some idea.'

He shook his head. 'Perhaps...'

'Yes?'

'Perhaps you ask her friend. Name is Roseanne, in bar at Crown hotel. Where Sheena drink.'

'Right. I'll do that. Thank you, Ramón.' She rose from the chair beside the old lady.

'Come...' Emily enunciated clearly, '...again.'

'I'd like that, thank you. I will.' This was the patient Alyson had said seldom ever spoke. Z smiled at Ramón as he saw her to the door. 'You seem to be giving your patient new confidence.'

'Miss Emily is lovely lady,' he said, and bowed as he closed the door on her.

Chapter Eighteen

There was a brief moment when PC Higgins confronted near-death. While the outer world froze, his mind leapt into infinity. Without his relatively short and uneventful life passing before his eyes, yet there was time enough to ask himself, *Poor Mum, who'll see to her...?*

Then basic training kicked in. Survival in a small hand-held radio. He waved it between himself and his destroyer. 'Back-up!' he croaked, then remembered to identify himself. The response from Control was level and totally relaxed.

Higgins gulped. Whatever else, he had to leave some lead behind for them. 'Car check!' and he gabbled off the licence plate figures.

They could be false, of course, but at least he'd tried. And still the threatening hulk in black leather had made no move, except to lean forward and peer at the blood-caked corner of the tartan rug.

PC Higgins retreated two paces. When ordered out, the man had switched off the engine, but the keys were still there. Higgins edged round to the driver's open window, reached in and pocketed them.

'Listen, son,' said the old and infinitely wise metallic voice in his ear, 'there's procedure to follow.' He gulped; desperately searched his brain. And complied.

'What the fucking hell?' the accosted driver demanded, eyes still focused on the rug and almost echoing Higgins's own first reaction.

'How the bloody blazes did that get on it?' But his belligerence was on the way out, as he recalled Sheena's bloodied face before he dumped her. She had floundered back on the rug, a quivering lump like a distressed, beached whale, hugging it to her.

'Hot cocoa, that's what!' he blustered. 'God, for a minute I thought it was blood. We took a picnic. Up to Halton ridge. Only it was too blasted cold so we got back inside.'

But by now PC Higgins's partner had abandoned the fuggy warmth of their patrol car and wandered round to see what the kid was getting so excited about. She lifted the rug from the open boot and ran an exploratory hand over the stain. A small chip flaked off as she scratched at it with a fingernail. 'What's all this, then?' She sounded unfazed.

A crackle from Higgins's radio prefaced the information he'd demanded. The car was registered to an Oliver Markham with a local address. It had not been reported stolen. Did PC Higgins still require back-up as first requested?

'I think,' Higgins said faintly, 'you'd better deal with this one,' and surrendered his radio to WPC Trish Carter.

Superintendent Yeadings had despaired of the accumulated paperwork and taken a turn round the corridors. He fetched up at the door of the CID office. Both his sergeants were there, and DI Salmon was perched on the edge of Beaumont's desk running through witnesses' statements before they were committed to the computer or the bin.

'Nothing that could be connected with Allbright, then,' he summed up. 'Unless he's the shadowy figure, sex unknown, who was deep in conversation with a kid on a bench by the boathouses a week last Wednesday. Or it may have been Thursday.' His voice was heavy with sarcasm.

'It's all we've got,' Beaumont reminded him. 'It was a school day, so it could have been Micky.'

'Or any local kid skiving off lessons. So can we assume the Kane boy hadn't arrived here until just before he was picked up?'

Perhaps he was content to shrug off the missing days as the Met's responsibility, Yeadings thought. 'Have we nothing yet on how young Micky travelled?' he asked, making his silent approach known to them.

Salmon looked round at the sound of his voice. 'Info's thin on the ground, sir,' he complained. 'Not many folk on foot in this weather, and road conditions are enough for drivers to keep focused.'

'Maybe there was nothing for anyone to see,' Yeadings suggested. 'If we can assume Micky did as "Hutch" recommended, and contacted him by land line, they'd have made some arrangement for a pick-up. Most probably by the famed Harley-

Davidson. The meeting could have been outside our area, and he'd be delivered straight to wherever he was to stay over.'

'Allbright's house,' Salmon said decisively.

'Well, his gear was left there,' Z put in, 'but we don't know he was there in person. SOCO haven't been able to pick up any dabs or hair samples.'

'And neighbours questioned about Allbright's comings and goings by bike haven't noticed any pillion passenger,' Beaumont added. 'So he used the car, or else...'

'...the boy was taken somewhere else entirely. Which has to be the warehouse. The "Hutch" computer will have to turn up there if we go on searching long enough.' Salmon was grimly hanging on to this belief.

'I don't think he could have taken him there directly,' Z objected. 'Micky left home as if to go to school. At about eight-thirty. If he knew already where he'd be heading, he wouldn't have wasted any time getting there, because I'm convinced he never meant to spend a night away.

'Because Allbright's a night-worker, he had the morning free to pick Micky up. He wouldn't have taken him any place that was buzzing with activity and where everyone knew him. So not the warehouse. He must have some hideaway we haven't discovered yet.'

'Or –' Beaumont felt he was scraping the bottom of the scenario barrel here – 'he took the boy joyriding until he was due to go on duty, and then slipped him in after day shift but before the night staff were due. We know he holds a key to the warehouse.'

'And if Micky wasn't willing,' Yeadings said sombrely, 'that's when recourse was had to the cocktail of drugs. But for how long was he held like that?'

They all sat considering this. 'An overdose,' Beaumont muttered. 'So maybe Allbright (or whoever) hadn't much experience of the quantities to use...'

'Or was just unlucky.' That was from Zyczynski.

'Or it was meant to be final,' Salmon decided. 'Just as it was later, bashing his head in and chucking him in the river.'

Yeadings sighed, shifting his weight from one foot to the

other. 'Well, if anything comes up, I'm in my office.' He left them to it.

In the canteen Higgins felt his ears burn as he queued with a tray, despatched for two teas, an almond Danish and a jam doughnut. Back at the table he heard their raucous laughter. He was the fool of the day. Never a slip until now, apart from the ribbing he'd received over carrying the ambiguous message to Inspector Ruby Winter, (and that was mild as initiations went). But now, expecting to bring in the local court usher on a charge of suspected GBH! That was priceless and he'd never live it down. As long as there were coppers on the beat the story would circulate and his name go down as a terrible warning to probationers who got above themselves and thought they were CID.

DS Rosemary Zyczynski was discouraged. The case was going nowhere, bogged down by lack of proof. She had no doubt it was Allbright they were after, but he seemed to be several paces ahead of the team. She stood on the kerb, letting the wind blow through her hair, but still mentally pent up in the office and wishing Max was here so they could go striding up the Chilterns and get some clean air pumping through their lungs.

But exercise was no fun on one's own, and it was another three days before her weekly aerobics class. *If* she was free to join it. Salmon had a way of sending her off on some wild goose chase whenever it came around.

She turned at the sound of footfalls behind her. 'Fancy a jar?' Beaumont invited, halting alongside.

It wasn't what she longed for, but, 'Why not?'

The Crown was their nearest pub; not the best, but she remembered then the name Roseanne, given her by the male carer Alyson had taken on. With any luck they'd find her on bar duty.

There were fewer than a dozen drinkers in there. The two sergeants settled on stools in front of the mirrored array of bottles. 'My shout,' Beaumont claimed.

'Thanks. I'd like a half of lager.'

The woman who served their drinks was slim, a hennaed redhead with an upturned tip to her nose and upper lip, revealing two long, rabbity incisors.

'Would you be Roseanne?' Z asked when there was a lull in serving.

'That rather depends on who's asking.' She darted a shrewd glance at Beaumont. 'You're a plain-clothes copper, aren't you? I've seen you around the courthouse. So what am I supposed to have done wrong?'

'Nothing. We just wondered if you could tell us something about one of your regulars.'

'And lose their goodwill, not to mention their custom?' She grinned along with the warning.

'Sheena Judd,' Z prompted. 'We understand she drops in here from time to time.'

'Sheena, yes. I know her quite well. She's a neighbour, actually. What's wrong?' She leant matily over the counter towards them.

'Nothing that we know of. It's more her boyfriend we're curious about.'

'Who would that be, then?'

'We thought you could tell us that.'

She regarded them both with her head on one side, her left hand reaching for a straying lock of hair which she absently laid over her upper lip like a moustache, then put its tip between her teeth. She shook her head.

'Look, I really can't help. Truth of the matter is, she's a sort of loner. Bit of a sad case, poor Sheena. Married the wrong bloke, got divorced, and then rather let herself go, if you know what I mean. Not that she wouldn't welcome a spot of nooky if she got half a chance. But she won't make much of an effort to set herself up, like.'

Not very much help, Zyczynski decided, sipping at her lager which was warm and smelled smoky, like the bar itself.

'Mind you,' and Roseanne broke off to mop up a puddle of spilt beer with a red-checked towel, 'I won't say she didn't fancy someone. But whether he picked up on it or not I couldn't say. You can't easily tell with orientals, can you?'

'Inscrutable,' Beaumont agreed, nodding like a mandarin doll himself.

'That's what I mean.'

'Ramón?' Z asked, to be utterly certain; ' – who used to work here?'

'Yeah. Nice bloke, a bit quiet. Got on all right with the customers, for all that. He's got a job as a nurse somewhere local, I was told. I doubt we'll see him in here again. Doesn't drink, see, except lemonade.'

'What goes around comes around, it seems,' Rosemary commented when Roseanne had moved off to serve a table with baguettes and tomato soup. We're back where we started. It was Ramón who put us on to Roseanne, who points us back to him. But if he's still looking after old Emily he's obviously not riding off into the sunset with his inamorata.'

'In amorwhatsit? Cor, how she do go on!' Beaumont complained in a Monty Python voice. 'Drink up, girl, and let's get out of here. There are better drinks to swallow, at better watering holes.'

'Not for me, thanks. But next time it'll be my shout. I think I'll get home. Today's been rather a waste of effort all round, to my mind. I'd hoped we'd make some progress.'

Alyson Orme sat hugging a mug of coffee. There was a rare lull in activity in ITU, allowing her mind to orbit other worlds: particularly the dining room of an Italian restaurant fifteen miles outside town. It should have been called The Subfusc, but the well-spaced tables stood out against the gloom, having crisp white under-cloths topped diagonally by pink linen. Not shocking pink; more flirty pink. And with pink-shaded lamps instead of candles.

Things she seemed not to have observed at the time came back distinctly to her now: Keith facing her, dark-suited and formal, unlike how she normally saw him. She wondered if her own appearance had seemed strange to him, out of uniform or the casual T-shirt and jeans she wore at home.

It was strange how people dressed themselves up for special occasions. As though they took on a carapace, had something to conceal. Well, she had. Not that it was shameful, simply inappropriate: loving Keith when he was powerless to respond. Waiting for someone to die, when both were dedicated to saving life.

Audrey, she thought. How awful it would be if she guessed. That, on top of everything else!

She hung on to the basin as the spasms ran through her. Keith was rapping on the door, but it was locked and she was safe from him. There was nothing left to come up but bitter, thin liquid, yet it hurt like hell, all through her body.

'Audrey, let me in,' he pleaded. 'Don't shut me out like this. We need to be together.'

Together. When were they ever that? Only in photographs. And they say the camera doesn't lie! That bloody wedding shot, all radiance and white satin; the groom dressed up like a fucking tailor's dummy. Lies, all lies. When had there ever been truth between them?

She slid to the floor already awash from when she'd tried to drench her pounding head. She wallowed there like a goldfish flung from an upturned bowl. Well, here was the truth then, the truth she couldn't find in her marriage. Pain and the long drag into death; alone, while Keith slavered over some other woman hot to fill her place in his bed.

So now there was no longer any shadow of doubt. She had proof, face to face with his treachery. She hugged her wretchedness to her as the only thing left of her own. God, she could not hate him enough. It should be him here, suffering as she did. She knew she'd been meant for something better than this, Daddy's little Princess. Oh, poor Daddy, why did you have to die? You'd have done something, rescued me, punished him.

She had torn up the restaurant receipt discovered in the pocket of Keith's best suit. Dinner for two. She knew the place well, the pinkness of it, the romantic shaded lights, the obsequious, discreet service. And afterwards, in the back of the car, or even an upstairs room – she could picture them at it. And all that while she was being held, drugged, in the psychiatric department, like a madwoman. That last night, Sunday, before she was allowed home.

Home? Just an alternative place for drawn-out dying.

'Cancer,' she said aloud, accepting it. But that was only a part of the truth. The greater thing was his treachery. That was why she must do it.

This time she would splendidly succeed. And everyone should know how he'd wanted her gone!

She pushed the shredded paper back into the jacket pocket and hung the suit again on its rail. It was safe there, her precious evidence that she could visit and revisit to feed her resolve on.

Chapter Nineteen

It had struck DS Beaumont that Z was being uncharacteristically casual about following up the name which Roseanne had offered as Sheena Judd's love interest. And any opportunity to get a step or two ahead of his rival sergeant could do him a power of good.

Ramón, he recalled. Foreign, Spanish-sounding. Well, there were a lot from those parts employed in the service industries in the South-East counties. Nearly as many as Cypriot waiters. Decent types for the most part, and he'd prefer them any day to the scruffy home-bred variety who sneered at your ignorance of the menu and muttered over the paucity of tips.

A visit to the nick's canteen, channel of all available gossip, reliable or otherwise, might bring to light where the man was working at present, at what Roseanne thought was a private nursing job.

He wasn't to be disappointed. Sergeant Charlie Wise, who laboured to live up to his name, had worn out the elbows of several civvy suits at the bar of the Crown hotel. He told Beaumont that the barman, who had worked there only a short time, had left them in the lurch, not having been bound by contract. The assistant manager, one of Wise's cronies, and probably a snout to boot, had complained loudly, particularly over the unrealistic wage being offered by the rich old lady at the one-time show penthouse.

Beaumont, not a local himself, had to be directed to it. 'Not that they'll let you in if they don't like the cut of your jib,' he was told. 'There's a spy camera on the door. One of those hi-tech security things.'

Thus warned, he repaired to the Gents to check himself in a mirror, combed flat an obstinate quiff which his son said made him resemble a tufted duck, and polished the top of each shoe with a nifty rub up and down the back of alternate trouser legs. It could pay to have a wealthy old lady batting for you. If she was susceptible to a Spanish barman she might well un-bosom herself to a personable British copper. Purely in the confiding sense, of course. Anything more literal wasn't on. Not with old ladies.

It was Alyson who answered his buzz, caught clearing the lunch things. Beaumont announced himself, displaying his teeth widely towards the camera, together with his warrant card.

'How can I help you, Sergeant?' the young voice asked.

Why do they say that? Beaumont wondered, not for the first time. For one thing it's always when they're holding you at arm's length, like on the phone, and for another they'd probably floor you if you said what it was you'd really like from them!

'I'd appreciate a word with you concerning the employment of Ramón Nadal.'

Alyson felt herself wrong-footed. She had put off contacting Social Services about Ramón, and already here was a policeman asking about him. She felt obliged to let the man in to settle the matter. She pressed the door release. 'Take the lift to the seventh floor,' she directed him. 'I'll be waiting for you.'

'I'm Alyson Orme,' she said as he stepped from the lift. Of medium height, lean, with fair hair cut short to curve in below prominent cheekbones, she looked stylish and confident. 'I look after Miss Withers who's an invalid. One of your colleagues told me how to check up on Ramón, but I haven't got round to it yet. He's here at the moment, if you want to speak with him.'

They seemed to be slightly at cross purposes. 'A colleague of mine?'

'Detective Sergeant Rosemary something.'

'Her name's Zyczynski. A lot of people have trouble with the name. We work together.'

'Jijinsky?'

Beaumont printed the name on a page of his notebook, which he tore off and handed to her. 'What exactly did she tell you?'

Alyson explained. It was about Ramón's background.

'Let's have him in,' Beaumont suggested, 'then he can account for himself.'

Ramón had been reviewing his finances at the writing-table in his bedroom and presented himself in a newly acquired sweater and tweed trousers from the Oxfam charity shop. He eyed the plain-clothes policeman guardedly before returning to fetch his identity papers. Beaumont looked through them, nodded and passed them to Alyson Orme. 'So you're not actually Spanish?'

'From the Philippines. Spanish is one language we speak. People make that mistake.'

'And how long have you been in the UK?'

'You can see here. I am asylum status. Refugee. All OK.'

'When did you leave the Philippines? And why?'

'Eight years back. Not to be killed. By both sides.'

Beaumont knew little of oriental current affairs, but he remembered there had been successive revolutions involving political assassination. A centre of turbulent politics, it was another place where way back the Americans had stepped in to stop further bloodshed. Not that they'd penetrated all the smaller, wilder islands. All the same this man's explanation sounded shaky. He fixed him with a challenging stare. 'Are you wanted there on any criminal charge?'

'By the government. Yes. A child, rebels capture me. Pirates. Bad men.'

'And you joined them?' As Ramón nodded, he pursued it. 'So why do the rebels want to kill you?'

He shrugged. 'Later, doctors save me. Rebels hunt and kill all against them. I live years with doctors, work there, but...' He frowned, trying to find the right words in English. 'They good but not – they have wrong politic. Cannot save me. I run away, sail to Hong Kong, work there, years again.'

His protectors had had no clout during the ding-dong changes of government. Liberal do-gooders, they'd likely stepped out of line, protested against injustices. Poor little bugger, Beaumont thought: pillar to post and back again. Then when Hong Kong became Chinese he'd moved on once more. 'But why come here, to the UK?'

'Not for weather.' At last Ramón smiled.

'Why not Spain? You speak the language.'

Ramón was instantly serious again. 'Spanish are Catholic. Catholics in Philippines raid south islands and kill too.' His face showed disgust. 'Some good people there, like doctors, but many bad. Always fighting, pirates, murders.'

'I had no idea,' Alyson breathed, listening appalled. His sparse account must cover a lifetime of misery and dangers. Such a quiet, contained man.

'I wait here long for papers,' Ramón said, pointing to them. 'All legal now.'

Beaumont nodded. 'Good. And you were employed as barman at the Crown hotel. So how do you come to be working here?'

'Customer invite me to apartment. I help with old lady Emily. Then Nurse ask me stay.'

'This customer at the Crown. Would that be Sheena Judd?'

'Sheena, yes.'

'Your girlfriend.' It was a statement, not a question, and Ramón was quick to deny it.

'No. New meeting her. I come for teatime only.'

'Sheena told me,' Alyson explained, feeling obliged to help him out. 'She had to get a prescription made up for her mother. While she was out, my patient's granddaughter called. Ramón impressed her as competent, so when Sheena let me down I called on him to help out. Those doctors in the Philippines trained him well. He's very good with Emily.'

Beaumont was watching the man's face. He was giving little away. 'It's convenient for you, her going missing. So where is Sheena Judd now?'

'With man friend, I think. They meet in Crown hotel bar. He visit here.'

'Do you know his name?'

Ramón shook his head. 'I serve him beer. Sometimes whisky. Roseanne say he work in police court.' He frowned over recalling the word, then his face brightened. 'Usher, yes?'

Beaumont recalled the man, raw-boned, humourless and surly: Oliver Markham. No great catch for a girl, but from all accounts she was an also ran herself. Court was over for the day, so he'd probably be at home. Not that chasing him up was a priority. Salmon was concentrating all efforts on the Micky Kane murder. Z would have to take on the missing girl. The missing girl was relegated to Z's charge. He could leave her to get on with it.

He put a note on the office computer and added his initials. Might as well get any credit for naming Sheena's man-friend.

Superintendent Mike Yeadings distrusted coincidences as heartily as any other member of CID. So, when his scanning of all reports for the past day, however minor, produced the name of Oliver Markham in two unrelated incidents, he sat back and pondered what he recalled of the man. Vaguely unappetizing, his body language spoke of a chauvinist and a bully. Yeadings had spent time enough in court for the man's attitude to come across. And just recently, it seemed, he'd been replaced as usher, or even pressured to resign. As yet it wasn't known whether he had alternative employment.

Yeadings phoned down to the incident room where Salmon was closing down the Micky Kane investigation for the night. 'This missing young woman, Sheena Judd. Do we know what blood group she was?'

Whatever the question, Salmon was instantly on the defensive. 'Is she officially a Misper, sir?' he barked back. 'Not a minor, I understood?'

'No, and as an adult she has every right to wander off without informing her family. I am aware of that, Inspector. But I'm curious. The boot of her quoted man-friend's car was found to contain a rug with suspected bloodstains, so I ask myself who was bleeding. Especially since he tried to pass the blood off as dried cocoa, during a routine road check for speeding.'

'That'd be Traffic's concern, sir. The report hasn't been passed to CID.'

'Understand that I'm passing it now. We need to know the missing woman's blood group. So send someone to her address and find out.'

'Everyone's gone home, sir. I'll send Zyczynski in the morning.'

He supposed tomorrow must do, but examination of the stained travel rug was more urgent. 'I'll send a patrol car to pick the rug up. Even if Markham hasn't a washing machine there are overnight launderettes. He could be destroying vital evidence. How fortunate you've stayed late, Inspector. The lab is open tonight until 7.30. Ring through and warn them there's evidence on its way. Full DNA can wait, but I want to know what blood group we're dealing with.'

Fussy old codger, Salmon fumed. Young women went missing all the time: anything to attract attention. Didn't mean anything had happened to them. Still, he'd have to do as instructed. God knows when he'd get finished, and today there'd been shit-all progress on the current main case.

He made the call, authorizing the cost, and decided to pick up a takeaway on the route home. He closed down the computer, dragged on his coat and went for his car. Driving across town, he noted that lights were on behind the lowered blinds of Callender, Fitt and Travis. More time and energy being wasted over the affairs of the thriftless and shiftless. Same old, thankless grind. And to think that once, decades back, he'd believed becoming a copper would leave some mark on the world!

Timothy Fitt waited until young Monica had finished making noises in the outer office and put her head round the door to say goodnight. 'Thank you, Monica, for staying on. I'm afraid I'll need you in on time in the morning, but perhaps you'd care to get home an hour earlier tomorrow.'

'Ooh, thanks, Mr Fitt. G'night.'

She was a steady girl, didn't mind extra little jobs dropped on her, like going out to get that new key cut. It was always a shock when things like that went missing, and in this case the client was specially vulnerable. But perhaps no real harm done. The lost key, although unusual, had held no number. There had only ever been two of them to that strongbox, and now there were two again. He wrapped the newly cut one in a strip of bubble wrap, together with a short handwritten note and put both in an envelope, adding a first class stamp. The package was light enough to be covered. He remembered the address, even the post code. He would mail it himself on the way home. From the main post office, to be on the safe side.

Putting on his velvet-collared black overcoat and tucking in his muffler, he wondered how Emily was. Such a formidable woman once, but now a mere shell. Still, she was well looked after, well guarded. He had done all that could be expected of him. It could have been disastrous if the key fell into the wrong hands.

Over at the college, with lectures finished and the refectory officially closed, Jim Anders considered the place needed extra
guarding. There were three club meetings scheduled, and god-
knows-what clandestine jiggery-pokery going on besides. He
took his duties as night porter seriously and had few illusions
about modern youth. He timed his rounds at random. Armed
with a heavy torch, he toured all floors, switching off unnecessary lighting and noting noise levels at the more boisterous club
affairs, alert for romantic couplings in secluded corners and discarded syringes or evidence of other illicit activities. On his third
round, when most revellers had departed and only the Fine Arts
crowd still worked on posters for the coming Rag Week, he made
his way up to the top floor, using his key to gain access to the
roof.

This was out of bounds for students, but he remembered occasions when security had been outwitted and inappropriate articles
hung from the college's ceremonial flagstaff. Tonight, as he ventured out on to the starlit, frosted flats, he could appreciate that
the pole had not been violated.

In the shelter of the central air vent from Training Kitchen I,
he reached in a pocket for his ready-tamped pipe, struck a match
to it and remained contentedly smoking for the duration of his
authorized break. Finally he crossed to take a look over the town
centre. Traffic had dwindled to the normal midweek level for this
hour. Pedestrians were sparse and unaware of his godlike vantage
point. Moments like this were compensation for the minor irrita-
tions of the job.

Laughter and raised voices reached him as a group of youngsters left by the main doors: the last of the poster artists on their
way home. He leaned over to scan what lights they'd left on and
thought there was something odd about the portico below. It
projected some twelve feet, relieving the modern building's
severity. On its flat roof the dark lead cladding showed paler
markings. Something more than frost or the remains of snow.

Anders sighed: these silly young people with their passion for
tossing toilet rolls! A heavy downfall of rain might finally flush
the stuff away, but as yet the cold snap showed no sign of letting

up. He supposed that the job of disposal would fall to him. It would involve climbing up by ladder from the forecourt, because in winter all windows on the front elevation were sealed shut.

He took the staff lift down to get a closer look from just above.

It wasn't as he'd thought. The pale area was a human body, curiously twisted and lying face down.

One of those crazy kids had been up and jumped off the roof.

Dealing with that wasn't within his remit. He went, sickly, back to his cubby hole to phone the police.

Chapter Twenty

Yeadings had taken Nan to see a play at the theatre in Aylesbury and, unlike one other in the audience, had turned off his mobile phone. So it was only on reaching home again that he learned of the body fallen from the college roof.

'It's female,' Salmon said shortly. He was chilled to the bone, called out after already being two hours later back for supper than expected. He'd no sooner eased his boots off and thirstily sunk half his pint at the table than the summons had come.

'Some bloody student's topped herself,' he'd told his wife. 'There'll be all hell to pay, so there's no escaping. Stick some of that beef between two bits of bread and I'll eat it on the way in. Beaumont's coming to pick me up.'

Tight-lipped, his wife had done as instructed. Her moment for retaliation would come later. It hadn't pleased her one little bit moving to this part of the world, away from family and such friends as her complaining nature hadn't turned against her. She took some pleasure in plastering horseradish on so thick that he'd have no chance to notice the cold. A superb cook – her one virtue – she bridled at a hot meal wasted, and saw unpunctuality as a personal insult.

And now Salmon found himself obliged to stand inactive while the SOCO team moved about the restricted space of the portico roof like white-clad ghosts, until the arc lights and generator were in place and a plastic tent erected. Not that their work would be visible from the road, but higher floors of the hospital tower overlooked the site and already there were faces peering from lighted windows in the apartment block across the way.

His mouth still stung from the vicious relish in the sandwich and he could still have done with another layer of wool under his sheepskin car coat. But for the fact that accepting Beaumont's suggestion of a lift left him without individual wheels, he would have passed this scene over to the DS and returned home. He had a grim suspicion that that idea might have been behind the man's offer all along.

'Quite a drop,' he commented sourly. 'So, harder for identification. Did that missing Judd woman have any connection with the college?'

'Not that we know of,' Beaumont told him. 'But a lot of people get in by invitation and for open lectures. Let's hope she wore something distinctive that someone'll recognize.'

'If it is Sheena Judd, she could have been here since Sunday. You'd better get hold of the porter and find out when he last took a look down here. Actually I'll come along too.' Indoors, it would be out of the wind. They'd keep it brief tonight; haul the man in early tomorrow to give a full statement.

In next morning's bright sunlight Audrey Stanford lay tucked in a rug on a sofa by the window, quietly seething. Edna Evans, thorough enough but so noisy, had spent hours slamming around in the kitchen. It was useless to demand she should be quiet. That could slow her down and prolong the annoyance. Audrey wished she'd just shut up and go home.

Wishing, ever wishing. Wishing she had company around her, then longing for everyone to leave her in peace. Enduring the endless nights wishing for dawn to break, and then, exhausted by the tedium of day, yearning for dark and oblivion. Which was futile, with final oblivion so close.

It had taken her a long time to believe that, and now she did. The evidence was irrefutable. Believed, but could not accept. Death happened to others who were old and worn-out, or had lived wild lives and so brought it on themselves. But she wasn't like that. She'd never deserved this. Still young, there had been so much living left to do, places to go, people to meet, joys to experience. Not that she could be bothered any more to make the effort. Any move left to her now was towards becoming nothing. And the world would go on turning just the same, as though she had never been.

In the kitchen there was sudden silence. Audrey waited for the rumble of the roller towel as Edna finally dabbed soap suds off her fat arms. Then the fridge door opening and slamming as she checked the contents against a shopping list Keith had made out. 'You'll want more Marmite, love,' she shouted. 'I'll add it on, shall I?'

Audrey pretended not to hear. The very mention of any food was nauseous now.

In the comparative quiet as Edna struggled into her outdoor clothes a fresh sound emerged. Steady and regular as waves breaking on the shore came a screech-scratch of Keith raking the drive's gravel.

You'd think it was deliberate, meant to irritate. He must know that any activity of his mocked her disability. All right, he had to be somewhere: it would be too callous if he didn't stay home. But did he have to keep reminding her of the great gulf between them; how he was fit, would continue *active* when she was no more? Whenever she saw him, every time he did something that she'd once done but was beyond her now, there was this rush of bile in her throat and a scalding hatred in her heart. She could only loathe him for it, wishing the same could happen to him and then he might understand.

If he had to face what threatened her, experience this gradual and inevitable falling apart, how would he feel?

There was a gentle tap at the window as he laid the handle of his rake against the glass. He leaned in towards her. 'OK, love?'

She wasn't, and he knew it. She wasn't his 'love' either. That was a meaningless word that the cleaner used. Perhaps she'd never been his real love, and all that romancing in the past had been deception too, while he waited for the big thing to come along. It would be some young locum they'd take on in the practice. Or a woman doctor at the hospital, someone *suitable*. Because she hadn't been much use to him, couldn't face illness – her own or any other's – didn't share his wretched work, was a sickly letdown.

All the same she didn't deserve to be left alone to die like this. Dying would be less awful if they could have ended together, in each other's arms. But he was to go on. She resented every breath left to him and the future she was deprived of. And, with someone ready to replace her, in a matter of weeks, even days, all memory of her would be lost. He'd had erotic moments enough with all those absences, ostensibly for his work. All those late nights recently when he'd come home late not wanting a meal. How often had he deceived her? Meant to go on deceiving? She turned away from the window as tears squeezed out between tight eyelids.

The house phone cut through her miseries. He'd heard it from the garden, mouthed at her through the window, 'I'll go,' and waved her to stay put. Not that she'd any intention of moving. The calls were always for him. That's all his replica woman could use to reach him now, since he must stay on guard-dog duty at home.

She turned on her side, straining to catch any part of his conversation in the hall. He seemed tense, listening, now and again grunting agreement or demanding clarification. There was little there for her to construct what was under discussion, or to guess who was on the other end. Just a few isolated words and one more urgent enquiry.

'Who was it?' she demanded when he'd rung off and came in to ask if there was anything she wanted.

'Just Dougie, about some patients. The locum who's supposed to come fell off her horse and can't come for a couple of weeks. So he's badly pushed.'

'You want to rush back and fill the gap?' Her voice was acid.

'No. My place is here with you, love. They'll simply have to manage. Still, I can't help wondering just how.'

'Who's Emily?' She had picked up the name from his conversation. The question was abrupt. She heard the suspicion in her own voice but couldn't contain it.

'One of my special patients.'

'What's special about her?'

'She's very frail. I like to keep in touch.'

'Normally you see her every day?'

'As often as I can.'

'Is she beautiful?'

He smiled. 'Yes, I suppose she is.'

Watchful, she didn't miss the brief wistfulness of his eyes. *I hate her*, she decided. Beautiful, frail, loathsome Emily, if I had a rag doll I'd make a pin cushion of you. But he can't see you now. I am the one he sees every day. And I won't relinquish him.

'She's nearly ninety-four,' he said, turning away, so he never saw the bitter scorn on her face at his words.

As if she'd believe anything he said! His face had given him away. Such treachery, pretending he'd never looked at any woman but herself. That last thing he'd said was a lame attempt to put her off the scent. But at least she was named now, the woman he visited every day, cared for, made love to, deceived her with. A strangled sound escaped her.

He turned, ready to give comfort, but met fury in her eyes and was rebuffed. He couldn't take her in his arms when she was like this. He knew there had to be these moments of fierce rebellion. He'd seen it in other patients faced with finality, but here it was too close to him. He was involved and could not cope.

'I'll see what Edna's left out for our lunch, shall I?'

She said nothing, screwing her fists into the cushions, and he went away.

He was clever. That was generally accepted. And this clever man had kept his affair from her until now. Surely somewhere hidden among his things there must be more evidence of his deceit? Letters, love tokens which this Emily had given him. If she mattered so much that he had to insist Dougie look in on her, surely they'd have exchanged gifts or sent notes.

Later, if she wasn't feeling too awful, she would look through his desk and the cupboards in his dressing-room. Only she'd have to make sure he wasn't around. She'd send him out shopping and make it sound urgent. For something special she couldn't trust Edna to choose for her.

Oh yes, two could play at being clever.

Thirty-six hours of searching the stationery warehouse had produced no traces of Micky Kane having been there, and permission was given for normal business to resume. The computers were still with Thames Valley's own technical experts who were trying to access connections between the boy and Allbright. Their time had been eaten into by the necessity to find two replacement computers and download current stock lists from hard disk for transfer to them.

Chief Superintendent Perry was almost apoplectic over fears of a lawsuit for malicious harassment, demanding compensation for loss of income. The public were so litigious these days. It was bound to ensue if no valid case was ever made against any employee of the company.

As a result, relations between him and Yeadings' team were in a delicate state of balance, which Salmon's bullish style was in hourly danger of upsetting. Nothing would persuade him that Allbright, once in his sights, should be allowed any benefit of doubt, although they'd had to release him after questioning. The investigation appeared to have stalled for lack of evidence.

It was at this point that a late sighting of Micky Kane was claimed by an anxious woman just freed from the bedside of a heavily pregnant daughter with pre-eclampsia. With the baby now successfully delivered, the relieved grandmother had been able to catch up with back issues of the local newspaper.

'It was him all right,' she told the duty officer. 'And I didn't like the look of it. If the lad hadn't got away by scrambling over a fence I'd have felt compelled to protest.'

'So you're sure this boy was the one found floating in the river next morning?'

'Oh, without any doubt. It was his clothes, see? Just like it said in the paper. He looked as though he had his dad's trousers and jacket on. And an outsize dad at that.'

'Was he wearing shoes?'

'Well, of course. Or maybe boots. Big clumping things. Like I said, he went over a fence, but he hardly made it because of his bulk.'

'If you'll just take a seat, I'll get someone from CID to see you.'

It was Beaumont who took the call and came straight down. He showed her into a vacant interview room. 'Mrs Durrant? Can you give me a time for this sighting?'

It was, she was sure, about 7.30, at latest 7.35, on the Saturday evening. That was when her number 334 was due in at the bus station, and it had been right on time when she picked it up in Mardham village. It was only ten minutes' walk to the hospital from where it dropped her off, and this was about half way, by that vacant lot behind the Odeon car park. Visiting hours had been extended for her because her daughter was so ill.

'And the boy was running away? Can you describe the man chasing him?'

She shook her head vigorously. 'Oh, it wasn't a man, Sergeant. It was a woman. I suppose that's why she didn't go over the fence after him. She had a longish skirt on, see.'

'A bit inconsiderate of you, Mike,' Prof Littlejohn had boomed down the telephone. 'This is high season for poor old pensioners going down with pneumonia. I don't need you cluttering up my morgue with your gratuitous bodies. Still, since you ask so nicely, I'll find a slot. How does 10.30 tomorrow suit you?'

'Policemen can't be choosers.'

'Ungrateful beggar. Everyone at home doing well?'

'Flourishing, thanks. And your lot?'

'Ginny's picked up a verruca at the leisure pool and for some reason thinks she should be immune. Seb's pockets must have even larger holes in them now he's up at Oxford. I guess that's par for the course.'

Yeadings laughed and rang off. The pathologist, tragically widowed eight months back, was immersing himself in the twins' activities as compensation, choosing to make a comic saga of their exaggerated misfortunes, and covering real grief with a carapace of determined cheerfulness. The daughter, kind child, had opted for a gap year before taking up her scholarship at UCL, and Yeadings guessed that there was a pact between her and Sebastian to keep their father bolstered with gossipy trivia.

Remind Nan to invite the Prof for dinner soon, he wrote on his desk pad.

'Did you get that?' he asked Beaumont. 'Tomorrow, at 10.30. It could be a long session, in view of the state of the body.'

'Disjointed data,' was the inescapable pun. 'I guess it'll be me attending,' the DS complained.

'Meanwhile, follow up this latest thing on Micky Kane. What do you suppose he'd done, to be chased by a woman?'

'Could she have recognized the clothes he was wearing? Maybe family or a neighbour of the man he'd pinched them from? But what was he doing down by the Odeon car park?'

'Making for the vacant lot? Coming *from* the cinema? How much money had been left in the clothes he made off with? This sighting was roughly three hours after he got away from the hospital. Where better to spend the time anonymously on a bitterly cold night?'

'I'd go for that, sir. There should have been three fivers and some loose change in the man's pockets. If Micky was desperate he wouldn't have hesitated to use the money. And in the Odeon he could get a snack to tide him over. Anything to put off contacting Allbright again.'

'So perhaps he didn't. It could be someone else who raped and killed him, and we've been barking up the wrong tree. Get down there with a PC who's familiar with the beat. Find out who hangs around that waste ground; if any tramps doss down there. It's meant to be fenced off, but there could be ways of getting in. Since Micky left no fingerprints at Allbright's house, this is possibly where he spent the intervening time.'

'And where he got the drugs?' Beaumont slid off the corner of his desk, patted his pockets and reached for his sheepskin. Sergeant Bird kept the beat records and would recommend a local man. It seemed a worthwhile angle to follow up.

DI Salmon thought he had a cold coming on. Sweating, he'd turned the heating down in his office, and now he couldn't stop shivering. Also his throat felt it had been scraped with sandpaper. With two ongoing major investigations begun, this was no time to feel under the weather.

This damned female suicide. At least they'd a suitable Misper to fit that. He had stayed on last night until the body was photographed and delivered to the morgue. There he'd watched her clothes bagged and had brought them away with him. Now he expected Beaumont to list and check them against what the Judd girl had last been wearing.

Snag One was that the mother hadn't seen her leave the house and had only the skimpiest idea of what hung in her daughter's wardrobe. Snag Two was that Beaumont had gone off on some errand for the superintendent and wasn't answering his mobile.

That meant using Zyczynski. Better she should burrow through the unpleasant garments than himself. Women's things, after all. Where was the wretched girl? Got in the way when there was work to be done, and now when she might have been of some use she'd gone missing.

He rang through to Yeadings' office. 'Is Zyczynski by any chance up with you, sir?' he demanded.

'Not at present, but I was thinking of sending for her. You sound as if you could do with a coffee, Walter. I'll start the machine up.'

Slightly mollified by the use of his forename, Salmon admitted that a large mug of Yeadings' special mocha wouldn't go amiss. By the time he was seated with this in his shivering hands he found his nose was irrevocably blocked.

The Boss noted his pallor and snorting speech. He reached into his lower drawer for the bottle of single malt, uncapped it and waved it at his DI. 'It's a bit early, but it'll help you get through the rest of the morning.'

A light tap on the door announced DS Zyczynski. Salmon opened his mouth to despatch her to listing the clothes, but was overtaken by a fit of sneezing.

'Have a seat, Rosemary,' Yeadings invited. 'Your coffee's on the windowsill. I thought we should have a meeting.'

It wasn't time wasted. Salmon, listening intently, had to admit that the Boss had it all at his fingertips. He dealt the new death a dismissive 'nothing we can do until we've an ID. Apart, of course, from a meticulous search of the college and questioning of all in the building from Sunday pm onwards. Someone there must have seen her at some point. It would help if we knew how long the body had lain there. Due to sub-zero night temperatures that won't be easy for the professor to determine.'

He then went on to summarize progress on the Micky Kane investigation. 'We're badly in need of witnesses. There's little doubt that Allbright was the enticer codenamed "Hutch", and it's vital that we find the computer he used to communicate with the boy. It's possible he has got rid of it or had the hard disk replaced. He's had time enough. And I agree with the assumption that he

met Micky on the same morning he skived off school and
brought him back here either by car or on the bike. But not,
apparently to the house. Wherever he took the boy, he appears to
have relieved him of his schoolbag and the things in it. It's likely
Micky had changed out of his uniform before they met up.

'We have to find the alternative place Allbright took the lad,
and it's there we just might find the computer, if it still exists. So
has the man access to a country cottage, or a lock-up garage, an
allotment shed, or workshop: somewhere that he's managed to
keep in the dark? What were his hobbies outside the home? The
search has to go on, spread wider.'

'There's this gap,' Z said as Yeadings paused. 'Four days
between his leaving home and being picked up drugged and
unconscious. His parents had tried to keep it low key, hoping
he'd come back on his own. The Met police were informed, but
it was kept out of the papers. A pity, or we'd have been on to him
more quickly. I've spoken again with the nurses who looked after
him in ITU. They'd noticed no evidence of sexual assault. But
then they hadn't specifically looked for it. They'd enough to do
with detoxing him and keeping him going.'

'So you're suggesting that up until then Allbright had been
guilty of no more than abduction of a minor?' Salmon sounded
to be choking equally with indignation and catarrh.

'It's a possibility,' Yeadings gave as his opinion. 'Professor
Littlejohn stated that the abuse was recent. It could have happened after he escaped from the hospital, either before or after
the woman was seen chasing him. Beaumont is checking on that
area now. Until we know more we can't assume that Allbright
ever caught up with him again.'

Salmon looked as if all the stuffing was knocked out of him.

Chapter Twenty-One

Alyson slept late, having been restlessly awake for over an hour from some time after two, and then visited with disjointed, disturbing dreams. Waking, she had no precise memories of them, only a vague sense of unease. She supposed that Sheena's disappearance was connected with it.

Smelling coffee and warm yeast as she came out of the bathroom, her hair in a terry turban, she found Ramón had laid the table for breakfast and heated some flaky croissants.

'This is pleasant,' she said, sitting down. 'But you mustn't feel you need to work out of hours.'

'I eat too,' he said simply and took the chair opposite.

They ate in silence until something came to mind that she had meant to ask him before. 'Ramón, that first evening you stood in for me, Sunday. Was there anyone else here, besides Sheena, when you arrived?'

He seemed to consider this. Perhaps, she thought, 'stood in for' was an idiom he had difficulty with, but no, he was nodding his understanding.

'There was nobody,' he said.

'I see. In that case he must have left already. Or else he never came.' The only person to know would be Sheena. Except that, surely, the art valuation man would have been in touch with Fitt after his visit. She could ring his office later and set her mind at rest.

'Emily is bright,' Ramón volunteered. '*Brighter*, you say?' He had a way of rolling some of his 'r's.

'That's right. Bright, brighter, brightest.'

'We dance,' he told her shyly. 'Slow, with wheelchair. And she laugh.'

'She has a great sense of fun. It's good for her to laugh.'

'And sometimes cry.'

Did he mean that that too was good for her, or – ? 'Emily cries?'

He nodded. 'Sad life, she tell me.'

It startled her. In all the months she had been here Emily had never confided that much. Or indeed spoken as much as she had done over these last few days. Ramón was bringing her out, rather as Keith had done. Perhaps it was men's company that stimulated Emily.

It should have occurred to her before, what was missing. Although Emily never married, there had certainly been men in her life. Fitt had implied as much. And there had been the illegitimate child born when she was seventeen, which made her run away from home. There must have been so much in her past that no one could guess at. If now she was remembering and speaking of it, did that mean she was regaining strength, or must it be seen as an intimation of the approaching end?

'I wish I knew more about her,' Alyson confessed. 'She's my great-aunt. That's my mother's mother's older sister, but none of us knew what had become of her until Mr Fitt tried to get in touch with me.'

'Mr Fitt?'

So she explained. The solicitor had represented Emily for a very long time and knew all her family. There had been a daughter Eunice who lived in Edinburgh, had married and had the daughter Rachel, whom Ramón had met when she called. A distant cousin to herself, Rachel had mentioned an older half-brother and half-sister, Eunice being the second wife of their father.

'I'm afraid that's rather complicated,' she apologized. 'The trouble is I don't know any of them really; and little enough about them. But I gather Mr Fitt considers that Emily's better off at a distance from them.'

But that was only his opinion. She remembered now that Rachel had voiced criticism of the solicitor; some doubt about his management of Emily's affairs. It was a serious thing even to hint at a professional's dishonesty. Alyson quite liked the man; and why not, since he'd sought her out and set her up here? So did that mean she was partisan, being under an obligation to him?

And then, she hadn't cared for Rachel at all, on the brief occasion that they'd met. And afterwards Mr Fitt had opposed the family getting in touch again. Could he really do that? Had he any right?

Certainly it was time he came out in the open with her. There was no reason why she shouldn't ask him to call, ostensibly to see Emily's progress and check on her employment of Ramón. An old-fashioned solicitor, he might even disapprove of Emily being intimately cared for by a male helper. Whatever the outcome, she would insist he took her into his confidence. There had been altogether too much taken on trust between them.

Beaumont had trouble catching up again with Mrs Durrant. He rang the hospital's maternity unit to hear that she had visited earlier that morning and left shortly after ten. No one answered when he rang the bell at her address. Then, advised by a neighbour, he ran her to earth at her daughter's house where there were two older children under school age whom she'd moved in to look after.

Yes, she assured him; it was certainly a woman she'd seen; not a priest in a cassock or one of those students who wore long arty-crafty coats. The street hadn't been well lit, but she'd known it was a woman by the way she ran.

And now that she'd thought about it, she was pretty sure the woman had shouted something at the boy's retreating back. She was breathless and the wind blew the words away. Maybe 'Stop! Come back!' Something like that. And the boy hadn't taken a blind bit of notice. Just ran on.

Mrs Durrant would be a good witness in court, Beaumont considered. If it ever got that far. But still he had to meet up with off-duty Constable Jarvis and get the lowdown on the locality.

They met in the Odeon cafeteria which opened for lunches before the afternoon film show. Jarvis, large and ponderous, was halfway through a pineapple milkshake. Beaumont went across to join him with a cappuccino. 'They expect you to eat,' he was warned, 'but they know me here. You'll be all right.'

Bloody patronizing for a mere plod, Beaumont considered. 'So what's the lowdown on the vacant plot past the car park?' he demanded.

'There's a lotta local politics,' the PC warned him. 'That's where the old council offices used to be before the clearance. A developer made a bid for the site, only he had a brother was an alderman, so they musta bin afraid it could look dodgy. Anyway, they decided to hold it over for a bit. Only nobody else has been allowed to make a bid since. A bit of an embarrassment all round. So if there's any complaint put in about what goes on over there, they don't really want to know. A case of everyone lie low and say nuffink. Sort of Brer Rabbit, see?'

Beaumont saw. 'So what does go on over there?'

Jarvis noisily sucked on his straw until the last of the milky sludge was drained off. 'Not a lot. A bit of rough dossing down, but there's no harm in the old fellers. These cold nights they build themselves a fire. I don't enquire where they get the timber from. They've sense enough not to pull down the fence that hides them.'

'Are they dealing?'

'Drugs? Nah. Old winos, most of them. A bit of meths when the cash is low.'

'Any kids there?'

'Runaways, you mean? I never saw any. That's not to say they don't stick them under some tarpaulin when they see I'm on me way.'

It was clear that PC Jarvis took a relaxed view of policing. Beaumont guessed that for him his wage packet and a full belly were the mainstays of life. Beyond that, no hassle. And, a bluffer, maybe he had clout with others on the beat, which was why mention of this setup hadn't penetrated to the upper echelons. And had that silence even contributed to Micky's death?

Ironically he thanked Jarvis and rose to go.

'I thought you wanted an escorted visit.' He sounded indignant.

'That'll do for now. It all sounds harmless enough.' Beaumont was damned if he'd be trotted round there like an exhibit by this load of lard. Better to wait for dark and turn up in scruff order with a half of scotch to share. They might sniff out that he was Old Bill, but he guessed he'd get more from them than would a man in uniform.

'When you're out shopping...' Alyson had said. And he'd felt diminished in her eyes. But he saw she hadn't meant it that way.

Keith Stanford sat on in the car, debating with himself. After lunch he'd gone for the curtain cords and tassels Audrey had suddenly decided were vital. Whether sending him shopping was some whim of hers to humiliate him or an example of the mental aberration of a patient nearing the end he couldn't tell. Anyway he'd discussed colours and silk twists with an androgynous assistant in the furnishing store and was satisfied that what he'd chosen would match the rather shabby old curtains in the lounge. Now he was free.

Parked in one of the designated spaces for doctors at the hospital, he looked across to the stack of apartments above the car showrooms. There was a low light on in the penthouse as the afternoon darkened. Behind the wide window he made out the shape of a man standing, and the head and shoulders of someone a little lower: Emily, in her wheelchair, gazing out. He could go and see her.

Or he could drop in at the ITU.

He knew which he most needed, but he had no excuse. After a moment's uncertainty he leaned forward, switched on, put the car in gear and eased off the brake. Return dutifully to Audrey; try to shore up her whimsical interest in brightening up the lounge.

She heard the clang of the garage door closing, and still she stayed crouched on the bed, his suits scattered all round her. In her hands, torn and scrunched up, was the retrieved piece of precious evidence: the receipt from the restaurant *Da Roma* – two starters; two main courses; one dessert; two coffees; a single bottle of wine, but an expensive one – dated Sunday. Her last night imprisoned in the psychiatric unit. And his last night of freedom, as he'd have seen it.

His best jacket lay over her thighs. He'd worn it for his whore. He'd taken her where they'd once dined together: the pink place with low lights and discreet service. She guessed there would be bedrooms upstairs, but she'd never ventured that far. Every detail rewound like a loop of film in her mind, and at each showing she held fast to it with searing relish.

She heard the front door open and he called out, 'I'm home!' She crouched lower, stuffing the treacherous, shredded paper in her mouth and gagging as it soaked up all the saliva, making it impossible to swallow.

'Audrey! Where are you, love?'

That *love* again! She clamped her jaws together, gulped once more and the wad passed over her tongue, lodged in her dry throat. She was choking. His infidelity would kill her! But not here, like this. There was a better way.

Footfalls on the stairs. He was almost upon her. She tried to scream, sobbed, and part of the wad moved farther down.

'Audrey, what on earth?' He took in her distraught state, the jumble of his own clothes strewn about the bed and on the floor. She was crouching, with fear and open venom in her eyes. He couldn't deny the vindictive intention. She'd meant to destroy his things, but hadn't managed to find the scissors.

'Don't touch me!' she screamed. As he went forward she stumbled from the far side of the bed and made for the open bathroom door. He followed and held her as her body was racked with convulsions. She vomited in the handbasin, and seemed to be bringing up confetti.

Eating paper. She was demented. He should never have brought her home. She would need sedation, and then he must get Dr Ashton across to assess her.

DC Silver unwrapped another mint humbug and popped it into his mouth. 'They'll think you've been drinking,' his partner warned, leaning forward to clear the misted window. 'How the hell long do we have to keep this up? He's having a long lie in. We're on to a dead end here.'

'Thank the Lord for small mercies,' Silver mouthed around his champing jaws. 'We're out of the Salmon's reach here and a negative report's less bother.'

'Uh-uh!' They both tensed. Although the bedroom window remained curtained, a burly figure in leathers had materialized from the side passage to the house and was at one of the double garage doors, removing the padlock.

'Dressed for the bike,' Silver whispered.

Allbright went inside, to reappear wheeling the Harley-Davidson. Silver reached for the ignition and gave one or two encouraging but subdued bursts of acceleration. If the man went burning rubber up the motorway they'd be in for a hair-raising chase with little chance of keeping up. As the bike turned into the road their unmarked car slid out of the shadows and fell in some distance behind. Allbright was making for the town centre, circled the central island and turned right for open country. 'Good,' Silver decided as they climbed among trailing traffic uphill.

About eight minutes of steady driving brought them to winter-bare fields and sparse farm buildings. Three vehicles ahead the Harley signalled left and turned into a narrow track. The Ford continued past, and fifty yards farther on pulled up by the gate to a ploughed field. From there they'd need to walk back. Silver hadn't missed the *No Through Road* sign at the track's opening.

Untrimmed hedges prevented their view of anything beyond the lane's twists and turns. It led down to a shallow ford which they splashed through, breaking its fine shell of ice over the grass verge. Then a steep rise and they came on a dilapidated barn with an abandoned cartwheel leaning against its crazily hung timber door. They might have gone past but for the fresh, wet tyre tracks that led along one side and to the rear.

'What now?' his partner asked Silver in a low voice. There was too much risk of their being discovered and blowing the operation.

'We report in, and come back when Allbright's returned to work. This could be just what we've been looking for.'

Back in the car DC Silver radioed in to Control and was put through to CID office where Beaumont had just come in. 'Better hang around until he emerges,' the DS advised. 'See if he's moving anything out. Then follow him back home. He'll need to turn up for the night shift at the warehouse.'

Two of the six beds in ITU had come vacant, due to a death and a stabilized arrythmia. Alyson took advantage of the brief lull to ring Fitt's office from one of the public telephones in the hall. 'What can I do for you, m'dear?' he asked.

She explained that the art evaluation expert might be able to answer a question that had arisen about her missing care-worker. If Mr Fitt would give her the man's phone number she would make the enquiry direct.

There was silence at the far end of the line. Alyson waited. Surely she wasn't demanding a breach of legal discretion?

'A missing care-worker? So you are understaffed at present?'

'No, Mr Fitt. I've found a substitute. Rather a better one, in fact. That's something else I wanted to talk to you about. But I'm not happy about what's happened to the helper I had before. Nobody seems to know where she's gone.'

'She left without giving notice? There was no disagreement?'

'It came completely out of the blue. And she wasn't paid up to date.'

'I see. That is disquieting.' He paused. 'But this art evaluation expert. Who was he?'

'He's the one you wrote to me about.'

'Miss Orme, there appears to be some misunderstanding. I know nothing of any such person. Nor have I written to you recently. Am I to believe that someone claiming to have those credentials has actually visited Miss Withers?'

He sounded alarmed. But not as appalled as Alyson, gripping the phone so tightly that her hands started to shake. 'Yes,' she whispered. 'That is what happened. I believed you'd authorized the visit. And he was to visit on Sunday afternoon. The day Sheena Judd went missing!'

It was his wife's bridge evening, so Timothy Fitt would be dining out in any case. The sight of onetime allies engaged in cut-throat recrimination after a game had strengthened his determination never to be drawn in. There were still in his life a few whose friendship he valued unconditionally. One of these was Emily Withers, once so redoubtable but now needing his protection.

From Alyson Orme's alarming phone call it seemed that Emily's valuable paintings were attracting criminal attention. He would need to strengthen security at the penthouse. Any break-in could endanger Emily herself. It wasn't clear whether the incursion had been only exploratory or if a theft had already occurred. The collection would need fresh verification.

Recently there had been other suspicious happenings which couldn't be passed off as coincidental. Within his own office, loss of the key to Emily's strongbox, for one thing. And could not Emily's missing care-worker be connected?

Alyson had insisted that the art expert had authorization in writing. The forgery of Fitt's own signature on the firm's headed notepaper must surely involve someone inside Callendar, Fitt and Travis with access to their stationery; so too did the missing strongbox key which normally was kept in his own locked desk. It seemed unlikely that any client visiting the office would have the opportunity, or be sufficiently familiar with the internal lay-out.

He pondered what precautions he should take, while lifting the succulent white flesh off his sole grilled on the bone, and sipping a pleasing Montrachet at the Conway Restaurant. Perhaps the time had come when he should be more open with young Alyson regarding her family's quite appalling history. She had fulfilled his intentions regarding Emily's welfare, and he hoped the girl was well-balanced enough to accept the revelation of past scandals.

He took out a pen and notepad, to jot down from memory some of the relevant dates. It had all happened so long ago, and most of what he knew was hearsay, gleaned from his own father and the original Callendar who founded the firm.

Henry Withers, Emily's father, had considerable wealth inherited from his shipping forebears in Bristol. They had brought back treasures from the Far East, and were involved in the lucrative transport of slaves from Africa to the New World. He, a Victorian autocrat, had been equally callous towards his own kith and kin. Emily, the elder daughter, had been seventeen when she fled his roof, unaccountably pregnant. He had not allowed her name to be uttered in his presence again.

Timothy Fitt sighed, gently dabbed the linen napkin over his greying moustache and nodded to the waitress that he was ready to settle the bill.

Although Mrs Judd had been unable to recall what her daughter had been wearing when she left the house for work on the Sunday, Zyczynski was able to pick up a recent photograph. It did away with asking the woman to identify the body at the mortuary. Sheena had been fleshy and big-boned with short, fair hair. According to Beaumont's description the dead woman was dark, thin and possibly older too. DI Salmon was going to spit blood when he couldn't connect this body with the missing care assistant.

Mrs Judd couldn't say what blood group her daughter belonged to, but she knew she had it written down somewhere, if only she was given time to search. It was with all that stuff about inoculations and so on. Maybe later on…

Zyczynski returned to base and reported direct to Yeadings while waiting for Beaumont to phone in Prof Littlejohn's preliminary findings from the post mortem. So far no similar missing person had been reported, and the college had failed to claim the dead woman as a mature student or member of staff, yet it was unlikely that a total stranger would walk in off the street for the purpose of jumping from the roof. Some knowledge of the building would be needed. She hoped that a press notice would bring a response from the public leading to an ID.

A call from Control switched her interest to the Micky Kane case. The two DCs detailed to keep a watch on Allbright's house had returned after tailing his Harley out to a farm building some eight miles north of the town. Informed of this, Yeadings began organizing a team to examine the building after dark when Allbright would be on night duty. He dispatched DC Silver to a magistrate to obtain the necessary search warrant.

'Are we likely to get it?' Z doubted.

'It depends whom we ask,' Yeadings said blandly. Which probably meant that he'd added his weight to the request.

When they met up with the DI, 'I want to be in on the search,' Z insisted.

'Just myself, Beaumont, if he's back in time, and one of the DCs already involved,' Salmon said shortly. 'You stay with the college body, in case anything comes up.' It seemed she was to blame for supplying proof that the suicide wasn't Sheena Judd. 'Shoot the messenger,' she murmured under her breath.

She looked towards Yeadings for a reprieve, but he was gazing elsewhere. When she left the CID office he strolled after her. 'I've just heard informally from the Prof,' he murmured, falling into step alongside. 'In advance of tomorrow's post mortem report, it seems your lady couldn't have jumped. Death was from manual strangulation. Which must have taken some finding, considering the state of the body. So we have another murder. It struck him we could make a move on that while he's tied up with cataloguing all the breakages and internal injuries.'

He cast a cautionary glance over his shoulder. 'I suggest we visit the college.'

Getting a step ahead of the DI on this one, Z hid a smile. The Boss relished any opportunity to abandon his desk and get to the coal-face. And, for herself, there could be advantages in being sidelined from the other case.

Mr Fitt had arranged to visit Alyson at half past eight. She came straight home off duty, checked that Emily was comfortable, then asked Ramón to stay on and meet the solicitor. After that he'd be free to go out if he wished.

Ramón picked up on the hint and decided he could afford to see the blockbuster film advertised at the Odeon. With this in mind he went to remove his coat from the airing cupboard where he'd left it damp with snow. The woollen scarf was still hanging there, which Nurse Orme had said was the doctor's. And towards the back there was something else quite unaccountable. He stood staring, and puzzled over what it could mean. Then, as the buzzer sounded for the front door, he retired to his room to await being called in.

Emerging from the lift, Mr Fitt had his briefcase with him, and followed Alyson through to the lounge, declining her offer of a drink.

'Before we talk business,' she told him, 'I'd like you to meet the care assistant I've taken on in place of the woman who left. He's a Filipino and I've looked at his work permit. Everything seems to be in order, but you may like to check for yourself. As I said, he's very efficient, and Emily has taken to him well. In fact she's been quite talkative of late.'

'Thank you. Certainly I should like to see the man, yes. And I'll look in on Emily, of course, before I leave.'

Ramón appeared to pass muster, having changed into a fresh uniform jacket for the interview. He was hesitant, as ever, in answering the solicitor's questions but gave a good account of himself, Alyson stressing the years he had worked for the two doctors in Manila.

'I hope he will prove as suitable as he appears,' Fitt said when he had been dismissed. 'One drawback is his limited command of spoken English, but his comprehension seems adequate. Now, my dear, tell me again, in as much detail as possible, about this bogus insurance man who claimed to have an introduction from myself.'

He examined the letter which Alyson produced, and hummed doubtfully over it. The signature was certainly false, but not the stationery. This was disquieting.

'And the only person who could describe him to us is the missing Miss Judd? How very inconvenient. What steps have been taken to discover her present whereabouts? Have the police been notified?'

Alyson explained how they assumed Sheena had gone off with a newly acquired man friend. 'Her absence may have no connection with the other business,' she said. 'I'm afraid she was very slack about some things, though this does seem the limit, even for her.'

'I've been thinking,' Fitt said, broaching a new subject, 'that I should confide to you some of the background to Miss Emily's – er, unusual life. You are aware, I believe, of the circumstances of her leaving home as a young woman?'

'My grandmother did mention it, but I doubt she ever knew very much, being just a child at the time.'

'And then being sent to live in Italy with her mother's sister until the outbreak of World War II.'

'For so long? I'd understood it was no more than a prolonged holiday. But after she died I did come across her marriage certificate to my grandfather. On it her maiden name was given as Adriani. Elena Adriani. When she should have been plain Ellen Withers.'

'Her name was changed by deed poll. That, and the removal to Italy, was to shield her from the publicity of her father's tragic death.'

'I knew nothing of that. What happened?'

Fitt, clearly discomfited, gave a little nervous cough before embarking on the story. 'I'm afraid he was murdered; in his home; bludgeoned with the base of a silver candlestick. Yes, quite shocking. The more so because the police believed it a family matter. For a while his widow, your great-grandmother, was thought to have been responsible. Then Emily, by then barely twenty, suddenly reappeared and claimed to have visited him that night in secret, been attacked and had killed him in self-defence. Whereupon her mother disputed it and pleaded guilty herself.

'It was a very difficult case to investigate, with two independent confessions, no witnesses and no material evidence. The candlestick had been handled by the butler and the local constable first on the scene.

'Emily claimed that she had meant to heal the family breach, bringing photographs of her baby daughter, but her father had become violent and she struck him in fear for her life. Eventually her story was accepted. She was tried and found guilty of manslaughter, not murder, but sent to prison despite her tender age. She stayed there for over eight years, until her mother's death when a servant came forward to testify that she'd overheard a passionate argument between the couple shortly before Henry was found dead in his study.

'The case was reviewed, Emily was granted a royal pardon and released. One is left wondering how many were unjustly found guilty and actually executed in those days. Because of official embarrassment and the scandalous nature of the full story the matter was hushed up, as was possible then.'

'Do you mean the fact of Emily's illegitimate baby?'

Fitt paused, looking at her with weary eyes. 'More than that, I'm afraid. I hadn't intended telling you so much, but perhaps you have the right to know. It concerns the parentage of the child. It appeared that Teresa, Mrs Withers, discovered that her husband had been paying considerable sums of money every month into a secret account in his daughter's name, despite her supposed banishment from his life.'

'So he had actually forgiven his daughter and was supporting her in her exile?'

The solicitor shook his head. 'I'm afraid it was something much less charitable than that. Teresa became convinced that her husband had fathered his own daughter's child, and had been abusing her from childhood.'

'Incest?'

'And statutory rape. Emily has never denied it. I once was bold enough to ask, but she simply smiled and said, 'I was a bad girl.'

'I suppose I shouldn't be astonished. We hear enough about child abuse today. But *then*! People appeared so proper.'

'Henry was a dyed-in-the-wool autocrat, incapable of seeing himself in the wrong about anything. He was raised in a period when hypocrisy was prevalent. No; if anything amazes me it is that Emily had given in to him. Such a firebrand rebel, as I remember her. She must have been very young when he first seduced her.'

'Rigidly brought up to honour her father. And afterwards it would have taken enormous courage to run off as she did. To face everything alone and damned in the eyes of respectable people.'

'Indeed, such condemnation seems unthinkable in these days.

Her child, a daughter, Eunice, was a timid little thing with none of her mother's spirit. But undeniably beautiful. At twenty-five, in 1957, she became the second wife of a much older man, an art collector in Edinburgh where she had been at school and lived with Emily.'

Alyson nodded. 'And their only child was Rachel, whom I met when she called here to see Emily. She told me there were a half-brother and half-sister, twins from her father's first marriage.'

'It was a curious, extended ménage, since Emily and Howard's first, divorced wife also made up the household.'

Alyson frowned, remembering. 'Rachel said the twins were cruel to Emily after the others died; that the boy, Martin, teased her and used to lock her in a dark cupboard. I'm inclined to believe that, because sometimes she remembers it and shouts to be let out.'

'She was getting frail by that time, after her first stroke. But I'm disinclined to believe that version of the story. Rachel, if anybody, was the one who resented her. This is why she must never be allowed in here again. She is the only natural descendant, and too eager to inherit. As Emily once ironically reminded me, she has bad blood in her.'

Alyson stared at him. Normally so hesitant, weighing each word, he was suddenly forthright, even risking slander. The mild, kindly face looked grimly decisive. 'And now,' he demanded of her, 'what are we to do about this other unwanted visitor, with his interest in Emily's art collection?'

'Is it so valuable, then?'

He smiled wryly. 'It is a clever mixture of the genuine and the fake. I have access to a catalogue with full provenance and valuation of each piece. When one of the two keys to the strongbox containing this went missing I took the precaution of relocating the box elsewhere. And I informed a senior policeman whose discretion I trust.'

'So you believe that the bogus insurance man was also involved in taking the key? But if so, why would he need to come here and re-value the pictures himself? And is he planning to steal them?'

'So many questions. I wish I had the answers. None of the

papers contained in the strongbox was missing, but they might have been copied. There is no way of knowing, but I am sure the photocopier in our office was not used for this purpose. A tally is kept of all documents put through the machine. So perhaps the window of opportunity never occurred, and whoever took the key was unable to make use of it.'

'But some of your stationery was removed, and a specimen of your signature was obtained.'

'Pointing to someone on my staff; which I am loath to believe. Or else our security has been breached from outside. That is why I have asked for discreet help from my police – er, contact.'

'Do you suspect professional art thieves?'

Fitt ran a hand over his chin and hesitated; then, 'Perhaps. Or amateurs about to become professional.' He fell silent again.

'How did Emily come to have such a collection in the first place, Mr Fitt?'

'Her son-in-law, Angus Howard, the father of Rachel and her half-siblings, was a dealer, with a gallery in Edinburgh. Some of his exhibits Emily bought or was given at various times. Other, contemporary pieces, she acquired direct from the artists or their agents. She had a keen eye for what was marketable, and used to attend auctions all over the country.'

'That explains why she's so fond of some of the pictures.'

Fitt smiled. 'Not that those she values most would necessarily be genuine or would fetch a high price. Emily admired a good imitation. She might cherish it from a mischievous pleasure in the skill of the forger. Nothing about Emily is simple, you see. She will always remain an enigma.'

Chapter Twenty-Three

Oliver Markham had found a slot to park the new 4x4 right outside his flat. It meant that the old Nissan had to be left in the yard at the stationery warehouse until the man who'd shown some interest made an offer. The police patrolman, sent for the rug which Markham had stuffed back in the boot, interrupted him frying an early supper before visiting more defaulters. While he argued on the doorstep his smoke alarm, oversensitive to bacon, went off.

'Hadn't you better answer that?' the constable suggested as Markham faced him out, fists balled.

'Buggrit,' Markham snarled. 'Wait a bit.' He slammed the door in the PC's face. He was no sweeter-tempered when eventually he reappeared in his leather trench coat and with a smear of tomato ketchup on his chin. The patrolman had returned to the warmth of his car, prepared by now to be awkward.

'My car's not here,' Markham began, not intending to lose his 4x4's kerbside parking at this time of day.

'So?'

'It's across town. You'll need to give me a lift.'

The policeman replied with a long, uncompromising stare.

'Unless you're not bothered about the bloody rug anyway.' Markham bit off a further sneer, furious at the way 'bloody' had shot out automatically.

'Get in. Mind your head.' His partner climbed out of the front passenger seat and went round to sit beside Markham as if he was under arrest. Show business for the neighbours' benefit. A customer emerging from the nearby greengrocer's looked across incuriously as the car door slammed. Markham gave the driver directions to the warehouse yard.

'Elston's,' the driver muttered. 'What's your car doing there? That's not public parking.'

'I used to work in the warehouse way back.'

'You got a current permit?'

'Not as such. There's an understanding.'

'Funny, that. They've asked us to check on unauthorized use

of the yard. Getting tired of old crocks being dumped there.'

'If they were really bothered they'd fit a gate and CCTV.'
Markham sat back, surly and resentful. At the yard he unlocked
the Nissan's boot and handed over the rug. 'Much good will it do
you.'

He might have guessed they'd drive off at that, leaving him
stranded.

At the college Yeadings met the Principal who passed him over to
the senior porter, Alex Crowe. Jim Anders was, understandably,
resting at home and accorded leave after the shock of finding the
body.

Together Yeadings and Zyczynski were given a tour of the
main building with an explanation of access and prohibited areas.
They reached the roof by a series of staircases, the final one lying
behind a locked door on the top corridor.

'How does this meet fire precautions requirements?' Yeadings
asked.

'The lock's electronic. All members of staff have a card-key
like mine. And we've a buzzer in the porters' lodge. The Principal
had to balance student safety against fire hazard. The system has
been passed by the local authority.'

'Yes, I suppose the roof would present a challenge to some of
the wilder youngsters. How often do the access cards go missing?'

'Perhaps two or three times a term somebody reports one's
lost. Usually that happens during a check, after students have
gained entry to the roof for smoking or some kind of minor mischief. There's not been any serious trouble until now.'

Yeadings nodded. There was never going to be a foolproof
security system. He thought he'd seen all he needed here.
SOCO's report would cover any fine details regarding the roof
itself. It remained only to return to the Principal's office, thank
him and pick up the full list of students and staff which his secretary had been printing out.

As he was leaving, the superintendent turned back. Doing a
Columbo, Z noted, hiding a smile. 'Does the name Markham
mean anything to you?' he asked.

'I'm afraid not. If he was ever here it must be before my time, Superintendent. I was appointed Principal only eighteen months ago, but I pride myself in knowing everyone here by name, if not always by facial recognition.'

'I recall Mr Markham,' the secretary confided, showing them out. She was in her late fifties, tidily old-fashioned in her dress and with keen, black boot-button eyes. 'I would need to look up his year of admission, but it was some considerable time ago. He took the shorter Civics course. I remember him because afterwards he was appointed as usher to our local police court, and I was pleased he'd made something of it. Rather an unprepossessing young man, he'd struck me.'

It all seemed to be coming together. Next morning DI Salmon was almost purring with satisfaction when told of Markham's familiarity with the college, especially since Allbright's country hideaway had yielded evidence of someone having slept there in what was a large, quite cosily insulated workshop with all mod cons. A computer with access to the web had been brought back for examination by a police IT expert.

So, Salmon considered, with two murders about to be rapidly solved in parallel, this would look good on his annual assessment.

Cars were sent to bring in both Allbright and Markham for further questioning. On arrival the former refused to speak beyond demanding a solicitor. He was tense and freely sweating, seeming almost relieved when sent to wait, alone, in a cell.

Markham's interview was also delayed, until Beaumont was free to share it with the DI. He had brought with him the eagerly awaited lab reports, one giving the blood type of the woman pushed off the college roof. This was the of the rare *AB, rhesus negative* group. The second, an analysis carried out on the rug sample, had revealed two types of blood: not only the same rare *AB negative* but also the commonest *O positive* group.

'Two different victims,' Salmon barked. 'We could be getting a serial killer!'

'Unless Markham himself bled on to it,' Z warned. 'But if so, why didn't he simply claim it all as his own blood? We know *O* wasn't Micky Kane's blood group, and his is our only other body.'

'What we do have,' Yeadings pointed out with ominous calm, 'is two unsolved murders, not necessarily connected, of a male adolescent and an older female; plus a reported missing female who may, or may not, have been abducted. And hers is an unknown blood group. I suggest DS Zyczynski rings the mother again to find out if she's chased up that information yet.'

Z found the number in her notebook and the others waited while she got through. Her approach was friendly-casual as she worked towards the crucial question. 'So you still have no news of Sheena? I'm sure you've no cause for concern, Mrs Judd. As you said yourself, daughters nowadays don't confide everything to their mums. And she is, after all, of a sensible age.

'I've checked that Sheena's not been taken to any of the local hospitals and we're still asking around generally. Perhaps, as an added precaution, you'd give us her blood group? If it's turned up yet?

'It has? And you're quite certain? All of you the same? Your ex-husband too? I see, thank you. I'll be keeping in touch, Mrs Judd. Try not to worry. Take care.'

She rang off and faced the others. 'For what it's worth, Sheena's was O, *rhesus positive*, just like the second sample found on the rug. But, for all we know, it could still be Oliver Markham's.'

'Blow that for a dandelion seed,' Beaumont put in doggedly, 'at least we can bring him in for the college death, whoever the woman turns out to be. If he's shaken enough he may put his hand up for Sheena Judd as well. And tell us where he's disposed of the body.'

'Meanwhile,' Yeadings reminded his DI, 'the Micky Kane case is dragging on. You'll need to get Allbright talking as soon as his brief turns up. Since Beaumont has something else to follow up, I want Z to sit in with you on this, as the only one of us who met Micky alive.'

'So what's your new line?' Z asked Beaumont, on her way to collect sealed tapes for the interview-room recorder.

The Pinocchio face was at its perkiest. 'You wouldn't want to know. There's this lowlife old queer I met half-stoned last night. He dosses down at a squalid little shack down on the vacant lot beyond the Odeon that's home-sweet-home to the local derelicts. I think that's where young Micky ran off to.'

She couldn't miss the smug tone. He couldn't bear her not to know he was way ahead of her on this one. And apparently Yeadings had been informed; had sanctioned this new angle. 'Let's hope it works,' she said. Forewarned, she felt a niggling doubt about the approaching interview with Allbright and his brief.

As they gathered across the fixed steel table in Interview Room I Salmon nodded to her to set up the recording. She switched on, inserted the two tapes, gave date and time, introduced the suspect and his solicitor, then herself. Salmon snarled his rank and name before starting a frontal attack.

'I want to volunteer a statement,' Allbright interrupted him. His face was white and taut. His cuboid figure seemed somehow less substantial. The solicitor gave him a reassuring nod.

So they had it set up. Z's premonition strengthened that the case against the man was going to fall apart. Allbright could slip out of the frame.

'It's about my chatline friendship with Micky Kane. That's all it was. Nothing nasty in it. It's just terrible what happened to the poor kid. If I'd ever dreamed...it could end up like it did...' His voice was choked with emotion.

'You'd what?' Salmon demanded. 'Have slugged him less hard? Have packed him off home to his mother?'

'DI Salmon,' the lawyer warned, 'this is a voluntary statement. Let my client continue. I must ask you to refrain from questioning him at this point.'

Allbright closed his eyes and drew a deep breath. 'I'd never have got in touch. Never said anything about the Harley. God, it makes me sick to think what...'

Z was already convinced. He's going to get away with it. We've got the wrong man.

'It's my hobby, see? Well, more than that, I suppose. There's something very special about a Harley. You've only got to say the name…It's sort of magic. There's other owners feel the same way. We meet up, talk bikes, go runs together. Only they're already – already *there*, if you know what I mean…I needed to tell someone else, someone new.' His voice changed, grew awed. 'Sort of spread the gospel.'

'Wanted to brag,' Salmon muttered under his breath, earning a hard stare from the brief.

Allbright seemed not to have heard. He continued. 'There are these chat lines. Well, you know all about them. I got linked up with this kid. He seemed kind of lonely, bored out of his mind at home. And enthusiastic. I wanted to *show* him. He was keen to ride. We arranged to meet up. It meant he'd have to skive off school. I was to pick him up on his way there. I'd got a spare skid-lid and leathers for him. He changed in the WCs near the town hall and we did the M4, M25, M1, hit over a ton and got pretty high on it.'

He stopped, suddenly aware of his audience. 'It was mad, I know. But it was like we had something between us. Like he was me, only younger, with it all yet to come. I wanted everything good for him and he really seemed to like me, thought I was the goods.'

He sighed, slumped over the table. 'We came back here and I dropped him in the town, while I went home to fix us a meal. He had my debit card to get some money for the train journey home. I really meant him to be all right with his folks.

'Only that's when it all went wrong. I waited, and waited, only he never turned up. I thought maybe he'd cleared off with my money, and I got really mad. So I went out to find him. He wasn't at the station and I thought he'd gone. But it wasn't like that. He was really sick. I found him down by the river, lost and half out of his mind. He said he'd snorted some angel dust he bought off a man near the bank. I guess he'd been watched at the cashpoint and looked an easy target. They'd have leaned on him to try it. Maybe he thought it would round off a perfect day.' By now Allbright was close to tears.

'Can we take a break there?' the solicitor asked. 'My client is fatigued. Perhaps a hot drink would be in order.'

'I'll see to it,' Z offered, noted the time and stopped the tapes. Salmon said nothing, glaring, frustrated, at the two opposite him.

When they resumed, Allbright shook his head. 'What could I have done? He couldn't travel home in that state. I was due at work later and I didn't dare leave him alone in my house. If he got rowdy he might do anything. The neighbours could get to hear him. He could run amok and set fire to himself. Drunks I can cope with, but with someone like that...

'So I took him by car out to my workshop. You've seen it. He was all right there, locked in. It's got heating and water. There's some food in a fridge and a divan bed with a sleeping bag, because I sometimes stay over, making adjustments to the bike or surfing the net.'

He paused, biting at his lower lip. 'I'd missed out on my day sleep, so I was exhausted when I got off work next morning. I went home for a bite to eat and I fell asleep over the table. I meant to go and see how he was, but I got scared because I couldn't see how all this was going to end. His folks would have panicked when he didn't come home from school the day before, and by that point he'd been away overnight. I didn't know their address or his real name; only what he'd called himself on line: Explorer. Just as he called me Hutch.

'I had a drink to make me feel better. And another, and so on. I was still starved of sleep from the previous day and in the end I just crawled off to bed. There wasn't time to go out and see him before I was due again at work. By next morning I guessed he'd be well over the worst of the drugs, and I went straight up there.'

Again he paused, covering his face with his hands. Then he leaned back, face drawn and a little tic quivering under one eye. 'The boy seemed quite different, older and – harsh somehow. He said let them worry. His parents, he meant. They'd never made any attempt to understand him, and maybe the shock would bring them round. That's what people did when they thought their kids had been abducted or run away: went all lovey-dovey and swore everything would be different from then on. So he was staying on and they could just wait on his pleasure.'

Allbright looked in appeal to the two detectives. 'Bravado, see?

Not a bad boy, but he felt hard done by. It was his first taste of freedom. Of rebellion. He'd got over being sick from the drugging, and he saw himself in a position to make demands. I tried to make him see sense, but…' He shook his head. 'It went on for another coupla days. Then, next time I went up there, he was gone. He'd broken out.

He appealed to them, pleading damp-eyed, 'I never meant any harm to come to the poor kid. It wasn't abduction, see? It started with him skiving, and then he just insisted on staying on. A friendly arrangement that just went wrong.'

Beaumont left the squad car halfway down the alley. Overhead there was a distinct line of grey cloud moving in from the west. Little warm flurries plucked at discarded food wrappers dropped in the gutters. A white plastic carrier escaped to go cartwheeling down towards the river, frisky as a Jack Russell pup. Rain on the wind. The cold spell was finally breaking up. Now they'd be in for days of drenching Atlantic weather.

He walked back up the cobbled way to where the fence slats hung loose, moved three aside and squeezed through into the wasteland of rubble. By daylight the place looked even more derelict. And the same went for its human life.

Among the collection of cardboard cartons huddled in the corner by the shack, one or two still had lumpy figures curled in them under old blankets and waterproofs. The others had lost their owners to pavement corners where they'd staked out their begging territory. He doubted that any of these here were fit to recognize him as their drop-in of last night. The stolen watchman's brazier they'd sat around held cold embers now, the scent of wood smoke no longer covering the stench of unwashed bodies and the aftermath of raw spirits.

He pulled aside the double sacking curtain of the shack and went in, stepping gingerly between the three bodies and their stacked possessions. 'Wakey, wakey!' he shouted and kicked at a zinc bucket to get his message across.

A stream of curses came from one corner.

'Oh, steady on,' quavered an older voice. 'No need to get unpleasant.'

That would be the old queen they called Fanny. Beaumont crouched beside him. 'Thought you might be on for breakfast, mate,' he told him. 'Bangers and beans and sunny-side eggs with slabs of bacon and crisp, fried bread. How about it then?'

'Bubble and squeak,' said the old man wistfully. 'They don't seem to make that any more.'

'Might do, if they've got the right leftovers. How about we try?'

The white-whiskered man struggled to sit up. 'Who are you, friend? Sally Army, is it?'

'Nuh. Just another empty belly. Only there's this place I know, see? They'll let me bring one mate in.'

He was being regarded by faded blue eyes with faint memory stirring behind them. 'Do I know you?' And then dawning suspicion. 'I've nothing worth taking.'

Beaumont placed a hand on his bony old shoulder. 'Pass up the offer if you want. I was here last night, remember?'

'Thought I knew your voice. Can't see a lot, though.'

'So, hungry enough to believe me?'

'Ah, there's some good people left in the world. Help me up, eh?' The old man dragged on his arm and they rose together. There was muttering from the far corner. Beaumont caaught the tail end – '...to bad rubbish. Sodding old queer.'

They went out into the muted light of day. 'Gonna rain soon,' Beaumont offered. 'Let's get inside before it does.'

As they emerged into the alley a uniform officer fell in to either side of them.

'Nicked?' quavered the old man.

'Just a few questions.'

'But *breakfast*?'

'Definitely,' Beaumont promised, 'with all the trimmings. Only talk to me first.'

Ramón finished dressing and looked at himself in the long mirror behind the door. He was wearing the new (new to him) outfit from the charity shop and wasn't displeased with what he saw. He wasn't on duty until after lunch but he knocked on Emily's door and looked in to wish her good morning. Alyson was bent over her, wiping some slop off the old lady's chin with a napkin and smiled back at him. Emily's smile was slower and lasted longer. She gurgled something throatily. Her voice hadn't yet got going for the day.

'You'll see him later, Emily,' the girl promised. 'Let him go and have breakfast now.'

He made fresh toast and helped himself from the cafetière, waiting for Alyson to reappear. He had made up his mind he must tell her, wasn't sure how much would have to come out, but knew the coat had to be produced. Sooner or later she would come across it, and nobody would ever imagine such a fashion item had belonged to Sheena.

When Alyson sat down to her own breakfast, across the bar from him, he asked, 'I show you something, yes?'

She looked up from sorting the post he'd brought up earlier. 'Show me what, Ramón?'

He rose. 'I get it.'

She heard his trainers squeak across the polished wood of the hall floor, and then a sharp click as he opened the airing cupboard used for a cloakroom. When he came back he laid a bundle of supple black leather and fox fur on the bench beside her. Puzzled, she opened it out.

'Ramón, where did you get this? It's beautiful.'

'Belonging,' he said, 'to lady visit Emily. I remember.'

'Yes, of course. Emily's granddaughter, Rachel Howard. She wore it on the following day when she came to see me. But I don't understand. She certainly had it on when I saw her out.'

'Perhaps she come again, leave coat.'

'And went off without it? In all that cold? I don't think so.'

He left it to her to work out.

'Has this something to do with Sheena? Did Rachel give her – no, surely not. And then Sheena disappearing. Was that when…?'

It was really weird. The coat must have cost an awful lot. Designer label, beautifully cut, lined with pure silk. If she put it on it would reach almost to the floor. But then Rachel Howard had been taller than herself. It was undoubtedly hers. So why was it here, and why hadn't she sent for it?

'I think,' Alyson said, 'something's very wrong.' She didn't want to call Fitt and burden him further when he was already worried over Emily's affairs. Perhaps it was a police matter, if only as found lost-property. She recalled the woman detective who'd been interested in the OD boy in hospital. Sergeant Rosemary Zyczynski. She would certainly know what to do. She'd actually been here when Rachel Howard called that second time. Her card with a phone number was still tucked into

Alyson's daybook.

'Who's Beaumont's fragrant friend?' DC Silver asked, passing Z as she burst from the CID office.

'Who? Where?'

'In the canteen, glugging tea by the bucketful. He didn't tell you? Seems some old tramp he's brought in.'

Tramp? And last time she'd seen Beaumont he was grinning like the Cheshire cat over going to visit derelicts down past the Odeon. So he was on to something. She was torn between following that up and passing on the puzzle that Alyson Orme had just dropped on her: the fashionable, arrogant Rachel Howard from Edinburgh turning up again at the penthouse, then going out into freezing wind with no coat on? And while Z hung on at the phone, Alyson had checked that no other outdoor clothes were missing.

You could almost suspect the woman was still there in the apartment, hidden away somewhere.

DI Salmon was in one of the interview rooms and couldn't be approached. He wouldn't welcome any interruption to what he so clearly saw as man's work.

Just suppose…a striking, thin, dark-haired woman unaccountably gone missing. Then the unidentified body Beaumont had been called to at the college… Similar age and appearance, according to him. So, the same woman?

As Z weighed the connection Yeadings turned the corner in the corridor and was ambling towards her. 'Sir,' she called, 'I think I've got a name for the murdered woman.'

'Lost your little lad, wasn't it?' The queer they'd called Fanny raised his beaky nose from the mug of hot tea. Fascinated, Beaumont watched the transparent drop of liquid hang on its sharp end, wobble an instant, fall and become unidentifiable in the dark, steaming brew.

'Name of Micky. Thirteen years old.'

'Don't know what they called him.' He raised the mug in both hands, warming them through, and drank thirstily.

'*They*. Who'd that be then?'

'Two men. None of us.'

'They didn't doss down at your camp? Had you seen them before?'

'No. On the street. Separate. Selling stuff.'

Hanging around near the banks, Beaumont guessed; watching who used the cash dispensers. Looking for custom. That's when one of them had seen Micky Kane flush with Allbright's handout, and on a sudden fancy he'd handed some over for a final kick. 'These guys were dealing?'

'I don't know what you mean.' He managed to sound offended.

'Oh yes you do, you old fraud. What was it they gave Micky? You saw.'

Fanny looked wildly around, decided there was no way out, and hung on to the promise of breakfast. The delectable smells escaping through the kitchen hatch confirmed everything the detective had promised.

The old tramp sniffed. 'Little packets. Could have been anything.'

'And then what?'

'Then they went away.'

'Taking the boy?'

Fanny looked uncomfortable. 'There were two of them. Young, tough.' His voice was plaintive. He had guessed what they wanted of the boy. It was a world he'd grown up and grown old in, and he'd no illusions. He'd seen it all before: kids snatched to make into call-boys, child prostitutes, street dealers.

'I'm not blaming you,' Beaumont told him. 'There was little you could do. But the boy had spirit, at some point must have tried to get away. So he ended up dead, with his head bashed in and thrown into the river. You could have been quicker telling me what happened.'

The old man stared down into his empty mug. 'You're a copper,' he excused himself.

'Yeah. I get to clean up the messes. Can you write? Because you haven't quite finished yet. I want it all down on paper before you get a bite to eat.'

Of course he could write. The man had obviously been educated and had a career of sorts at some time. Beaumont had come across his kind before, inadequates who finally couldn't face up to being rubbished by others walking a straighter route. So they gave up and joined the garbage they were condemned as.

'Let's get upstairs and find you a pen,' he offered.

'You'll discover I'm a bit shaky. I'd do better with a typewriter.' He was clinging to remnants of dignity.

'Ever tried a computer keyboard?' Beaumont asked, almost matily. 'No? Well, now's the time to try. Then I'll print it out and you can sign it.'

Fanny got shakily to his feet. 'It's some time since I did that. Let's hope I can remember who I am.' But he was weakly smiling.

Zyczynski and Beaumont had joined the Boss in his office for coffee. 'The DI has reported a negative interview with Mr Allbright,' he told them. 'And Beaumont's statement from Arthur Goodenough, aka "Fanny", has confirmed that we've little enough to hold our Harley biker on. Encouraging a minor to skip school, and failing to report a runaway aren't major crimes. It's well short of abduction, and Crown Prosecution would never look at it. The disruption at the warehouse and blame arising from it are probably punishment enough to make Allbright wiser in the future.'

'The DI...?' Beaumont ventured.

Yeadings busied himself over the filter to hide an appearance of smiling. 'Is far from gruntled. He'd had high hopes of putting Allbright in the dock for the Micky Kane murder. He's with uniform branch at present, organizing a sweep to pick up the dealers, if they haven't fled the scene. Mr Goodenough, despite claiming poor eyesight, gave a very useful description of the two who took Micky away. As local distributors they'll have more important connections, which Drugs branch have doubtless been surveying. This may signal the end of their Nelson's eye policy on the small fry involved.'

He switched on the coffeemaker and returned to his desk while it began to burble. 'As for Miss Rachel Howard, I've been in touch with her brother Martin in Edinburgh. He confirmed that she has been absent from her own apartment in the family home for over a week. He is flying down, due in at Heathrow this afternoon, to identify our body. Which, in the circumstances will be difficult visually. Dental information will be needed as well, until they've processed the DNA sample.'

He waited until they were sipping his special-blend Mocha before he dropped his bombshell.

'Professor Littlejohn has given me a rundown of his final deliberations on the post mortem findings. He is now satisfied, from further analysis of the trauma, that although the cause of death was manual strangulation, the fall from the college roof was by no means a simple event. Like the ladies' fractures, it was, in fact, compound.'

Beaumont suddenly sat up straight. 'Sir, d'you mean...?'

'I mean she fell off more than one roof.'

Uniform were working in conjunction with Drugs branch and Beaumont had gone along as an interested party. DI Salmon was happy to let them net the abductors of Micky Kane. He could then take over with the more serious charge of murder. Arthur Goodenough, aka 'Fanny', was happily ensconced in a cell for further questioning and regular meals. It was hoped that he would eventually pick Micky's captors from an identity parade. He had lingered a moment at his cell door, modestly delighted to see his full name being written up outside in chalk capitals. 'Yeah, it's nice to be wanted,' the custody sergeant said, 'if only for vagrancy.'

Meanwhile DI Salmon resumed his interest in Oliver Markham. To satisfy Crown Prosecution that this suspect was a double killer he would require a deal more hard evidence than a bloodstained travel rug. Seating himself again opposite the wretched man, who appeared to have shrunk in the interval, he was determined to extract a confession.

'Let's start again at the beginning,' he invited, baring unlovely teeth, 'where you first met Miss Judd in the saloon bar of the Crown. What attracted you to her?'

Markham stared unhappily back. She'd been on her own and that was all. He'd been bored and thought he'd take a rise out of her. She was big and sloppy and undesirable. But she was there, and that had been enough. He would need to watch his words.

'She looked lonely,' he said carefully. And then he remembered. 'I think she fancied the barman but he wasn't taking her up on it. Not then, anyway.'

Trying to shift suspicion, Salmon noted. Understandable move, that. 'Remind me: what he was he called.'

'Ramón. A Spaniard, or South American or something.'

Filipino, Salmon recalled. Quite different, he'd look more oriental. It might be worth getting this Ramón's angle on Markham. He'd left questioning him to his sergeants. Time he checked on the barman himself.

'Go on. How did the relationship develop?'

'She invited me to visit her at the penthouse where she worked, so I dropped in one afternoon. I was sorry for her, is all. She was keen to have someone to talk to. This was before she got Ramón to go and work there.' Markham had revived a little, warming to the image of himself as a kindly friend.

Ramón again, now as a co-worker. He'd certainly be worth looking into. 'So there was some competition between the two of you, for her favours?'

'I wouldn't say that.' Markham denied it heatedly. 'She just used me, I guess, to get at him.'

'But you did have sexual relations with the woman?'

Markham paused, remembered the police had the rug. There could be other stains than blood on it. 'Well, Sheena was pretty desperate. Any man would do.'

'Did you pay her?'

And so it went on, slowly, inexorably, tying him in, working towards the Sunday afternoon when she'd begged to go out in his car, and he'd driven her out to Coombe Hill. Yes; he agreed she'd officially been on duty at the penthouse, but somebody had stayed behind in charge. And anyway the old lady would be asleep for hours. It was what she did every afternoon, so Sheena said.

'That would be this Ramón on duty? You both left when he arrived?'

Markham considered his answer. It would be easier if he knew what statement the other man had made. Best perhaps to stick to the truth. Or somewhere near it. 'He was nearly due, and he's a punctual sort of bloke. In any case the insurance man was there, looking at the pictures. He said he'd be staying on an hour or two and he offered to let Ramón in.'

'Sheena Judd trusted him to keep an eye on the old lady?'

'Like I said, she was asleep.'

'So you drove the woman to Coombe Hill, where you had sex. And were the last to see her alive.'

Markham shot upright. 'Who said she's dead? She was perfectly all right when I left her.'

'Left her where? And exactly when?' Salmon's fishy gaze fixed on the man's hands which had jumped like electrified rodents.

Markham clenched his jaw. From that point on he'd have to resort to fiction.

Salmon listened while he explained how he'd dropped her at a bus stop because he'd clients to see. They were slippery beggars and the house had always been deserted. But early on a Sunday evening he'd hopes of catching them at home.

The DI leaned back in his chair unimpressed. Leave him to sweat while still on the hook, he decided. Follow up a sideline. 'So this insurance man you mentioned, what would his name be?'

'How would I know? He was someone the senior nurse had made the arrangement with.'

'A total stranger, then. Right.' Salmon lowered his eyes to the notes in front of him and let a silence build before he pounced. 'And Rachel Howard: how did you get to meet her?'

'*Who?*' Markham stared back in what seemed genuine amazement.

Slumped against the wall, Keith Stanford crouched with his head in his hands and tried to understand what had happened. Part of him saw it all from the outside, like something he'd been called in to deal with. As police-surgeon: violent death. But it was Audrey, his wife, and he couldn't believe that she was actually dead; and dead in this way.

Only twenty minutes earlier she'd called him, wanting a plastic bag to put her ankle boots in because they'd got uncomfortable and she'd be sending them to a charity shop. So he'd indulged her whim, like all her other little oddities.

Then, without warning, this. It was obscene. She'd have hated anyone to see her like this.

Now he must get to the phone. Talk to the police, the coroner's office. Someone other than himself would have to confirm death. And maybe the pathologist would want to come and view the – view her in situ. Suddenly so much to do which hadn't been needed minutes back. But that is what death did. Changed everything, irrevocably, in a flash.

The news reached Yeadings in a roundabout way, by a phone call from Nan. She had been driving past and saw the blue lights turning in at the Stanfords' gate. Being neighbourly, she'd followed them in. She found Keith, taut-faced and pale, being dissuaded from re-entering the house. Whether suicide or not, it was now a secured police scene accessible only to the experts.

She put a hand on his bowed shoulder and he let her lead him next door. Nan had guessed that word of this would take time to percolate through to Mike from police sources.

'Should I come home?' he asked when she phoned.

'It would be good to have a man here on standby. Keith's taking it badly.'

'In half an hour, then. There's not much I'm needed for here at the moment. I'll get a note to Z and she can warn Salmon I'm away.' Nan would know how to treat a man in shock, better than he would himself. Poor devil, this was the second attempt his wife had made on her life, and this time it seemed she'd succeeded.

He sorted the papers on his desk, switched off the coffeemaker and heaved himself into his overcoat, remembering that this morning Nan had advised him to take a raincoat instead. And been right. He left by the front entrance, passing two stout women who were coming in, arguing. The older one's words stopped him in his tracks.

'Sheen, you've got to tell them. There was a real fuss made when you let Miss Orme down.'

Yeadings halted. 'Mrs Judd?, can I help you?'

It didn't surprise her that he knew who she was. A policeman, after all, although he wasn't in uniform.

'We've just come to say my daughter isn't missing at all. She'd gone to stay with a friend of her old auntie out Wendover way. And they haven't a phone, you see.'

He smiled. 'Good of you to let us know, Mrs Judd. I wish everyone was as cooperative.' He turned to the younger woman. 'You appear to have been in the wars.'

The remains of a black eye was flowering yellow, purple and green alongside a misshapen and bloodied nose. A liberal application of cake makeup failed to cover what must still be painful injuries.

'Got mugged, didn't I?' she claimed sulkily. 'And it's no good asking what he looked like because it was dark and he had a scarf over his face.'

'So when and where did this happen?'

'Coupla days back. In the lane near auntie's friend's bungalow.'

'I hope you reported it to the local police.'

'Fat lotta good that'd do.'

'Well, speak to the officer on the desk, and ask to see DS Zyczynski.'

'That's the nice young woman I told you about,' said the mother. 'She'll tell you if there's any way of getting compensation.'

'No harm in trying,' Yeadings encouraged, raised his hat and felt rain plop on his forehead. 'Better get inside before the downpour.'

'What is it?' Salmon snarled as the duty sergeant knocked and put his head round the interview room door. 'We can't be disturbed.'

'Phone for DS Zyczynski, sir.' He watched the DI's face go purple, and got the punch line in before he exploded. 'From the super, sir. He's phoning from his car.'

'We'll take a break,' Salmon growled.

Z formally closed the interview for the tapes and switched off.

'Don't be all day.'

'Right, sir. I'll get some tea sent in.'

In the corridor the duty sergeant was grinning. 'Actually it's a verbal message. The missing Sheena Judd has just walked in, large as life and twice as ugly, face covered in old bruises. I couldn't give it to you in front of the suspect. He's probably the one who clobbered her.'

'Sweet heaven,' sighed Z. 'And the DI's just had his other case blow up in his face. It's just not his day. But thank God the woman's alive. Look, write the gist down for the DI, would you, and let him have it along with the tea. But give me a chance to talk with her myself first.'

'My pleasure. They do say wild salmon's the best sort, don't they?'

Sheena still wasn't being forthcoming and it was getting her mother distinctly annoyed. Z had taken them through to the canteen where they sat together at a corner table with a tray of tea and some Danish to help the talk along.

'Look, you do know who did this to you,' Z insisted. 'You'll find it's easier in the long run to explain what happened rather than have to remember what tall stories you made up instead. Believe me, I've been there.'

'It was that man she went off with, only she won't admit she goes for the wrong sort every time.' Mrs Judd had her mind made up on this.

'It's nobody's business but my own. You can't force me to...'

'But why protect him? You can't like him after he done this, surely?'

'Mum, you don't understand.'

Z put a cautionary hand on her wrist. 'If he does this once, he's likely to go on doing it until we stop him. He's a danger to other women as well. Could someday kill one. Do you want that?'

'I don't deserve this,' wailed Sheena, near to tears. 'It's not my fault. He's an animal. I told him no, no, no, no! Only he wouldn't listen. So I kneed him in the nuts and tried to get away. But he came after me and did this. Then he drove off and left me. I had to walk miles on me own in the dark. I couldn't let anyone see me like that.'

'Did he – did he, I mean...?'

'Not that time. But just taking me out in his car doesn't give him the right, Mum, does it?'

'But you'd done it before? Had sex, I mean.'

'Well, sort of. Only he's rough, and I made up me mind I wouldn't let him again.'

'Well, you are a fool,' her mother said. 'You should know by now what most men are after, and he doesn't sound the sort to play games with.'

'I never did,' Sheena wailed. 'I knew you'd go on like this. That's why I couldn't come home. I wish I'd never met the bloody man, and now I suppose he's made me lose me job as well!'

Yeadings recognized the mortuary van and patrol car, but the classic MG was a new one to him. He decided to drop in and see how things were going before he had to encounter the tragically widowed Stanford.

'Sir,' the patrolman greeted him. 'The doc's looking at the body now. His name's Holland-Prees. Very young, sir. Enthusiastic.'

But taking it seriously, Yeadings considered, walking in on him. He introduced himself and saw interest light in the man's eyes. 'Superintendent?' he queried. 'Bringing in the big guns? Are you expecting something suspicious?'

'It happens I'm a neighbour. The dead woman's husband is next door with my wife, who was a nurse.'

'I see.' The sprightliness left the young man's face. 'Actually I've done more than confirm life's extinct. I took a little look, as well as body and air temperatures. But otherwise I've left her as she was.'

Audrey Stanford's head was still enveloped in a plastic bag, her face cyanosed, mouth agape. Yeadings stared down to where Holland-Prees was pointing.

'It's not very distinct, but I'm pretty sure the wrists are chafed. If a ligature was used the bruises will take time to come up. That's why I didn't remove the bag. It was clearly too late to save her. The body was already cooling.'

Yeadings crouched to look more closely, reached into his over-coat for his reading spectacles and grunted. 'You think she'd been tied up?'

'Restrained in some way. Then released. Presumably after death.'

'I see.' He rose to his feet. This was unexpected. The young medic had done well not to interfere with how she'd been found. He went out to where the patrolman was leaning against his car. 'Was there anyone else in the house?' he demanded.

'Just the husband. He was pretty cut up. He came in from dig-ging the garden and found her. Said she was supposed to be sleep-ing after lunch. He's gone next door with a neighbour.'

'I'll see him there. Secure the scene. I'm sending SOCO in.

Make sure no one else is allowed inside.'

He reversed his car and drove the few hundred yards to his own driveway. Before getting out he made two phone calls, the first to SOCO with detailed instructions and then pressed out the Prof's University number, waiting while Littlejohn was fetched to the phone. 'I've something that will interest you, I think,' he told the pathologist, and gave him the address.

'Hmm,' the professor remarked to his clerical assistant. 'That was Mike Yeadings with the offer of a new body. If I didn't know what an old hand he is at it, I'd have said he sounded upset.'

Beaumont came in grinning. The drugs bust had been successful enough to merit exposure on the evening TV news. It had yielded several thousand pounds-worth of Class A substances and a list of addresses, at one of which a coordinated raid on a Met's patch had produced two local men who'd fled there after Micky's body was taken from the river. Now the DS and DI Salmon were to interview them as soon as they arrived under escort.

In the Boss's absence it was left to Z to deal with Martin Howard and drive him to the mortuary. Even prepared for the worst, his reaction when the sheet was turned back to reveal his half-sister's broken face was startling. The mortuary assistant was there as he collapsed and, helped by Z, supported him from the room.

'We did what we could in the time allowed,' he admitted afterwards, 'but there's a limit to how much you can cover up. Would you say he recognized her?'

'Almost certainly. He's taken it badly. They must have been close.'

Watching the man, she thought he had come round some time before he opened his eyes and murmured, 'Yes, I'm almost sure it's Rachel. And that necklace: it was her mother's.'

'There's an overcoat she left behind at her grandmother's apartment. You'd better see that too. I'll take you there later.'

'Where did you say she was found?'

Zyczynski explained. 'We don't yet know why she was at the college at all, or how she got there. It was bitterly cold that evening and she wasn't wearing the coat. Did she come by car from Edinburgh?'

'No, she took the train.'

'Are you sure?'

He hesitated. 'I guess she must have said she was going to do that. But she might have hired a car when she got here. Listen, it's all been a terrible shock. Do you mind if I go to my hotel for a while?'

He told her where he'd checked in and she arranged to pick

him up two hours later after he'd rested. 'I don't suppose you have a photograph of Rachel with you?' she asked as she dropped him off.

'Actually, yes. I brought it to help with identifying her.' He reached in an inner pocket and produced a studio portrait. It was certainly the woman Z had seen at the penthouse claiming to be Rachel Howard.

'May I borrow it?'

'If you think it's of any use.'

Z was almost sure it would be, though it had taken a leap of imagination to see quite how. Back at the nick she looked up an address from Beaumont's computerized notes and set off to track down Mrs Durrant.

'Could well be,' was the nearest the woman would admit to. 'Like I said, she was running, sort of hobbled in this long skirt.'

'Or could it have been a coat? An ankle-length, black leather one with a big fox fur collar?'

'Yes, that's what it was. The fur. I remember that's why I didn't get a proper look at her face. I'm quite certain now. That's the woman who was chasing the lad in the outsize clothes.'

So now Rachel Howard had a link with Micky Kane after he'd fled from the hospital, but Z couldn't see what that implied or where it was leading. Had he, in desperation, tried to snatch her handbag? Whatever the reason for her chasing him, neither of them could explain it now. Both were dead, by widely different means; but possibly killed within hours of each other. So was that because of their connection?

'Never rains but it bloody pours,' Salmon snarled, bustling in as she settled again at the terminal. 'We've another body. Looks like the husband did it. Straightforward domestic asphyxiation with a plastic bag. You'd think a doctor would find some subtler means. Must have suddenly seen red and just gone for it.'

'Who's this?'

'Woman by the name of Stanford. Her husband's a partner in a local practice. They're bringing him in for questioning. If I can't reach Beaumont to sit in, it'll have to be you.'

She'd known more genteel invitations, and had to excuse herself. She was already involved with taking Rachel Howard's half-brother to the grandmother's apartment.

'Well, there's no great haste. Stanford can sit and sweat till we're ready. Doctors should understand waiting-rooms. Let's hope he'll break and confess. An open and shut case. The woman was tied up first to keep her quiet.'

Not exactly instant passion, then, Z thought; but it was Salmon's case and she doubted her opinion would be asked for. She looked at her watch: 6.28. There was time to pack up Micky Kane's effects and write a covering note to the parents before picking up Martin Howard again. They could have a meal together somewhere and she'd find out more about the family background. This was the man Rachel had said used to be cruel to Emily, locking her in a cupboard. When she took him to the penthouse flat they must be kept apart for fear of alarming the old lady.

When he suggested they eat at his hotel she found him urbane, seeming interested in her work and divulging only that he'd joined the family business on leaving art college at twenty-one. Asked if he'd met his second cousin Alyson Orme, he said no; in fact, he'd not known of her existence until Rachel spoke of her. Emily was fortunate to have skilled nursing from someone close.

They timed their visit for when Alyson had returned home and had time to relax, but it was Ramón who let them in. Alyson's greeting was understandably cautious. 'I'll get the coat,' she offered and brought it in sheathed in transparent plastic.

He appeared embarrassed. 'Why don't you keep it? I'd only send it to a charity shop otherwise. I'm her executor, you see. Her nearest relative, apart from Dolly, my married sister in Aberdeen. She wouldn't want anything from Rachel. They didn't get on well together.'

'And you did?' Alyson asked, her face expressionless.

'It was a case of having to. She's – she *was* – a fellow director in the firm.' He was interrupted by a low buzz from the direction of the kitchen.

'More visitors,' Alyson said.

Ramón came and stood in the doorway. 'It is missing lady,

Sheena, downstairs. I let her in?'

'I suppose you'd better, or she might vanish again.' She turned again to Martin Howard. 'It must be years since you last saw Emily Withers?'

He hesitated. 'Quite some time. We all used to live together, you know, in the old family home. Rachel and I still have separate accommodation there. We neither of us married or moved away.'

Z heard the lift doors open and voices out in the hall. Then Sheena Judd walked in, blinking at the unexpected company. 'Sorry,' she said, gauche as her air of defiance was punctured. 'I thought you'd be on your own.' Her eyes passed over the DS and rested on Martin. She looked surprised, then mildly provocative. 'Oh hello, you're back again. How did you get on with the pictures?'

In the momentary silence that followed, Z watched all colour drain from Martin Howard's face. 'Oh God!' he gasped and sagged in his chair. It was a repeat of his collapse at the mortuary and she moved forward to help him, but Alyson was there first.

'Do you have any medication?' she asked, supporting the lolling head.

'Breast pocket,' he managed to get out.

Z left them to it: Alyson was the professional. Her own interest was centred on Sheena. 'Where did you meet him before?' she demanded, already more than half sure of the answer.

She'd guessed right. Martin Howard had been the bogus insurance assessor, visiting to check on Emily's art collection. And she remembered Alyson speaking of the 'family firm', a gallery in Edinburgh through which Emily had originally obtained some of her treasures. But his action had been deliberate deceit. He could be charged with theft of stationery from Fitt's office, forgery and possibly intent to steal valuable art work.

Ramón reappeared and helped Howard to a sofa, where he lifted his legs and pushed a cushion behind his head. Alyson came across. 'He'll be all right shortly. He's diabetic. Can't stand shocks. I'm not sure I can either.'

She turned to Zyczynski. 'You see, I'd met him before too. In the snowy street. He helped me with my parcels when my umbrella blew inside out. I thought what a kind man!'

'He is not bad man,' Ramón declared. 'I know. Sometimes Emily call me Martin. Then she hold my hand and smile.'

They all stared at him.

Martin Howard stirred on the sofa. 'I didn't mean...' he whispered, '...to kill her.'

Z moved nearer, bending to listen.

'She would have...smothered Emily.'

'With pillow,' Ramón said, scowling fiercely. 'I find pillow on floor. And with bed all...' He twisted his arms about. 'Window is open in glass wall. I think now perhaps woman fall out.'

'Rachel Howard,' Z said quietly. It all fitted: Rachel who'd 'fallen off more than one roof,' and whose cause of death had been manual strangulation.

As soon as Howard recovered and Alyson said it was safe, she'd have to arrest him for murder.

The team were kept busy with paperwork until late into the night, then Salmon and his two sergeants met up in the Boss's office to unwind. Yeadings produced a bottle of single malt and announced, 'taxis home on the house. It's a tad late for mocha but let's hope the scotch will damp down the caffeine.'

Salmon nodded. 'After a day like today no one'll need rocking.'

'But how did the dead woman get from where she fell to the rooftop of the college?' Beaumont pursued.

'Presumably in Markham's car,' Yeadings offered. 'But it needn't have been him driving. There were smudges from gloves on the steering wheel and bodywork.'

'There was no more than a dribble of her blood on the rug.'

'So the body was wrapped in something waterproof first, but it leaked at one corner.'

Z nodded, remembering the way Alyson had wrapped the black leather coat. There would be no shortage of sheet plastic in a house where an elderly patient was being nursed. She guessed it would be regularly used to cover the mattress against spills.

Perhaps when they questioned Martin Howard further he would explain how he'd moved the body, using the old Nissan dumped in the warehouse yard near where Rachel had fallen. For the time being they were kept at bay by medics at the hospital. The man was in a poor state. She wondered how he'd managed to carry the woman's dead weight all five floors up to the top of the college. And then one further narrow staircase to the roof. Would a stranger from Scotland know how to access the college lift?

Salmon rose to his feet. 'All reports on my desk by eight in the morning,' he decreed. 'And you'll find mine there before you.' His grin looked more of a leer, Yeadings thought; but, despite its unpromising beginning, clearly the day had ended on a high for him.

Sitting alone at the huge window with all the lights left on behind her, Alyson stared at the room's image thrown back. Her mind was in turmoil. Before Martin Howard had been driven off by Rosemary Zyczynski he had asked to look in on Emily. She had still been reluctant to take the risk, despite Ramón's defence of the man.

Emily had been dozing and barely opened her eyes as they came in. Alyson had watched life come back into them as her slow smile spread. 'Martin,' she breathed, focusing on his face. Her eyelids drooped, closed, and she was asleep again, silent and serene.

If she could believe all he'd said, this was Martin who had always 'got her out of there' when she was shut away. So it was the treacherous Rachel who used to lock her frail grandmother in a cupboard, and then, just days ago, tried to smother her in her bed.

Now, with Ramón on hand, perhaps Emily would emerge further from silence and begin to speak of the past, even describe what she'd seen when Martin arrived in time to save her life. So often after dark she had sat in her wheelchair staring at the great window, as Alyson did now, facing the room's reflection with herself at its centre. And unspoken emotions had fleetingly lit her face. Maybe on this screen she was seeing herself younger, among old friends and rivals, defying the social conventions that condemned her wildness; rekindling her contempt for the bullying father who had seduced and betrayed her.

Met with hauteur and blame when she attempted a reconciliation for her bastard child's sake, it was surely Emily, not her mother, who, enraged, snatched the silver candlestick and struck him down with a single blow.

But proof of that was beyond reach now. She had once spoken of her granddaughter's 'bad blood' but, with black humour, must have included her own part in it, with her father as its source.

Driving home, Zyczynski's eyes still burned from concentrating on the computer's screen. So much had happened in so short a time that she felt herself hurtling towards the last bend of a helter-skelter. They knew now who had killed Rachel, and it seemed certain they held the men responsible for Micky's tragic end, but there were so many small questions still niggling at the back of her mind.

Markham was absolved of any major crime, but he had still been violent to Sheena, and could be so again, yet she would not have him charged with assault. Ramón must have smothered his suspicions for days, and was guilty of concealing a crime, whether knowingly or not. Z sighed. And now, with most of the paperwork done, they had this new domestic murder to work through, a husband killing his terminally ill wife – but never a mercy killing, and not at her demand. Otherwise why the need to tie her hands?

Z was glad she hadn't mentioned the case to Alyson when the nurse phoned earlier to declare her faith in Martin Howard's good intentions. Dr Stanford, she remembered, was the doctor Alyson had praised for treating Emily with such compassion. How easily people deceive us.

Driving past the college she saw the penthouse lights still blazing and a figure seated by the great window. On an impulse she pulled up, got out and buzzed for admission.

'Is it too late to call?' she asked of the entry phone.

'Oh good, it's you. No. Come on up.'

Alyson put out glasses and opened a bottle of Merlot without asking. 'Pointless to go to bed,' she said. 'So much has happened. I can't believe it. To think of Emily being in such danger. And this was days ago.'

Z nodded. So perhaps Alyson hadn't yet heard about Dr

Stanford. No need to pile that extra agony on.

They drank in companionable silence, and then the buzzer sounded again.

Alyson went through to the CCTV viewer. 'It's Mr Fitt, of all people,' she called back, going to let him in. Z listened as she met him stepping from the lift.

'You've heard?' Alyson said. 'I'm so truly sorry.'

'Mr Yeadings rang me, so I came at once. I must apologize for the late hour, but I needed to reassure you, if I can.'

Coming through, they appeared to be countering apology with apology, each of them taking blame for what had been allowed to happen.

'This is Detective Sergeant Zyczynski,' Alyson introduced her.

'We have met. I'm glad to see you here, my dear. This is a distressing time for Miss Orme.'

He took the seat between them. Alyson produced a third glass and poured him wine. 'I feel terrible,' she said, 'allowing all these people to get in and put Emily in danger.'

'The blame is mine,' he insisted. 'I so regret not warning you fully,' and he explained how security had twice been breached at his office; once when Emily's strongbox key disappeared, and again when Martin must have got in on some pretext and taken the headed stationery.

'When you told me that Rachel Howard had been here at that time I guessed she had used some excuse to visit the office in my absence and help herself to the key, using a false name. Then the bogus insurance man visiting to view the collection: another deceit I should have been able to prevent. It seemed logical to me later to suppose Martin was behind it, checking whether Rachel had occasioned any mischief here. He is in a curiously ambivalent position, being a co-director with her in the family firm, but well aware of her animosity to her grandmother.

'I decided to trust him, and sent him a duplicate key to the strongbox, against the possibility of my not being in a position to defend it.'

Z leaned forward, 'Couldn't it have been Martin who helped himself to the original key?'

'If he'd done so, then he'd have had no need to check that
Emily's collection was the same as when she left Edinburgh with
it. No; his concern was for her security.'

'This key,' Z considered. 'I believe it featured in another case,'
and she explained how she'd found one such hidden in Micky
Kane's trainer.

'A few days later a witness saw the boy being chased by a
woman answering to Rachel Howard's description. Suppose he'd
somehow acquired the key – snatched her bag or picked it up
when she'd dropped it. Despite the different way the boy was
dressed later she could have recognized him as someone being
close when she lost the key. But he got away over a fence and she
couldn't follow.'

'So where is this key now?' Fitt asked.

'I have it, together with the clothes he wore when he was first
picked up unconscious. I was about to send them back to his parents, but I could drop in tomorrow and show it to you.'

Days passed while early March falsely promised the arrival of Spring. Martin Howard was to be arraigned on a charge of manslaughter. He was proving cooperative and to a point his story made sense. Warned by Timothy Fitt of Rachel's first visit to the penthouse, which coincided with the loss of Emily's strongbox key in his office, Martin had employed an Edinburgh PI to watch her closely, fearing some move against Emily whose principal heir she was.

Alerted to her second visit south, he had followed her from Edinburgh, forged the letter of introduction to Alyson by photocopying the firm's headings from Fitt's letters, and faked his signature. His concern was to ensure that Emily and her valuables were adequately protected.

He later admitted his deceit to Fitt who had guessed the identity of the self-styled insurance appraiser and posted to him the replica key, while retaining the strongbox with its catalogue of the art collection and Emily's latest will. Recent occurrences had convinced the old solicitor that his office was not as impregnable as he'd believed.

Martin had hidden nothing about attacking Rachel as she attempted to smother the sleeping Emily with a pillow. Nobody had witnessed her enter the apartment. Perhaps Sheena and the man hadn't properly closed the door behind them on leaving. Or Rachel had some means of picking the lock. Absorbed in appraising Emily's pictures, Martin had known nothing before a sudden clatter from the bedroom. He'd gone in to find her there, bent over the old lady, intent on murder.

He had seized her violently by the neck from behind, shaking her until she dropped the pillow and slumped, unconscious, at his feet. Desperately he had tried resuscitation, but without success. The woman was dead, with Emily staring wide-eyed at him as he bent over the body.

He had panicked, seeking some way to hide what he'd done. He couldn't carry the body out into the street. It had been mad to push her from the window, but he wasn't rational then. He still denied any further involvement. He had fled the penthouse in horror, leaving Emily unguarded with the door wide open and the woman's body God alone knew where down below...

And the window open, Ramón had claimed in his statement. He had gone in, found no one in charge and closed the gaping glass panel for fear Emily should take a chill. He had not reported the circumstances to Alyson Orme because he was new to the job and did not know what would be expected of him.

This had not satisfied the detectives interviewing him, but Ramón stood firmly by what he'd said, and collusion with Martin Howard was unlikely. The man was a foreigner and had poor spoken English in any case. The situation as he'd found it could have been too complicated for him to describe at the time. Strange, all the same.

It still remained to find who had discovered the body in the warehouse yard, broken into the Nissan and used it for transport to the college. Some knowledge was required of the layout there, and that the porter's lodge had electronic control of the staff lift and roof access. Although once an external student, Oliver Markham had pleaded ignorance of this. Also he had been elsewhere that Sunday evening, and eventually Sheena had provided his alibi. Not that the body had to be removed that same night. Weather conditions made it impossible to tell with any accuracy how long the body had lain unnoticed among rubbish in the dark corner of Elston's yard.

The post mortem on Audrey Stanford confirmed that a ligature had been applied with some force to her wrists. Examination of the plastic bag brought up only one set of fingerprints. These proved to be her husband's, and a search of the Stanfords' home produced a pair of corded curtain ties with tasselled ends. These had been purchased by him on the day before her death and paid for with his credit card.

'How could he have been so stupid?' Z asked.

'Bought them before he knew how he was going to use them,' Salmon overrode her. 'It was a crime of sudden passion. He used whatever came easily to hand. There's no doubt at all. Stanford killed her.'

Yeadings lingered over the specimen bag containing the cords. 'One is cut through,' he observed. 'Presumably when it was removed from her wrists.'

'Path lab found on it microscopic flakes of skin matching the dead woman's,' Salmon claimed promptly. 'We've got it all sewn up.'

Yeadings returned to the computer terminal in CID office and read back the report on finding the cut cord. Both cords, together with the scissors used, had been found crammed at the back of a drawer near where Audrey's body had lain.

Yeadings sat pondering a while. He hadn't known the Stanfords as well as Nan, but he'd agreed that Keith as a killer was a hard one to swallow. 'Audrey,' Nan claimed, 'was one very mixed up lady. There was a streak of malice there which her illness had done nothing to improve.'

Yeadings reminded himself of that earlier suicide attempt, genuine or not. Malice, he considered. Well, why not?

He rang through to the DI. 'I haven't seen the scissors listed among the exhibits for the Stanford murder case,' he said. 'Do we have them?'

'They weren't considered necessary as an exhibit for court,' Salmon told him. 'Beaumont will know what became of them.'

'Yessir, they were bagged and then put aside,' Beaumont confirmed when Yeadings went to the CID office to tackle him. 'I could probably find them if it's vital.'

They arrived on Yeadings' desk still in the original forensics bag, with contents and provenance printed on the label. 'Send them to fingerprints,' he ordered. 'This shouldn't have been overlooked. I won't accept sloppy practices.'

Dr Stanford, distraught and confused, had been held twenty-four hours for questioning and then allowed to return home on bail with his passport confiscated. He knew that by then his arrest would be common knowledge throughout town. His immediate concern was for his patients, and Emily among them. But above all he agonized over what Alyson must think of him. If she accepted the police view of Audrey's death, then he was truly past all hope.

Alone in the house – become an alien place, no longer home – he considered, and abandoned, the idea of phoning. Alyson must not be dragged into his disgrace. Anyone learning of his interest in her could distort it into further scandal.

The police searches had left the place in disorder but he hadn't the heart to start putting things straight. He supposed that Edna Evans would automatically have abandoned the household at the first scent of suspicion. Under steady rain the garden looked sodden and uninviting, and there was nothing to busy himself with in the garage because both cars had recently been serviced. He had no alternative to facing the situation he was in and trying to account for it. He went through to his study and surrendered himself to bitter recrimination.

The shrilling of the doorbell startled him. He was in no mood for company, but a glance from the window showed Nan Yeadings's people-carrier in the driveway and he couldn't turn her away.

'I don't want to bother you,' she said, 'but I guessed the fridge might need some restocking.' He took the heavy carton she'd dumped on the doorstep and waved her ahead of him into the hall.

'No, I'm not staying. I've got young Luke with me, and sorting this lot will give you something to do.'

Briefly he marvelled that she understood, but then suddenly he needed the sane ordinariness of her. 'Please stay,' he said. 'Bring Luke in. If you can spare the time, that is.'

He made coffee for them both and unearthed some Jaffa cakes to go with the little boy's orange juice. Between them they sorted the groceries and put them away, all normal activities that made him feel almost human again.

'It's a nightmare, isn't it?' Nan said, and again he was overwhelmed.

The phone rang and he had courage enough to answer it. 'Alyson? How are you? I've been thinking so much about...' Too late he knew he should have taken the call elsewhere. Nan would think the worst. A police superintendent's wife! He really knew how to condemn himself.

He forced the animation from his voice. 'It's kind of you to ring,' he said formally. 'Good to know some people still have some faith left in me. How's Emily?'

She had picked up the change in tone. 'Of course we believe in your innocence. The whole thing's crazy. Emily's well, considering we've had quite a little showdown here with a member of her family. It's too complicated to explain now. I just wanted you to know how sorry we are and we're with you all the way.'

They said goodbye and she rang off. 'One of my patients,' he excused himself lamely.

'Well, I must be off. Thanks for the coffee, Keith. Luke, what do you say?'

The little boy grinned. 'Thank you for my orange juice and the bikkit.'

'I've made you a beef casserole and set the right temperature. All you have to do is switch on and put it in when the red light goes out. Give it forty minutes. It should last you two days.'

'Nan, I don't know how to thank you.'

'Just be certain it'll all sort itself,' she said briskly, gathered up Luke and departed.

Will it? he wondered. Was that an oblique message from Yeadings himself? There'd need to be plenty of sorting. Audrey had been so clever in tying him into her death.

Ramón had made lunch, sliced chicken breasts and mixed vegetables tossed in a wok. Facing him across the kitchen table, Alyson was still uneasy about his part in the Rachel business. So preoccupied with the awful situation Keith was in, she hadn't at the time properly considered the explanation Ramón had given to the police. It alarmed her that he had kept silent about the unguarded apartment, the disarray in Emily's room and Sheena's absence when he arrived to take over.

He hadn't exactly lied, though. When she'd asked if the insurance appraiser was still there, he'd said, 'Nobody was there.' The strict truth, but a little short of what he should have said. And once she had started to doubt, she remembered something else: that when she was considering employing him he'd told her he attended an English for Foreigners course at the college. He'd started some weeks back, so surely he'd be familiar with the building's layout? Even know how to reach the roof?

No, she told herself; it was too fantastic to imagine that because he'd closed the panel in the window, he'd gone further in tidying up, and removed the body. It was the inscrutable face that gave her such ideas of secret planning going on behind.

'I'm home!' Yeadings called, letting himself in, dripping rain. Nan and the children came from the back of the house where they'd finished watching a video.

'Good day?' Nan asked as he bent to kiss her cheek.

'Quite productive. How was yours?'

She gave an account of various encounters at the school gate and in the supermarket while he fixed them drinks. 'All very small fry,' she excused it. 'And I dropped in on Keith Stanford who's feeling pretty down.'

'Wouldn't you, in his circumstances? Actually he'll soon have cause to perk up. There's good news on its way.'

'You can't leave it at that, Mike. What's come up?'

He teased her, shaking his head knowingly. Then, 'Audrey's fingerprints on the scissors used to cut the cords off her wrists. Hers and no others.'

'But only his on the plastic bag, Mike.'

'Quite easily done if she handled it through some kind of fabric. And as for the business of cutting herself out while tied up, I had some practice this afternoon with Z.'

'Bondage with junior officers? I hope you didn't have your wicked way with her.'

'I'll show you. Sally, love, pop up and get the cord belt off Daddy's dressing-gown, will you?'

When she brought it he folded it double and wound it round Nan's joined wrists. 'Now do it yourself. Thread the loose ends through the loop and pull tight. Right. Now imagine you've tied the ends to something above your head, and slumped long enough to cause the cord to bite into the wrists and later leave marks on the flesh. Now when you take the pressure off, the cord will shake loose because there's no knot. Finally you cut through the cord at some point and hide both cord and scissors. Who's to know you weren't tied up and released by a second person?'

'Can you prove she did it herself? Suppose those weren't the scissors used. She could even have used a knife.'

'But she didn't. There was a silky thread from the curtain ties caught in the join of the scissors. This was a clever attempt to pass suicide off as murder.'

'Clever, yes, but wicked too. How bitter she must have felt to do this to her own husband. Even if he was looking sideways at someone else.'

Yeadings grimaced. 'I never heard that, Nan. I only hope there's a chance of happiness left for the poor beggar. He deserves it after all this. And if, as you imply, there's someone he's fond of, I just hope they make it together as well as we do.'